Heatwave in Berlin

HEATWAVE
IN BERLIN

Royston Millmore

CANONGATE

Edinburgh and Vancouver, 1978

First published in 1978
by Canongate Publishing Ltd,
17 Jeffrey Street,
Edinburgh EH1 1DR,
Scotland

© Royston Millmore 1978

ISBN 0 903937 55 7

Printed in Great Britain by offset lithography by
Billing & Sons Ltd, Guildford, London and Worcester

To six million Jews murdered by the Nazis.

1

I looked at the calendar, and sweated. August first: rent day — and I didn't have the rent. But I did have a new pupil coming at three — a new, young, *female* and attractive pupil. More to the point, she would pay me fifteen Marks, which, with the fifteen I'd painfully put together during July — not without missing a meal or two — would just pay a month's room-rent in advance. And in a month anything could happen.

Many things, and not least the Depression, had taught me to be neither optimistic nor romantic. But I couldn't entirely suppress these emotions when I thought how I'd met my prospective pupil yesterday. Walking in the Kurfürstendamm, I had suddenly felt my legs bound together by a dog-lead and thrust against a slightly startled young woman. Instinctively, I'd apologised in English. She'd replied with an instant flow of eloquent German apology. It was not her dog but her father's, and such big dogs must be exercised, and . . . Suddenly she'd stopped. "But you spoke in English. Perhaps you don't understand German?" I'd assured her that I did, and half an hour and two cups of pavement-café tea later she'd said with delightful spontaneity that she would "respect the hint of destiny" and start taking lessons from me the very next day, in my room, at three.

The tea had taken all the money I carried, apart from one ten pfennig piece, but I considered it a good investment. What had really surprised me was her volunteering to come to my room, for I was under the impression that unaccompanied young German women did not go to the rooms of young men. But I'd gathered from her card that she was Elfrida von Steinfels, so had to assume that the rules were different for baronesses.

Now it was half past two and blisteringly hot, and my little room was as tidy as I could make it, considering its many functions. Would she come in such a heatwave? Would she come at all? It seemed rather doubtful, but the Germans usually kept their word. Well, if she didn't, I would have to call on David Whitaker again. If he was in funds, he would be very nice about it, and would probably remind me that being able to "lean on" him was part of the bargain that had brought me to Berlin. But I would hate it, and he would know that I hated it.

Now, if I were to go down to the entry, I would risk meeting our caretaker and being asked for the rent, though he usually waited till later in the day when people were back in the house. But I couldn't take the chance of her dithering in the entry, and probably being put off lessons altogether if she asked the oafish Goldgruber how to get to my room. Well, I would go down and risk it. After all, it was possible that he was stamping around Berlin somewhere in his Nazi Brownshirt outfit while his self-effacing wife was on duty, acting, unpaid.

At a quarter to three the entry was empty. I went into the street and walked to the corner of the block in one direction, then in the other, keeping the entrance under observation. Half an hour went by, and there was no sign of my pupil. I went back into the house. There was just a faint chance that a former pupil who owed me sixteen Marks might have dropped it into my post-box rather than face me. Holding the little key firmly so that it did not tremble, I opened the box. There was no money in it, though there was one of Elfrida von Steinfels's cards. On the back, in neat handwriting, it said: "Very sorry. The owner of the dog totally forbade the whole idea. Too bad. But perhaps some other time . . .? E.von S." So there were no special rules, not even for baronesses.

I pressed the ten pfennig piece into the house telephone and, luckily, got straight through to David Whitaker. "David," I said softly, "I'm broke — and it's rent day. Could you manage fifteen, under the Arrangement?"

"Certainly, I can, Eric. I'll bring it round in about an hour: certainly before six. Must go. I'm teaching." I hung up.

"Good day, Herr Yonson," said an unmistakeable voice in German behind me. "Still hellish hot, but a perfect day for a beheading, eh?"

I hadn't turned round, for I knew exactly what I would see. Goldgruber's odious, thick-necked, thread-veined face would be peering round the side of the caretaker's cubby-hole and smiling most unpleasantly.

Of course: August first — the day set aside for the execution of four Communists who'd fired on a column of his fellow Stormtroopers marching in "red" Hamburg earlier in the year, before the power-takeover, and before Hitler had re-introduced the axe.

But I must be prudent. "Good day, Herr Goldgruber," I said as I turned to go back to my room. "Yes, terribly hot. But any day should be good enough for an execution." I began to climb the stairs.

"Ah, yes — for the criminals. Good joke. Very appropriate."

Back in my room, I flopped down on the bed. So near the roof it

8

really was appallingly hot. My hand touched a small pile of newspapers on the floor. They had been passed on to me by well-meaning fellow tenants. I picked one up, but did not get beyond the date — July 25, 1933. New propaganda was bad enough; stale propaganda was insufferable.

I must have dozed off, for I jumped into apprehensive wakefulness at the sound of Goldgruber's voice booming up the stairwell. Was he on his round? Evidently not. He was addressing the house telephone in his sub-Hitler manner.

"It is clearly laid down in the Haus Roseneck window-cleaning contract," he rasped, "that the windows are cleaned at least once a month and more if requested. As it is now August and no windows were cleaned at Haus Roseneck in July, I will give you precisely two hours to make good your failure or to take the consequences." And bang, down went the instrument.

It was a poor omen for anybody a trace late with the rent. Yet there were amusing aspects. Even the ludicrous Goldgruber was unintentionally amusing in the way he brought the correct name of the house into almost every conversation. There wasn't a rose anywhere near, let alone a rose corner. But it was always Haus Roseneck for Goldgruber because he knew all the tenants called it "Haus Odol". It had a huge advertisement across its front for that popular mouthwash and our nearest Underground station, at Wittenberg Platz, had an even bigger one for Chlorodont Toothpaste dwarfing the station building. So our unofficial address was "Haus Odol, Chlorodont Platz".

Before I went to Germany, I hadn't thought it possible to mispronounce "Johnson". But I found myself more often "Yonson" than "Johnson". Goldgruber always got it wrong.

Not that he liked his own name. The "Gold" bit hinted at Jewishness — unthinkable in a long-standing Party member and Brownshirt. Besides, "Goldgruber" literally meant "gold-digger" or even "money-grubber".

If I'd been bolder — and heavier — I'd have deliberately tangled his name up one day and called him something inescapably Jewish, such as Goldbaum. But people who couldn't pay their rent couldn't play tricks, least of all with Nazi Stormtroopers.

What on earth was David Whitaker doing? It was after six.

I went to the window again and scanned the street, but there were only Germans walking in it, and looking very German.

Not that I disliked them, despite their remarkable lack of interest in learning English. I realised now that I'd arrived in Berlin with a small but fairly typical stock set of British prejudices, expecting to find square-headed men goose-stepping all over the town. Which, in a way, the Nazis were now doing. And quite a lot of ordinary German men *were* square-headed from the summer habit of having the side hair shaved off and the top cut very short and squared off. Some were totally shaved. These tended to be the fattest ones; so Berlin in summer seemed to have a brigade of resident Humpty-Dumpties.

But I'd found the ordinary Berliners very agreeable and surprisingly like the British. Though I had to admit they were taller, cleaner and more handsome. Except Goldgruber, who was very strong-looking but rather short and really a sort of caricature compendium of all the traditionally unattractive German aspects. ''That big-arsed, scar-faced, cripple-thumping, sausage-eating baboon'' was one of the more polite ways that David Whitaker and I referred to him, and not always outside his hearing, for he spoke no English.

In point of fact, Goldgruber was quite proud of his scar and was in the habit of standing or sitting so that the light fell on it. This, I'd soon found out, was not uncommon practice in Germany among university graduates, many of whom were said to have taken more care to get duelling scars than to get degrees, even to the extent sometimes of having a little help from a surgeon. What Goldgruber didn't know was that I had it from a reliable Haus Odol tenant that he got his scar from nothing more elegant than a broken bottle wielded by a Communist in a street fight.

Well, come what may, I'd have to have something to eat. I went on to the landing and peered down the stairwell to see if I could spot his hairy hand on the bannister, for all the tenants could now be expected to have come in. But there was no sign of him.

Slipping back into my room, I placed a wooden chair where it would check any sudden opening of the door. Then I sat on the other one and began my cooking routine, despite the notice on the back of the door that forbade it under the fire-insurance regulations. Indeed it was *''strengstens verboten''* under pain of eviction, attention being drawn meanwhile to the cooking cabin in the basement. But this, worked by gas, was four flights of steps away and — most important of all — needed a coin in the slot-meter.

I could have locked the door, but if I had done I would have roused his suspicions, which needed no stimulation — and he would doubtless have thought I was cooking, boozing and fornicating all at the same time.

So I sat in my shirtsleeves on the straightbacked chair, facing the chest of drawers, with one foot on the edge of the open bottom drawer. Inside it, resting on a small methylated-spirit stove, was an aluminium kettle of the sort that fills at the spout and has a folding handle. I'd bought it, equipped with a whistle which I quickly discarded, at the big

10

department store KDW. If Goldgruber were to knock and come in, I could have the stove out and the drawer shut before he knew what was going on. He'd still smell the spirit, of course, but I'd provided for that by having a bottle of it handy and a good excuse for it being there.

The kettle boiled. I took out a packet of tea and dropped a generous pinch into a mug beside the kettle, then turned off the stove and infused the tea. Next I pushed a Vienna sausage through the spout into the kettle. To one end of it was attached a length of string with which I would pull it out when the residual heat had sufficiently warmed it. This economical practice meant that my tea always had a tang of delicatessen, but I'd long since got used to that.

Another part of my collection of stage properties was a cheap vacuum flask. This was kept in a conspicuous position since it had to provide a silent explanation for any hot liquid I might be caught drinking. It was all a bit tedious, but part of the price of survival.

I must have daydreamed briefly, for I was suddenly aware of the sound of Goldgruber's jackboots in the corridor. A second later he had banged on the door and, with the rent book under one arm, was pushing the chair out of the way with the other. But not before I'd closed the drawer, picked up the bottle of spirit, and begun to rub some into one arm. My only hope now was to engage him in talk till David Whitaker arrived. As I expected, he was in full Stormtrooper kit: peaked cap, brown shirt and breeches and shining black leather jackboots. Reluctantly, I had to admit to myself that the Germans had a gift for effective uniform.

To try to keep him talking was a long shot, but fortunately he loved to talk, and never more so than when he and his fellow toughs had some small victory to celebrate. Today he had the executions. So he would be boringly predictable and odiously bumptious, but fluent — and it would help my German.

"Ah," he said, "alcohol." I waved him to the chair he'd nearly knocked over. He sat down, but quickly realised that his hope of a free drink was slender when he took in the fact that it was rubbing, not drinking, alcohol that he smelt. His affectation was that he had no more than a normal, masculine interest in alcohol, but I knew that he had been stinking drunk for a week at the end of January when the Nazis came to power. I knew, too, that he was now extracting a growing number of bribes of alcohol from the tenants.

As usual, he was sitting in such a way that his scar caught the light. "Sorry I can't offer you a drink," I said. "Wrong sort of alcohol."

"It's perhaps as well. I've a lot of work to do. The place isn't as clean as it ought to be inside. And I might have to find a new window-cleaner. That damned one-legged villain who's supposed to be our

11

present window-cleaner hasn't laid a finger on any glass in Haus Roseneck for more than a month.''

"Just a minute," I said, giving a last rub to my arm. "You did say 'one-legged window-cleaner' didn't you? How on earth can he climb ladders if he's only one leg?''

At this, Goldgruber howled with joy, beating a fat thigh with his fist. "Ha, ha, of course, being an Englishman you wouldn't understand. When I referred to his one leg, I meant his *middle* leg. You see, with a houseful of kids he evidently cares a damn sight more about keeping his middle leg busy than he does about cleaning the windows of Haus Roseneck.'' And again he burst into raucous laughter.

"Ah, yes. We have the same joke in England, sometimes. Especially with window-cleaners.''

"But not often, I should imagine?''

"No, not very often. Just occasionally, when it rains a lot.''

"Yes, of course. In England it rains very much. So you need a lot of good jokes in England — and window-cleaners.''

"Well, I don't.''

"Why not?''

"Because I'm here in Berlin.''

"Of course. To be sure. And you intend to remain?'' He glanced towards the rent book.

"If I get enough pupils.'' I'd long ago decided that any attempt to conceal my shortage of pupils would only make him more suspicious. There was also the remote possibility that he might recommend me as a teacher. After all, there were quite a number of people in Haus Odol, and he was likely to have caretaker friends in contact with more.

We had held this conversation, or something like it, fairly often. But Goldgruber never seemed to tire of it. So I prepared to go on to the next stage of my standard conversation with him which started by my asking after the health of his gracious lady wife and he, in return, inquiring of the wellbeing of my gracious lady mother in England. But this time, with only the first inquiry made, I was thankful to hear the telephone ring again and see him rise to go and answer it. Apparently the gracious Frau Goldgruber was out. Well, this gave me a little more time.

When he had so confidently sat down, the heat had made him unbutton his uniform Brownshirt. Then, to my surprise, he had unhooked it from his trousers and I saw that it was in fact a stiff jacket made — without laps — to look like a shirt. So the famous Nazi Brownshirt, like much else in the Third Reich, was a clever sham. With a few simple movements, he fastened it all together again.

Thus restored to formidable normality, he strutted out, saying over

12

his shoulder: "I'll be back soon." He seemed to smirk as he said this and I suspected that he knew I couldn't pay the rent.

I slid open the drawer. The tea was just nicely infused, and I drank it gratefully. God bless my gracious lady mother in England. For if she hadn't sent me a quarter-pound a week, in an open packet with a brass clip through the end and marked "Sample of No Value: *Muster Ohne Wert*", I should certainly have had no tea. Even so, a sense of gratitude didn't entirely blot out a sense of shame that I wasn't able to send her a penny.

When she was feeling inventive she would even put a fictitious lot number and description on the back of the packet where there was printed provision for that sort of information, the packets being designed chiefly for yarn samples for use in the local wool-textile industry. Indeed, I took a sort of pride in noting that I was supposed that very minute to be drinking "Lot 1578 Lapsang Suchong, Choice" or, to be more accurate, a bit of cheap blend from the local Maypole shop. In another minute, granted the usual eloquence from Goldgruber on the telephone, I would haul on the string and enjoy meat as well as drink. Things could be worse, much worse, though I could not quite blot out my longing for something really English, such as a kipper.

Although my mother and I were thus working together regularly in a nominally criminal conspiracy to defeat the terms of the International Postal Union, we did observe a certain delicacy of protocol. She would not enclose even a terse note, let alone a letter, with the alleged tea sample, any more than she would do so with the bundles of periodicals and newspapers she occasionally sent me.

But that *was* my mother. Her whole life was struggle, and she had plenty of excuse for taking short cuts with honesty, but never did. When my father had deserted her years ago, leaving her with me and my two brothers, she had just taken up the burden without so much as a sigh. "We'll manage somehow," was all she said. She was a clerk with the Providential Furnishing and Clothing Club, which sold credit vouchers to the poorest people in Britain and had its surprisingly large head office in Fogston. Her wage was thirty shillings, and she spent it every week like a general working out the strategy of a life-and-death battle.

When I was younger, I'd taken this for granted. But as I got older and the Great Depression deepened, I began to feel it as a personal humiliation, for I knew that she should have been able to lean on me, but couldn't. I'd longed to be able to support her, or at the very least buy her a few luxuries of the sort she'd never had. And now I was two years past my secret deadline of twenty-one — and penniless.

Anyway, by leaving England I'd spared her the degradation of having to submit to the Means Test, and myself of having to be kept by her: of all of us having slowly to rot, really. Besides, her job at what we always called "The Improvidential" was not at all secure, and the discipline there became fiercer as time went on. One of her friends had told me that ever since they'd had a man walking round with a stop-watch in one hand and a writing-pad in the other everything they did had a time allowance — including visits to the lavatory — and no visits without permission from the forewoman. And any talk had to be brief, softly spoken, and strictly about the work in hand.

My thoughts about my mother were suddenly interrupted by Goldgruber's yell up the stairway: *"Herr Yonson! Am Telefon."* Why he should have ignored the usual method of calling me by three short rings on my room bell I couldn't imagine, unless he considered the shout to be an extension of our recent conversation. I jumped up and ran quickly down the stairs.

"Hello, Eric Johnson here," I said into the instrument. The phrase had the merit of being the same in both German and English.

"Hello, Eric. It's David Whitaker. Sorry I couldn't make it. Something's cropped up that could do you a bit of good. By the way, how many pupils have you?"

"Three. Half my regulars are on holiday."

"Hell's bells. That won't even pay the rent."

"It doesn't. I need at least ten to make ends meet. What's happened, then?"

"Something that could turn out pretty good. Can you come round right away?"

"If I can give our rent-collecting caretaker the slip. If not, I'm stuck, and you'll have to come and bail me out."

As I hung up Goldgruber put his head out of his cubby-hole: "There was something wrong with your bell, Herr Yonson. That's why I shouted. But it's all right now. I've mended it."

"Thank you, Herr Goldgruber," I said, and began to climb the stairs. Then it suddenly struck me. Something wrong with my bell. Christ! Pupils or potential pupils might have been ringing it to no purpose. I ran quickly back. "How long has it been out of order?"

"Oh, not more than about twenty minutes. Somebody blew the fuse. Probably one of our lady tenants sticking a hairpin in the electric circuit. Ha, ha. See you shortly, Herr Yonson."

There was no mistaking what he meant, and, as I walked back to my room, I was sure that he was enjoying my sustained anxiety. I closed my door thoughtfully and went to open the drawer again.

But it was not to be. There was a sound outside my window and the head of the window-cleaner appeared. "Excuse me," he said, shutting

14

the window in order to rub it more firmly. While I suspected that he disliked Goldgruber as much as I did, I knew that, in a country full of informers, I couldn't risk anybody knowing anything to my disadvantage. But I knew, too, that I couldn't get out of Haus Odol to see David Whitaker without being asked for the rent. I went closer to the window and watched the window-cleaner work on it. He had an assistant standing with one foot on the base of the long extension-ladder.

When he had given the glass a last rub and swung the window open again, I said: "Good day. I see that our caretaker has compelled you to work overtime. I heard him speaking to you on the telephone."

"Yes," he said, "the brown-shirted shite-hawk." And instantly I knew that I must still have an English accent and that a man who would make a remark like that about a Stormtrooper would be likely to fall in with the plan forming in my mind.

"Listen," I said. "He's on to me, too. You see, I can't pay the rent, though if I can get out of the house without him seeing me go I know where I can get the money. Could I come down your ladder?"

He climbed into the room. "I know how to lock the window from the outside after you've gone. That'll fox him. Away you go."

I slipped on my jacket and was half way down the ladder before I fully realised what a dangerous thing I was doing — apart from leaving a stranger in my room. But it was too late to turn back. Anyway, the only thing of value that I owned — fifteen Marks — I had with me.

2

The soles of my shoes being thin, I was careful to keep to the flagged part of the pavement, moving on to the cobbled sections only to give way to approaching pedestrians. I began a sort of barmy instant analysis of which of them would gain from a knowledge of English.

The newlywed matrons clearly didn't need anything they hadn't already got; the fair younger girls — who cast down their eyes so engagingly — would never miss it, either. The young men, both in ordinary clothes and in the various Nazi uniforms, were so assured that any idea of self-betterment via English seemed irrelevant.

That ruled out half Berlin, so I moved up the age-scale. The Hausfraus were too busy at home — and their husbands too preoccupied seeking promotion. Anyway, everybody was now being carefully indoctrinated by Dr Goebbels, Minister for Propaganda, and his associates, to think that everything foreign was bad if only because it was foreign. England was particularly high on their hate list.

It seemed only the elderly were left to me, and they were beyond ambition — unless they were Jewish. They alone had good reason to want to learn English — to flee. But if rumour was to be believed, all the wealthier Jews were in concentration camps. So I hadn't a potential pupil in all Berlin. Ah, well, that settled that. I could now attend to other matters.

It was always pleasant to walk to David Whitaker's garden flat in the Meinecke Strasse, off the elegant Kurfürstendamm. As I walked through the neat little garden, I saw him standing in the entrance, backed by the graceful upward curve of the white marble stairway with its Turkey-red carpet.

"Hello," he said, "I was just drawing a breath. Berlin gets a bit close in August."

"It's close with me all the time."

He grinned. "Ah, well, we must see what we can do about that. Come in."

Turning, he opened the heavy door on the right at the foot of the stairs and walked in ahead of me. We'd known each other too long for

16

me to feel slighted or to need an invitation to sit down in the soft chair next to the coffee table. His splendidly Germanic glass coffee-maker made a discreet glug and infused the coffee. David popped a glass snuffer over the little blue flame and sat down opposite me. I needed a cup of coffee and I suspected he knew it. The buzz of the traffic in the Kurfürstendamm came in gently through the open French windows. "So you gave Goldgruber the slip."

"Yes, but I'd rather have given him the rent."

"I didn't realise how bad the unemployment was here when I encouraged you to come. I see Hitler claims it was six and a half million when he came into power in January, and, for once, he might be telling the truth."

"Could be. I see he's got. the poor sods. marching along with brightly polished shovels on their shoulders, all set to build the New Germany and singing cheer-up songs fit to bust. God help them!"

He glanced at the open french windows, then rose and went over to them. Parting the long net curtains, he looked out in both directions, closed the doors and returned. "Have some coffee. Help yourself." I poured two cups of coffee and handed him one. As he took it he said, "Hungry?"

"A bit." I didn't like to admit that I'd not eaten since breakfast-time.

"Should be something in the fridge." He got up and went into the tiny adjoining kitchen, where he made agreeable rattling and paper-rustling noises. I heard a light tapping on the french windows like somebody brushing the glass with the back of a hand. "David," I called, "I think there's somebody at the garden entrance."

He came back and said quickly to me as he moved towards the french windows: "A pity about that. He's come early — before I've had time to fill you in. But it doesn't matter really." Then, after looking through the glass of the doors, he opened them and stood aside.

An elderly, rather bent man with one hand pressed against his side came silently into the room, moving slowly but glancing quickly first at David Whitaker then, more intently, at me. He was very ugly, conspicuously Jewish, and seemed deeply perturbed. "Good evening, Herr Mandelbaum," said David, holding out a hand, which the other took tentatively, "This is an English friend of mine — the one of whom I spoke — Eric Johnson." I stepped forward a pace or two and greeted him similarly. "You're just in time for coffee. Do sit down," David went on.

Choosing a hard chair near the wall, the visitor seated himself and David poured out and handed him a cup of coffee. For a few moments

17

we all busied ourselves with the coffee, waiting for some sort of social atmosphere to establish itself.

"You teach the English?" said the visitor eventually.

I was tempted to say, "Well, I try," but checked myself in time and simply said: "Yes."

"That is good. While I speak, as you see, some sort of English myself, I am concerned for my wife to learn it, in spite of her age, which is the same as mine." Here he shot a searching look at David, as though seeking to know if he might speak freely.

"Herr Mandelbaum is apprehensive about some aspects of the future," said David.

"I'm sure he is," I said, then realised that the remark could be taken two ways. "So am I. So is every friend of freedom." It sounded trite — like a piece of propaganda, but it was better than suggesting that all Jews had every reason to be fearful of the future, and old ugly male Jews most reason of all.

"Yes, I would like her to go for a while to England or America." I didn't envy Frau Mandelbaum her sojourn in England, or America. Neither did I look forward to teaching her English. I had hardly expected a classful of beautiful virgins, but this was a very dusty answer.

We all fell silent for a few seconds; he was giving me time to get used to the idea, and I wondered as I considered it how much he knew of my circumstances. I was turning over the thought that the more people knew about one's background, the easier it was for them to misuse the knowledge. But I also knew — or at least thought I did — that David Whitaker would not have handed over any more weapons of that sort than was necessary.

Over the buzz of traffic in the Kurfürstendamm there came the sound immediately outside the flat of a car stopping rather suddenly with a small squeal of brakes followed at once by the impact of stout boots on the pavement. Mandelbaum jumped and began to shake a little. A car door slammed and the footfalls moved on. Herr Mandelbaum said: "I have been away in the country for a while: I have to get used to these city noises once more."

I picked up my coffee cup and drank slowly. Herr Mandelbaum watched my actions but did not watch me.

"Where would you want the instruction to take place?" I asked. He made a dismissive hand gesture and smiled again. He looked even uglier when smiling.

"What would suit you best?"

"At my place, near Wittenberg Platz."

"Ah, Chlorodont Platz." And now we all smiled, but uneasily.

18

I was conscious that there had been no mention of the fee, and didn't know if this was a good or bad sign. Usually it cropped up very early in such discussions. "But I do attend pupils in their homes or offices if they wish it. That costs more, though."

"Of course. Of course. I quite understand. But I should much prefer you to attend her at our home, in Teltow. You know Teltow? It is only a few miles away, on the edge of Berlin."

"No, I've only heard of it."

"It's easy to reach by rail. Assuming everything goes well, could you come every day but Saturday and Sunday? For a two-hour lesson? Starting with a trial week immediately?"

It seemed an excessive frequency and length of lesson, likely to impose nervous strain on both pupil and teacher, but I was in no position to turn down income.

"Yes, but we haven't discussed terms . . . ."

"No need. Your friend here has told me your usual charges. I agree to them. And if a trial week works out well, then I propose you shall be paid double the normal rate for lessons in your room because you will be accommodating yourself to our rather special requirements." My normal charge was one and a half times. He rose and held out a visiting card. "Details are on the back. Perhaps you would be kind enough to telephone my wife and arrange a suitable time." I took the card.

"Certainly."

"Very good. And now, if you don't mind, I am paying you fifty Marks in advance as evidence of seriousness. It will not be repayable in any case — though I am sure that the arrangement will work very well." He held out the notes, and I hesitated. Such generosity and trust was the reverse of all that I imagined to be Jewish. "Please, I insist." I took the notes and looked round for somewhere to write a receipt. "No receipt, please," he said, anticipating my intention, "there is far too much paper in the world already." Again he smiled his awful smile, shook hands with us both, said "*Aufwiedersehen*, gentlemen," and left by the way he'd come.

"Christ," I said, after he'd gone. "You weren't kidding, were you?"

David shrugged. "I've as many pupils as I need. I hope you like Jews."

"I don't. But haven't any choice at the moment."

"True. Come on, let's go out for something to eat."

We walked the hundred yards or so to the Kurfürstendamm and turned left, away from the costly end near the Kaiser Wilhelm Memorial Church and the elegant Café Trumpf, but stopped well short of the hamburger-and-sausage stalls round a corner about half a mile down. There was a wide choice of restaurants with inviting, well-lit enclosures coming out on to the pavement and we soon selected one. David handed me the menu. "Never mind the bits and pieces," he said, "pick something you can sink your teeth into. It's on me."

He was too kind to suggest that he knew that I was familiar only with the cheapest dishes, but I was sure that he did know. In fact, I was the resident expert on the subject, having long ago learnt which cafés and restaurants offered the best value in side dishes meant to be ordered with the main dishes and therefore underpriced. I simply dispensed with the main dishes, sometimes to the surprise of new serving staff.

"I'll have a Wiener Schnitzel," I said, "with all the trimmings — and maybe a glass of that white Berlin beer with a shot of raspberry juice."

"Not a Berliner Weisse," he smiled. "That's a tart's tipple. Why not have a litre of dark Schultheiss, and I'll join you? And I suggest asparagus among the trimmings with the Schnitzel. Berlin asparagus is very good — grown on the old filter-beds of the Berlin sewage plant, they tell me. Very German-efficient. Very appropriate, too; asparagus is a gross feeder, as the gardening enthusiasts say."

"I agree that it sounds like German logic, anyway. Yes, I'll have some, then." I wished I could say something graciously appreciative, but didn't seem able to find the words.

When the waiter had put everything on the table, I had a fleeting recollection of my poor Vienna sausage slowly congealing in the kettle at Haus Odol, but this only sharpened my appetite. Stein in hand, I turned to my friend. "Well," I said, "as the least religious man in Berlin sitting opposite to the second least religious, I never thought I'd feel like saying grace before a feast."

"That reminds me," he cut in. "Tomorrow's the Knabenschiessen Feast, also in Teltow — you know, the annual boys' rifle-shooting competition, with beer and a band and a certain amount of disorderly gaiety. If you can sort out your affairs with Frau Mandelbaum in time, then we might go there, eh? And what's more, I know a beautiful brunette in Teltow who might have a no-less beautiful friend. Now what do you say about *that*?"

"I say, so far as this mouthful of delicious Wiener Schnitzel, delicate decorum and a refined upbringing will allow, that I think it's a splendid idea and that I can only hope that your friend's friend turns out to be a beautiful blonde with big tits."

3

Goldgruber was not on duty when I got back to Haus Odol, for my ring on the front door bell was answered by the sound of Frau Goldgruber's voice from the little loudspeaker in the portico. I identified myself and immediately heard the buzz of the device that released the bolt as she pressed the button in the caretaker's flat. No doubt her husband was pounding some part of Berlin in his jackboots to the greater glory of the New Germany.

I pushed open the heavy door and paused a moment to hear it automatically lock behind me. A pity Goldgruber was out; I was looking forward to seeing his puzzled surprise as I handed him the rent money. Ah, well, that was a small pleasure in store for tomorrow.

My room was exactly as I'd left it except that the window catch was lightly "on". How the window-cleaner had done this from the outside must be one of the few secrets of the window-cleaning — and the burglary — trades. But I wasn't worried about my few rudimentary possessions.

The thought of dealing with the sausage in the kettle was faintly revolting; but if I left it there overnight I'd have to suffer particularly garlicky tea for some time. So I pulled it out, poured away the water down the wash basin, and rinsed out the kettle.

Not feeling quite tired enough for bed, I picked up a back issue of the *Fogston News & Intelligencer*, or the *Fogston Newt*, as we often called it at home. "Amateur Actress Weds Idle Tenor" ran the first headline I saw. While the report did not say so, I knew that she had once played a poor second lead in a presentation of a popular comedy put on by the Fogston Baptists' Amateur Operatic and Dramatic Society and that the bridegroom had twice sung in the chorus at the Idle Village Church Choral Society's annual offering of Handel's "Messiah". How curious the name of the village looked when seen from Berlin.

The adjoining item was headed "Cigs Go in Quick Raid". Evidently life was going on much as usual in the Fogston district, but I'd no wish to be there, except of course to see my mother, and brothers. I put out the light and went to bed.

I didn't look forward to teaching Frau Mandelbaum because I knew that old minds were hostile to new knowledge. But I certainly needed the money, so I rang her next morning at nine-thirty.

She was businesslike and to the point and asked me to call at four that afternoon if this suited me. It did, though it probably meant that I would miss the shooting at the Knabenschiessen. Well, so long as I didn't miss the evening with David Whitaker and the girls, that didn't worry me. I telephoned David immediately and he suggested that we meet at the Haus Maximillian beer-garden in Teltow at seven. I had two lessons to give in the morning in my room, so the day was set out. It remained only to pay the rent.

I went downstairs and found Goldgruber in his "office". He gave me only a scowling nod and picked up a sealed envelope from his desk. I returned the nod but not the scowl and laid the rent money on the desk, spreading out the notes. He asked no questions, simply separating the notes to make sure they came to the right amount. Then he crumpled up the envelope in his other hand and threw it into a waste bin before writing out a receipt for me with an indelible pencil, which he licked before using. As I walked back up the stairs, I pondered on the crumpled envelope. Had it been my notice to quit? I very much suspected so. Well, that pleasure had been denied him for at least another month.

I had no difficulty in finding the Mandelbaum dwelling in Teltow. It was a modest-seeming upper flat in a house of two flats that otherwise looked very much like an English "semi" except that it had two adjoining entrance doors.

Herr Mandelbaum answered my ring and let me in. I noticed as he did so that the other name above the second door-bell was not Jewish. We went up a flight of stairs to the first floor, through a small lobby, and into a pleasant lounge that overlooked gardens. The flat itself was small and rather over-furnished in that the furniture was too big and solid and the ornaments and paintings too opulent-looking. But this didn't surprise me; I'd often heard that Jews liked to show their material progress by their surroundings. A handsome elderly woman rose from a high wing chair and gravely nodded to me. "Rebecca," said Herr Mandelbaum, "this is the young Englishman of whom I spoke." He stayed with us long enough only to make the introduction.

As soon as we were seated, Frau Mandelbaum said to me, still in German: "What teaching method do you use, Herr Johnson?" I was a little surprised, and pleased, that she had not said "Herr Yonson".

"I have two methods: the traditional one of grammar instruction and practice sentences and the direct method of speaking only English and requiring the pupil to do the same. The first is the more pleasant, but slower. The second is sterner and less pleasant, but gets quicker results.''

"I am afraid,'' she said with a sigh, "that I have not enough time for the pleasant one.''

"Very well,'' I said in English, "then we talk English.''

Not for the first time, I was silently thankful for all the midnight oil I had burned learning my own language, suppressing my local accent, and for the much-tried determination to do this my teacher of English at Fogston Grammar School had somehow implanted in me.

It was a strenuous two hours, if a little less so then I'd feared. While Frau Mandelbaum had no English, she apparently had some knowledge of Hebrew. This, though totally unrelated to English, did mean that she had at some time in her life crossed the one-language barrier, so was psychologically prepared to accept other languages as valid and useful. For this I was thankful, even though I sensed far more strongly her deep resentment that she was really being forced to prepare herself to leave her native land. But nothing of this was expressed, or could be expressed, in any language.

I thought at times that we were making a little painful progress, then doubted it when she instantly forgot some simple phrase such as "How do you do?''

I was physically and emotionally exhausted when the session was over. She, poor woman, must have been even more so, yet she stayed erect in her chair and alert to the end and we then lapsed back into German only long enough for details of my next visit to be arranged. As I walked down the street, wondering where I would find the Haus Maximillian for my meeting with David Whitaker, I wondered if she — and I — would be able to withstand the strain of such an intensive daily course. I realised, with a little surprise, that her being Jewish was now an irrelevance; she was just an old woman submitting herself, as well as she was able, to an indignity.

Finding the beer-garden was simple, for it proved to be the head-quarters of the rifle-shooting club sponsoring the festival and was already crowded. The weather was fine, and much the busiest place was the spacious garden, where serving-maids in national peasant costume were rushing to and fro between the tables and the large trees balancing trays full of heavy beer mugs. I slipped into one of the few empty seats, and prepared to wait some time to be served.

Although I'd heard the music as I approached, there was now an interval and the members of the wood-and-brass band set about draining their instruments of spittle, easing the valves, sorting pieces of their curiously abbreviated music, and drinking beer in great gulps. They were wearing hunting-green national dress, but had already discarded the jackets because of the warmth of their exertions. All of them were, in greater or lesser degree, fat, and two of them boasted the famous "beer bellies" of which I'd heard even in England.

As I watched their perfect ease, I remembered how my grandfather used to talk of "German bands" wandering around England and had a fly-spotted photograph of one of these showing four lonely-looking middle-aged men obviously far from home.

One of the serving-maids, pink and sweaty with her work and looking all the more attractive for it, suddenly stopped in front of me and asked me what I wanted. A minute later she was back and setting down a stein of lager, picking up the money and slipping it into a sporran-like purse under her apron before rushing off with her still heavy tray.

The leader of the band stood up again and took his place, looking at the players but cocking an ear for a shouted request from the cheerful crowd. Soon he got one and the music began again. The standard of playing was more vigorous than skilful, but this was no surprise since it was clear that the band would play almost anything, whether they had music for it or not.

Yet they presumably had set pieces for, a little later, after some shuffling of printed music, they prepared to play one of these, but not before their conductor had stood for a full minute with both arms raised to indicate that a show piece was about to begin and that he expected relative silence for it.

As soon as the opening bars were played I recognised a favourite Strauss waltz, though I couldn't have named it. Typically, the opening was not in waltz tempo, yet hinted at it, and I realised for the first time why the Strausses tended to start their waltzes with introductory passages. It was to achieve a mood, to bring about a sort of mild musical intoxication after which the waltz itself was a climax of simple joy.

By now the band had reached the waltz, and everybody began gently to move in time with the lilting beat. On the tiny dance floor, those who were dancing were so close together that they could only sway and turn, quite unable to progress, but not caring. Even the many young children who were present in the garden finally caught the mood and were unselfconsciously included in the gentle swaying and humming at the tables, where some groups now linked arms. This, surely, was how music was meant to be enjoyed. I recalled the obligatory annual performance in Fogston of Handel's "Messiah", with the "big men at the church" jumping to their feet a split-second early, and bawling "Halleluja! Halleluja!" yet feeling nothing. Suddenly I felt very

English and alien, but was strangely content to be so.

Sitting there under a fine tree, sipping the bright beer and eating a pretzel that a previous occupant of the seat had left on the table, I was happy. David Whitaker must come soon, but even if he didn't, there was enough happening to keep me interested. All the same, I was a bit apprehensive about the impression I would make on the German girls he might bring with him. While I'd not yet been in Germany two months, he'd been in the capital for well over a year, so was probably on terms with quite a number of girls. He was taller and two years older than I was and, in his good English-teaching connection, had a far better basis for self-confidence than I had. I was pretty sure, too, that he'd been ahead of me in experience with women in Fogston before he left for Berlin.

Well, I would just have to work as well as I could within my limitations. I thought about the objective way some of them were set out in my passport. Born in 1910, five feet eight inches in height, brown eyes, brown hair, no distinguishing marks. Still, I did at least look English, and spoke German with an English accent. These considerations were supposed to be attractive to German women, though I couldn't imagine why, especially in Prussia, which had a tall blue-eyed Adonis on every street corner, if only selling newspapers.

As I gazed around, it suddenly struck me that there were more signs than usual of the presence of Nazis. Perhaps it was because this was a shooting festival. Quite a lot of men, including older men, were wearing the swastika lapel-badge that announced membership of the NSDAP, the Nazi Party, and there was a scattering of Brownshirts. At a nearby table were two very handsome young men in the elegant black-and-silver uniform of the SS. Although they were relaxed in the presence of two girls, they were obviously conscious of being members of an elite, so sat quite erect with not a button undone, the only concession to informality their two caps bearing the double lightning flash resting in the middle of the table. As they toasted each other, then the girls, their daggers swung gently to and fro in brightly plated sheaths on chains attached to their belts. David Whitaker had told me that the blades of SS daggers were etched with the motto "Blood and Honour" and, watching these wearers, I did not doubt it, though I did doubt his claim that they were prepared to marry any "pure Aryan stock" selected for them by their superiors in the corps — or to breed from them to order, without troubling about the formality of marriage.

"Well, Eric, how goes it?" said a voice behind me in German. It was David Whitaker. When I got up and turned round, I saw that he was accompanied by two good-looking German girls, one dark, the other fair. Turning to them, he said: "Allow me to present my English friend, Eric Johnson. Fräulein Helga Stern and Fräulein Anna-Maria Rantzen. Helga and Anna-Maria — Eric."

I suppose I ought to have bowed, but I shook hands with them instead, mumbling something about being happy to meet them, and doing nothing neatly or suavely, much to my private irritation. But they put me at my ease with a stream of gay chatter and much smiling and gesture. Very soon we were toasting each other in tall glasses of pale golden beer, nibbling pretzels from a plateful that David had ordered, and generally behaving as though the whole festival had been put on for our benefit.

I'd offered my seat to the blonde Anna-Maria, but she'd declined it with a wave. Fortunately, the party sitting next to me had risen and moved on only seconds before David and the girls arrived, so places at the table were not a problem. David slipped me a twenty-Mark note under cover of the table and I was bold enough shortly to ask if they would not prefer spirits to beer — I'd previously noted from the menu that they were not greatly dearer. But the girls would have none of it. It was, said the dark one, Helga, "a beer occasion — especially because it's so warm." The blonde one immediately agreed, adding: "Have you seen the target?"

When I showed puzzlement, she obviously wondered if I understood the word, for David must have told her that I had been only briefly in Germany. She pointed to a tree nearby. On it, about two yards above the ground was fastened a circular piece of wood on which was painted a hunting scene showing a proud stag sniffing the air in a forest clearing. "Oh, *that*," I said. "Yes, I saw that when I came in. Is it the target, then? Surely they won't shoot at it there?" At which both girls laughed gaily.

"Come," she said, taking my hand in hers. "The shooting has already happened, and the boy with the sash of honour at the table in the corner is the winner."

As we walked, hand in hand, to look at the target, I had a closer sight of the boy who had won the competition. Surrounded by smiling people, he was draped with insignia of several kinds, the most conspicuous of which was a broad blue silk sash with silver lettering reading "KNABENSCHIESSEN TELTOW 1933". I thought he looked a little embarrassed by all the adulation, but happy. "On the part of the sash over his back," said Anna-Maria, "it says 'Prize of Honour'." Her eyes widened in mock adulation. "I know because my young brother won it last year."

We had now arrived at the wooden plaque and I was able to see that about a dozen small round wooden pegs pierced it, each peg bearing a carefully lettered name. One was about half way along the body of the stag. ''That,'' said Anna-Maria, ''is where the winner's bullet went through. The others missed the stag and hit the landscape.''

''It seems a pleasant enough way to kill stags without doing any injury,'' I said.

My comment seemed to please her, for she called it *''ulkig''* — ''quaint''. She was still holding my hand when we returned to the table.

''Well,'' said David, looking up. ''Can you two understand each other?''

''Perfectly,'' she said. ''He speaks excellent High German like . . . like an Englishman. That's good.''

All the same, the fact that the two girls swapped a rapid stream of idiomatic German and that David and I were often included in the exchange showed that they did really take it for granted that we were familiar with the language. In the talk it came out that both girls worked at some government office in Berlin where they were telephone switchboard operators. For this reason, their chatter took in the whole Reich and places outside it where German was spoken, for they said they spoke no other language. So David and I forgot briefly that we were English, drank a little and ate a little, and toasted each other in elaborate toasts, hooking arms and drinking while looking straight into the clear eyes of these pretty girls, the sunlight-dappled flesh of their forearms firm before us and their eager bodies so closely within reach. And we danced to the band, closer still, and quite intoxicated. But not with what we were drinking.

In a few rare moments of North of England common sense, I tried to get a grip of my thoughts and tell myself that it was all a summer idyll, a waking dream, that would fade before the daylight did. But it did not fade; it became more intense and bewitching, and the band played more and more waltzes, Strauss waltzes. And we danced closer together on the crowded little floor as the light died gently away and the stars came out.

4

For reasons that I told myself were absurdly sentimental and irrational, I had not looked forward to Christmas in Berlin. Yet when all the signs were around me, I welcomed it. To be still there meant that I had survived more than six months.

But there was another reason — Anna-Maria. Wholly against my intention, I had come to need her, even to take so deep a joy in her that sometimes it alarmed me. But she brought far more happiness than alarm, so I continued to make my meetings with her bright signposts in a dull landscape.

The situation was not altered by my knowing that I was far less important to her than she was to me. Although she never put this into words or deeds, she was quite open about it. I was quite simply outside her plans, and I forced myself to accept this by an effort of will. At least I was in training for such a renunciation, I reflected sombrely, for if the Depression had taught me anything it had taught me that somehow I must put my normal expectations — and with them something of my manhood — into cold storage until the arrival of better times. I recalled a girl I knew in Fogston who worked in the Income Tax Office, and never went out with a man before she had looked up his income-tax position. That she had told me this made my own standing with her only too clear. Well, Anna-Maria was not at all like that, which was something for which I was truly grateful. She had granted me a short lease on her affections, no more; but it was a wonderful gift, even so.

I turned over this problem in my mind as I slowly honed a razor-blade on the inside of a glass tumbler, hoping to extract a few more shaves from it. Survived I had, but only by maintaining a hundred humiliating economies of which this was one. But Christmas was here, or nearly so. I discarded the blade, stripped out a new one, and shaved quickly with firm strokes. When I looked at myself in the mirror, I saw that I'd been too decisive, and now needed a good deal of dabbing at small cuts with a styptic pencil.

Well, I told my reflection, deliberately seeking a new thought-train, I should be thankful to see the back of 1933. Surely 1934 must be better. Surely the world slump must end sometime, if only by a spontaneous reaffirmation of the need of life to go on, in spite of the fumblings of politicians and economists who had competed with each other in uselessness. Yet to judge by the newspapers my mother was still sending me, there was still no shortage of resounding speeches from the leaders while the unemployed were bravely bearing their share of the common burden. In other words, were quietly, decently disintegrating. As I fastened my shirt, I shifted a shoe with a foot so that I could read the latest outpouring from Mr Ramsay MacDonald, the Prime Minister of our government, God help us, of national unity.

It was totally incoherent — all "on and on, and up and up" — despite the help that the journalists had doubtless given him. Well, I was a million miles from being any sort of a success, but at least I wasn't taking the bread out of my family's mouth by warrant of his "equality of sacrifice".

I pulled out my grey flannel trousers from under the mattress and put them on. They, too, could not last much longer, but replacing them was something I certainly didn't propose to worry about this bright December morning. Meanwhile, I'd managed to make my shoe-soles tolerably waterproof by spreading some rubbery stuff from a tube that my mother had sent me, as a "Sample Without Value" of course, over the holes in them. So long as I remembered not to slide my feet — which caused it to roll off — it did its job quite well. I gave quiet thanks for my foresight in buying a sports jacket with over-long sleeves that allowed them to be gradually turned up as the cuffs frayed.

How strange it was that my mother never asked me in her letters if I'd found a girl friend. When I was in Fogston, she'd taken it for granted that I couldn't afford one, and so had I. I'd friends who'd opted for love on the Dole, and they put as brave a face on it as they could. But it was not for me.

More than once, I reminded myself of the slow corrosion of my parents' marriage; that by staying free from any deep association with the other sex I was avoiding misery not only for myself but for somebody else as well. Sometimes I almost believed it.

Perhaps I'd been too susceptible when I'd met Anna-Maria. Now I had to remind myself that I was still penniless, though just managing to keep myself, and that she was German and therefore alien. I could not even say anything to her with true depth of feeling because this needed a more delicate command of German than I had. Yet each time I tried, foolishly, to tell her that I didn't trust my knowledge of the language enough to say some of the things to her that I would like to say, she just smiled and said: "Not necessary. Not necessary. I understand perfectly."

Sometimes, in the early hours of the morning, in the heat of the summer when I couldn't sleep, I longed for her presence there in the bleak little room: even got out of bed and stood at the window, absurdly willing her to come walking into view between the trees in the street, smiling up at me.

I looked out of the window now. Snow had fallen, but was being briskly removed by a seemingly endless supply of men with brushes and shovels. Every day the German national newspapers had a new picture of useful work now being done by men who were unemployed before the Nazis came to power. "Adolf Hitler Brings the Dignity of Work" said the issue of the *Voelkischer Beobachter* lying next to the *Fogston Newt*. And there on the front page was a smart little army of snow-shifters, shovels over their shoulders like rifles, to prove it.

Somebody knocked on my door. Maybe it was David, or maybe Goldgruber. It was a relief not greatly to care which.

It was David, carrying a circlet of laurel and holly. "Merry Christmas," he said. "A Christmas wreath for your door." And he slipped it over the coat-hook inside the door.

"Merry Christmas, David. And thanks." I was irritated with myself for not having given him such a token. Moving some books and a shirt, I waved him to a chair. "How are you progressing with Anna-Maria?" he said. "I take it you *are* progressing?"

"Well, yes, you could say that, I suppose. I see her about once a week and we get on very well together. I find her very attractive. But I don't kid myself that I make much impact."

"Hm," was all he said.

"And I am only a sort of foreign novelty to her. Apparently she's got a boyfriend in East Prussia." David simply raised his eyebrows a little. "Yes, I think he must be a semi-secret soldier in this semi-secret extra army they're supposed to have. She says she first met him when he was stationed in Berlin, but when I asked one or two questions, she shut up completely. Anyway, whatever he is, he's far away, thank God, at the far side of the detested Polish Corridor."

"Probably running around like a blue-arsed fly deep in the forest of some Junker, training with the secret New German Army or the even-more-secret New German Luftwaffe."

"Do you think they have an air force, then?"

"I'm bloody sure they have. One of my braver pupils says they fly in the mornings and go to the funerals in the afternoons."

"But they're only allowed gliders by the Treaty of Versailles."

"Yes, and you're only allowed to look at pretty girls before marriage

30

but that hasn't stopped you handling the goods now and again, has it?''

"I only do what they want me to," I said, grinning.

"Well, that's one way to put it. And I only do what they say they don't want me to do. Comes to the same thing in the end, I suppose. Anyway, I'm here to invite you to the English parson's for tea on Sunday, where there will be not the least trace of hanky-panky of any sort.''

"You can't be serious. Tea at the Vicarage. It's straight from Jane Austen. Not at all my cup of tea — to coin a phrase. Anyway, how ever did *you* get invited?''

"Simple. Every Englishman resident in Berlin and not conspicuously of the artisan class sooner or later gets an invitation. There's a sort of grapevine that sees to it. First it found me. Now it's found you. The fact that you're invited suggests that you're now considered resident. I suppose you are C of E? Not that it matters. You can be a liquorice all-sort and you'll still get an invitation, if you're English, and reasonably clean.''

"I suppose I'm C of E, officially.''

"Right, then. I'll call for you next Sunday afternoon at three-thirty and take you along for a sacred sup of tea and a 'oly bun.''

"I can't wait.''

"Fine. That's settled. Where are you going now?''

"To Teltow. Frau Mandelbaum asked me to go in the morning today if I could fit it in with my other lessons, and I can.''

"So she's still sticking it out?''

"Yes, it's amazing. Her accent's appalling, of course; but she *is* learning. And I'm learning, too, I suppose.''

"What?''

"Oh, all sorts of things. About being Jewish in Hitler's Germany for instance. And even a bit about Kosher food, which I find I quite like.''

What I did not tell him was that once or twice the English lessons had extended themselves into informal music sessions, with Herr Mandelbaum playing the cello and me playing the piano in some of the simpler pieces by Schubert and Schumann. Why I didn't tell him this I didn't know. Perhaps I rather treasured the experience as a sort of secret compact between the Mandelbaums and myself. Or maybe I thought it would somehow embarrass him as, in fact, it had embarrassed me at first — before I realised that the Mandelbaums not only found solace in the music, but also in having a link with the world outside "Fortress Germany" through my Englishness. And I found it a great pleasure to play their excellent Bechstein upright piano, so perfectly in

31

tune, and so different from our fretwork-fronted wreck in Fogston.

At the mention of Jews and the Third Reich I saw him ponder a moment. Then he said, "I had hoped that the anti-Jewish rubbish would fade away when the Nazis got into power, but it's worse, isn't it?"

I nodded. "Those disgusting glass show-cases advertising *Der Stürmer* make that clear enough. God knows, I'm not carrying a spear for the Jews, but I can't stick the *Stürmer*."

David sighed. "Well, at least we're not Jews. That's something to be thankful for. How's the teaching going? Got any more pupils?"

"Yes, a few. But I'm a bit anxious about the extent to which quite a big proportion of them seem to be learning English as a sort of fire insurance."

"You mean like Frau Mandelbaum?"

"Yes. Though in her case it's fairly clear. She's Jewish and old, so what possible purpose can she have in learning English but to escape?"

"She never says so openly?"

"No, never. And I'm glad. If she did, it would make me a sort of conspirator instead of an instructor. Anyway, it's clear enough, and her husband didn't conceal it, you'll recall. But you must have the same problem."

"I wouldn't quite call it a problem. The Nazis would be glad to see all the Jews leave."

"Yes — empty-handed."

"Ah, they've an explanation for that. They say Jews flooded in and robbed them at the time of inflation when a loaf cost a million Marks, or something. So to rob the Jews before turfing them out on a one-way ticket is seen as only justice."

"Do you believe them?"

He shrugged. "Most of it's just hate and envy. But the inflation did attract nimble-witted people from Central Europe who could smell an opportunity. Some of them were Jews, presumably because Jews move more readily than other people."

"But they're hard-working and clever. Surely the Germans valued that?"

"The hard-working bit, yes; but not the clever bit. You see, the inflation was largely contrived, to get rid of the war debt that the Treaty of Versailles had hung round Germany's neck. Hitler's turned the Treaty of Versailles round on us. He'd be lost without that bloody Treaty; it got him into power when he pledged himself to get rid of it by hook or by crook."

He sat brooding, then said: "The trouble is, Eric, that Hitler promised the Stormtroopers a chance to knock hell out of the Jews when he got into power and, by God, from what I hear he's kept his word. Every township in Germany has its building where they're tortured. Now they're building concentration camps all over the place.''

"Come on, David, let's go out." I put on my raincoat and we left together.

Every time I went into the street it seemed that there were more Nazi flags, emblems and portraits of leading Nazis. Today they were everywhere. Then I remembered that all supporters of the Nazis had been called upon to express approval of the Winterhilfe collection for the poor and needy by showing some Nazi sign. No doubt the leaders of the party had calculated that the sight of Nazi emblems together with signs of Christmas would somehow associate the Party with benevolence and the Christmas spirit.

"How useful," I said, "to have it made clear on every building whether or not it holds Nazi Party supporters. No wonder we can't see for swastikas.''

"Yes, very useful for keeping tabs on people. But it was the referendum confirming Hitler in power that really wrapped it all up. If you didn't vote, your absence from the polling-booth was noted. If you did vote, you received a voting paper bearing a big circle for you to make your mark for a 'yes' vote and a little one for a 'no' vote.

''And if that hint wasn't plain enough for you, well, you had only to take a look at the gang of Nazi thugs all around you. So, if you valued your liberty, and maybe even your life in some cases, you voted 'yes', openly, there and then. One rumour even had it that when you slipped your voting paper into the slot in the top of the ballot box, it fell straight down a chute into a basement where the way you voted was entered against your name.''

"Do you believe that?"

"Who knows what to believe these days? In the New Germany anything's possible.''

"I suppose so. But they'll never believe it at home. I think they know there are some 'Jews not Wanted' signs in Germany, but that's about all.''

"Perhaps they'd rather not know.''

"Perhaps.''

* * *

33

I took the train to Teltow, as usual, and was soon at the Mandelbaum house. On the door, roughly daubed in red paint, was a Jewish star of David and the word "*Jude!*" My heart sank.

If I rang the bell, would anybody dare to answer? Was anybody there to answer? Were visitors forbidden, or under observation? Had the flat been plundered? All these thoughts rushed through my mind as I stood there, one hand half-poised near the bell-push. Than it struck me that, apart from the star of David and the word "*Jude!*", there were no signs of smashing and destruction. I rang the bell. Nothing happened, and I rang it again, and again. No reply. Gaining some moral courage, I stepped back from the doorway and stood in the garden so that anybody in the house peeping out would be able to see and identify me. Then I rang the bell again. And still there was no reply. Cupping my hands round my mouth, I called into the crack of the door in German: "Frau Mandelbaum — it's me!" I was ashamed to find that I lacked courage to shout my name.

After quite some time, I thought I heard a sort of shuffling sound within. I called again: "Frau Mandelbaum — it's me!" Then, as though I had crossed some invisible but vital border, I heard myself shout: "Frau Mandelbaum, it's me, Eric Johnson."

A little later, from the other side of the door, I heard the voice of Frau Mandelbaum ask: "Are you alone?"

"Yes, I'm quite alone." The door suddenly opened; I almost jumped inside, and heard it close and lock behind me.

"*Gott sei Dank*," she said softly, and pointed the way up the stairs. "Go first." I went ahead of her and into the lounge.

To my relief, I saw that everything was in order, exactly as I'd last seen it. She watched me look around the room, my eyes finally coming to rest on her. I marvelled to see that she too looked exactly as she was when I left her the previous day.

"They took him," she said. "I don't know whether he is still at the Gestapo office or already in concentration camp. But I have no doubt that he will finish at the camp, as he did last time." She saw my surprise. "Yes," she continued, "he was in Oranienburg for a month, just before he first made contact with you." And suddenly I realised why he had jumped at the sound of the car stopping outside David's flat.

"He never told me."

"No. He hoped — as I hoped — that it would only happen once." She showed not the least sign of weeping or weakness. "But come. We must get on with our work." The last sentence she had said in English.

"But Frau Mandelbaum . . ." I was still speaking in German,

thinking — foolishly — that it was kinder.

"In English, please, Mr Johnson. In English." She moved towards a chair, then suddenly checked and looked at me. "Unless," she said, "you would like instead not to do?" I sat down and took out of my pocket a text book of English conversation that we had often used.

"I suggest we carry on from the top of page thirty."

She sat down and began to read out of her copy, which had been waiting on a little table beside her chair.

"'Does the King live in Buckingham Palace throughout the year, or does he spend only part of his time in the capital city?'"

"'He spends only part of his time there,'" I heard myself saying. "'Usually he goes at some time in the year to Scotland with the Queen.'" It sounded absurdly unreal — like an extract from a fairy story giving a glimpse of a never-never land of peace and tranquillity. Not in the whole of my life had England struck me in such a light before. Perhaps I was beginning to catch a sight of it as it appeared to countless millions outside its shores. Perhaps the very unreality of some aspects of life in Britain were now a comfort, and not only for the British.

Only when the lesson was over did Frau Mandelbaum lapse again into German. She apologised even then for speaking the language, excusing herself by adding that "unfortunately" it was her native tongue, so was inescapable for her.

She told me that they had previously lived in a much grander house in Berlin, in Dahlem, but had thought it wiser when the Nazis came to power to move to a far more modest house and one in a small township where they hoped the ugly passions of anti-Jewish feelings would be less likely to break out in actual violence. Teltow had seemed particularly suitable because her husband's furniture factory was there. They owned a small string of furniture shops. "After all," she said, "we are work-givers here in Teltow. Surely they can see that?" Then, reflecting a moment, she added: "But I suppose now it is impossible for a Jew to be seen as giving anything — but offence."

"Have you any family?"

"Alas, only a married sister. In Zürich in Switzerland."

"Well, there might be some comfort in that."

She looked out of the window towards the south, towards faraway Switzerland.

"There might. There is some anti-Jewish feeling even in Zürich. But the Swiss are a moderate people. Surely there will be no pogrom there."

"Have you any petrol or paraffin, or anything like that?" I asked, and she looked puzzled.

"I might have, but why?"

"I should like to remove that disfigurement from the front door."

She jumped to her feet. "Oh, you can't do that! No, no. You must on no account do that. Nobody must. If you took such a step it would count as interfering in the internal affairs of Germany and you would be severely punished and no doubt expelled. I am sorry. I much appreciate the kindness of the thought. But it is impossible."

"Then must it stay on indefinitely?"

For the first time she showed hesitation, raising both hands to her head in a gesture of infinite weariness, then quickly lowering them again.

"I don't know. I must be thankful, I suppose, that they have not smashed everything — and can only pray that my poor husband comes back soon and unharmed. I suppose that they did not break the place up because it would have also damaged the flat downstairs — if only by letting the rain go through. It is occupied by a member of Teltow Council. A blessing. A blessing. It was my dear husband's idea to take a flat above the councillor's flat."

I was amazed that anybody in such a situation could find any basis for blessings, but did not say so. All I could see was an old woman in a terribly weak and exposed position who didn't know where her husband had been taken, or even if he would ever come back. I wondered how I could tactfully suggest that she abandon the English lessons, since it seemed obvious that she would not want to continue with them.

"I want you to continue to come and teach me English," she said, almost as though she'd been reading my thoughts. "I think the discipline will help me." Her face clouded. "But you might not want to go on? Perhaps you might — with every justification — see it as unwise, indiscreet, even dangerous."

"No," I lied. "I see it as none of those. If you want to continue, so do I. Indeed, I consider it an honour . . ." I was fumbling for the right words, and could not find them in either German or English.

"I'm most grateful, Herr Johnson. Shall we say the same time, then, tomorrow?"

I had a moment of trepidation on leaving the flat. But there was no group of Brownshirts outside — only the ordinary people of Teltow walking along the pavement, casting uneasy glances at the anti-Jewish signs on the door, and at me. It was impossible to tell from their look whether they approved or disapproved, but I felt it hard to believe that Julius Streicher had many readers in Teltow of his odious anti-Jewish newspaper, full of hideous Jews holding sacrificial knives dripping with the blood of ritually sacrificed Christian babies. All the same, I was glad to get on the train and melt into the anonymity of the crowded carriages.

* * *

I had to decide whether to tell anybody about the events at Teltow. As the train moved towards Berlin I made up my mind. I would tell David Whitaker and nobody else, not even Anna-Maria. David, I felt, had to know, if only because he had introduced me to the Mandelbaums — and because he was my link with the outside world if events turned even uglier.

So I got off the train at the Zoo Station and walked the short distance down the Kurfürstendamm to his flat. Luckily he was at home. We sat close together and I spoke softly. He heard what I had to say in total silence, then offered me a glass of Korn, the cheap, powerful spirit that he knew I rather liked. "I'm sorry, Eric, damned sorry. There are aspects of the New Germany that stink to high heaven." He took a sip. "Mandelbaum hadn't told me that he'd had a spell in concentration camp. But then, I don't suppose he had any good reason for doing so."

"And quite a few for not doing so."

"Yes." He took another sip. "Are you afraid?"

"Yes."

"Quite right. Who wouldn't be. I'd be terrified."

"But you'd carry on with the lessons?"

"I like to think I would."

"Well, I have one very good reason for doing so."

"The money?" He smiled wryly.

"Yes, the money. I only hope to God she can afford it still."

"That's in doubt now. But I think she must be able to. Above all, the Jews are practical. And I do know that the Mandelbaums were well off before . . . before we got the New Germany."

It was doubly ironic that David and I had arranged with Anna-Maria and Helga to have a sort of Christmas party that evening at the big popular Berlin restaurant, Haus Vaterland. I turned this over in my mind as I sat there, twisting the glass. Whatever sort of company would I make on such a day? Yet the event could be postponed only by explaining the reason. "We must stick to our plan for this evening, " I said. "No point in trying to put it off. Nazi Germany won't go away."

David held up his glass in an ironic toast. "Agreed. To the

37

Thousand-year Reich! Though why Adolf should have been so modest in his expectations I can't imagine.''

I rose and moved still nearer to him until I was so close that I could whisper.

"Has it occurred to you that the time might already have arrived when it's no longer wise to say anything rude about the regime in your room or mine?'' He looked shocked at the suggestion of hidden microphones.

"You mean,'' he said, "you think we're so important?''

"I mean they think the Third Reich is so important.'' He reflected on the idea for a moment, then simply nodded and switched on the radio set near to him. Unlike the one in my room, which would receive only local stations, his was powerful enough to pick up signals from stations quite far away and we now talked to a background of bumpy laendler-type music from a Swiss transmitter.

"By the way,'' said David, "talking about frustration reminds me that the Vicar's tea-party is off and I'm asked to convey polite regrets to you on that account. It seems that the Vicar's wife has gone down with the flu and that the party will have to wait till she recovers.''

As soon as it was made clear by this information that there was to be no vicarage tea-party, I perversely wished to attend one. When David had first mentioned it, I'd feared being snubbed or patronised by supercilious English people more socially secure than I was. Now I saw it differently and wished to see if my stay in Berlin had toughened my social skin enough to withstand such a test. But I only said, "Oh, I'm sorry. I was beginning to look forward to it.''

I made a conscious effort to be sociable when we were settled around the table that evening in Haus Vaterland. So too did David, and I listened and watched rather enviously as he rattled out the idiomatic German phrases and even kissed the hands of the two girls. "Oh,'' said Anna-Maria at this, "don't be too German, David. I like you English, not ersatz German. Eh, Helga? Aren't they at their best when they are most English?''

"Definitely,'' said Helga. "As English as rostbiff and Yorksheer pooding. Do you feel like a rostbiff Yorksheer pooding, Eric?'' I grinned easily; it was a pleasant start.

Haus Vaterland was big and cheerful. Those who did not care to dance could eat heartily from an immense menu; or they could drink, or watch the cabaret. We decided right at the start to do everything. Just before I had set out, a letter had arrived for me from England in my mother's careful, clear handwriting. Not having time to read it, I'd thrust it unopened into my pocket. As my hand touched it now, I wondered what my mother would think of our party at Haus Vaterland, assuming she could understand what the place was like, for I'd never even heard of anything like it in England, and certainly not in northern England, where Methodism had so long restrained any hint of excess.

Curious, I thought, that I'd never felt English until I got to Germany.

I picked up my wine glass and toasted Anna-Maria: "To your eyes, to your beautiful, pale blue German eyes," I said. She smiled a delighted smile and David and Helga joined me in the toast, David adding: "And not forgetting the equally beautiful blonde German hair." Then, of course, he had to toast Helga's dark beauty in equally extravagant terms.

This set the tone, and from then on we vied with each other in toasting combinations of personal and national characteristics. One toast given by Anna-Maria was to "Eric's English coolness, and self-control", which I immediately offset by toasting "Things about Anna-Maria that make nonsense of my English coolness and self-control." Then we danced and sang to each other the choruses of the popular musical items that the big band played for dancing. *"Die Liebe"* — "love" — was the theme of them all, and we wanted no other.

The table service was as quick or as slow as we wanted, the waiters taking their cue from the diners without the least sullenness or reluctance and showing pride in giving service that pleased. This was done with a touch of theatricality that was new to me. I suspected that it didn't exist anywhere in England, even at Christmas time; it certainly didn't in Fogston.

And so the evening slipped away, in a sort of timeless quiet delight. None of us drank or ate much, yet we all had as much food and drink as we wanted. Though we spoke German, David and I sometimes spoke a slapstick mixture of German and English, which greatly amused the girls and, truth to tell, amused us too, and not least because we used for it the old familiar "thou" to match the German familiar *"Du"* that was now our way of speaking to each other.

For a long time I'd been anxious about these German formal and familiar styles, being sure that I should never know when it would be right to slip from one to the other. Yet Anna-Maria and I had done this quite unselfconsciously, to my great relief. She was astonished when I explained to her that there were no formal and familiar ways of addressing people in England, but was not surprised to find that it was the formal "you" that was used for both. "Ah," she said, "I should have known. That is so truly English." Obviously, it lined up with some strange stereotype of the English that she had. Maybe she had picked up her notion of England and the English from sources even more unreliable than those that had formed my early impressions of Germany and the Germans.

Was it my imagination or was it a fact that the band seemed to play a little louder and faster as the evening progressed, and the waiters behaved more extravagantly in their gestures and their neat use of delightfully idiomatic phrases of courtesy? Perhaps the gentlemen would care to run an eye over the selection of fish specialities; or possibly they might be pleased to find something a trace more suitable for the occasion among the meat delicatessen? Meanwhile, was it possible that the gracious ladies might like a little iced water, for it was getting hotter, was it not? And iced-water was so refreshing.

At one point David and I found ourselves climbing adjoining brightly plated metal poles topped with garlands of paper flowers near the ceiling. Even while I was straining so hard to make some upward progress I was telling myself that they were ridiculously decadent versions of the greasy pole; but I struggled all the harder and at last, at the very extremity of my strength, managed to pluck a paper flower and slide rapidly down again. Anna-Maria took it as though it had been a sheaf of lilies, touched it to her lips, and put it into the top of her dress, letting its long stem slip down between her breasts.

When, at last, it was all over, there was no thought of our each going immediately home. No, we must have coffee and a drink at David's flat before anything so absurdly ordinary was to be considered. So we took a taxi.

Soon we were waiting for the water in David's coffee device to boil and climb up the glass stem to infuse the coffee. When it did so, to some faintly suggestive comment from David and me, there were little squeals of joy from the girls. His radio was tuned to dance music from England — or so he claimed — and we held the girls and swayed to the rhythm, stopping only to drink the coffee and some brandy.

We persuaded Anna-Maria to telephone home and say that she was staying with Helga. David's flat offered the luxury of two beds — one in the bedroom and one in the lounge that doubled as a divan. The girls had previously made a solemn inspection and decided that there was room on the divan for both of them.

After a lot of talk and laughter, David and I went reluctantly into the bedroom and the girls prepared the divan. I took off my wrist watch and placed it on the polished bedside table near the lamp, using the letter from my mother, still unopened, as a support so that I could see the time during the night simply by touching the switch.

At last the lights were out, including the one showing under the bedroom door. But no sooner was all still than a ghost-like Anna-Maria appeared, dressed presumably only in a slip. "Helga feels a little queasy," she whispered. "Is there some soda-water?"

"Yes," said David, "in the lounge, in the bottom of the cabinet." She went back and made faint searching noises, but returned to say that she couldn't find it. "I'll get it," said David, getting out of bed, and going into the lounge.

"Are you asleep yet, Eric?" said Anna-Maria. I could just see the points of her breasts through the slip. I reached out and gently held her hand. She did not pull it away. I drew her down and into the bed, fearing none of the things I had expected to fear, but only that the thumping of my heart would alarm her more than it alarmed me.

She slipped between the sheets and her body came close to mine.

I thought all the anxieties would be hers, but they proved to be all mine. "Just don't worry, my dear, sweet Englishman," she said. "I shan't." She was so close I could smell the perfume of her breath through the darkness.

I realised that I had both longed for and feared this experience, beside which all my former furtive and hasty fumblings in Fogston were not merely nothing, but actually destructive of any sexual joy. So *this* was consummation: this blending of body and spirit in total happiness that overleapt time and space, country and language, even right and wrong. The night, and Germany and all else sank totally away.

When I awoke, it was almost daylight, and according to my watch, seven o'clock. Anna-Maria woke beside me without so much as a sigh, smiled at me, looked at my watch, then quickly slipped out of bed. She was naked, fair — and truly beautiful.

Realising that her clothes were in the other room, she fumbled briefly in the bed beside me, found her slip and put it on. Then, tapping lightly with the back of her finger-nails on the door panel, she moved into the other room and came back presently with a little bundle of clothes, and began to sort out the items. First she whipped off her slip with a single graceful swirl of her arms. Then she put on her brassiere, gently easing each breast into the waiting cup.

This done, she pulled on her knickers, then the stockings, which were of a type quite new to me, ending just below the knee. Half-dressed in these garments, she looked more female than anything my imagination had previously been able to supply. It seemed almost sacrilege when she put on the full-skirted gown. Then the silver shoes. "Washing and making-up I shall do at work, where I have day clothes in my locker."

Breakfast was a curiously relaxed affair. None of us knew what any of the others normally ate, and there was a slightly comic offering and passing, declining and accepting, of the few simple items on the table.

Soon it was over and, in a flurry of gay little waves and kisses and the click of the door-latch, the girls were gone.

As I was due to give a lesson at Haus Odol at ten, I was in no hurry and went through the washing and shaving routine — using David's equipment — with a sort of studied leisure, hoping that I looked sophisticated and worldly-wise, but suspecting I didn't. I was thankful that David made no direct reference to the events of the night.

I was back in my room before I realised that I still hadn't opened the letter from my mother. I quickly did so.

"Dear Eric," she wrote, "I have some rather sad news for you. Your father is dead. I have had a solicitor's letter, in French, from Monte Carlo. It seems he was there on holiday and died of typhoid fever. He has given me the name and address of a solicitor to see in Fogston who will sort out the legal side of it. But he makes it quite clear that we have no financial expectations. I suppose I'm grateful in a way. Having had nothing from him for so long, I want nothing now. But I'm sorry for you and your brothers' sake — and I don't just mean for the money. It's bad enough not to have a father at home, but it's worse not to have one at all.

"But don't worry about us. Fred's working now, thank goodness — twelve shillings a week. It's not much, but its's twelve shillings more, and a Godsend. Arthur would like to be trying to get a job as well, but he knows I've signed for him to stay at school till he's sixteen, and I'm determined that he'll stay, for I know he'll be grateful later. I could wish we were all together, especially at such a time. But I'm thankful we're all well. All my love, as ever. Mother."

I felt nothing. I could not even remember what my father looked like. I told myself over and over again that it was wrong that I should have no reaction to his death. But there was nothing I could do about it. As a father, he'd never noticed my presence, or that of either of my brothers — except occasionally to grumble about how costly we were to keep. I'd never once seen him kiss my mother, or so much as lay an affectionate finger on her arm. Then he'd simply gone. I pushed the letter into my pocket and set out the things needed for the lesson. As I did so, it occurred to me that my mother had said nothing about how she felt about my father's death, being concerned, apparently, only about its effect on her sons. I felt ashamed.

5

Although I'd heard about the "Continental winter" that affected inland Europe, I wasn't ready for the biting cold of January and February in Berlin. I soon found that I hadn't enough warm clothes and would have liked to ask my mother to knit me a pullover of good thick English wool, but didn't want to trespass on her brief spare time. Anyway, I was afraid the German customs would charge as much import duty as the garment would be worth.

So, after much cogitation, I bought a sort of crude knitted cardigan made of rough-teaseled heather-shade wool. It was hideous, but warm.

On the worst days I was not above packing a few old newspapers inside my shirt, relying on my trouser-belt to keep them from making an embarrassing reappearance. As "Hitler's own paper," the *Voelkischer Beobachter*, carried long reprints of the Leader's inflammatory speeches, I took a sort of facetious pleasure in using a few back issues of this, provided by Haus Odol, to keep me warm.

Frau Mandelbaum kept up the daily two-hour lessons for far longer than I had expected she ever would; then she reluctantly reduced them to one hour a day. Towards the end of February her husband was restored to her as suddenly as he had been removed. When I saw him I thought he looked haggard and cowed, but he insisted that he had not been beaten or tortured — "though they showed very little interest in my health". I could tell from his wife's nervous smile as he said this that she didn't know whether to believe him or not, and the more he made light of it all, the more I felt she mistrusted his reassurances.

He must have apprehended some of her doubts, for he gradually began to drop references to the concentration camp from his conversation as he returned to something more nearly like his normal appearance. Some of this I noticed for myself; more of it she told me when we were alone together.

On my many visits to the house I'd thought that the odious daub on the front door seemed to be fading. Was it possible that the Mandelbaums were occasionally rubbing at it a little under cover of darkness?

It was very unlikely and, anyway, they would never be able to remove it entirely — especially from their memories.

Not very long after her husband came back, Frau Mandelbaum said to me with genuine reluctance, and in English: "Mr Johnson, I would like to let the lessons rest somewhat now, if you please. My husband needs much of my . . ." She groped for the right word.

"Attention?"

"Yes, attention."

"I am sure he does, Frau Mandelbaum," I replied also in English. "I think you have done marvellously well to go on so long. Please don't worry about stopping the lessons. You can always start them again any time. You have my telephone number, or you could write to me."

She smiled a sad, grateful smile and looked for a moment as though she would like to say a great deal more. But, like so many others now, she hesitated even in her own home to say anything that could be considered anti-Nazi if overheard.

While this conversation was taking place, I presumed that her husband was in his bedroom. Now he came into the lounge and she told him, this time in German, what she had just said to me. He listened carefully, then simply shook his head slowly and said to me: "I am sure my wife is as sorry to suspend the lessons as I am. They have helped her in these — these difficult recent times, and both of us are grateful. You have been most welcome here, Herr Johnson, and will be again at any time in the future if we can ever pick up where we now feel we must break off."

They both went down with me to the front door, and opened it so wide that the disfigurement was less obvious. I thought they were genuinely moved as they waved a faint goodbye to me. I know that I was when I waved back to them and walked down the path and through the gate.

Parked about fifty yards further down the road was a drab looking old Opel car that I had seen there before and to which I had attached no importance. As I walked past it now I noticed that one man was sitting in the driving seat and another in the rear. They were in civilian clothing and seemed about thirty years of age. The man on the rear seat wore a black leather coat and was smoking. He had a hard and concentrated look that he turned on me as I walked past, and I was suddenly chilled and fearful. But neither stepped out of the car or gave any sign of specifically watching me. Even so, I was thankful to get into the train without seeing either of them at the station.

The loss of Frau Mandelbaum both as a pupil and as a friend was unfortunate, but I had to admit to myself that the daily journey to

Teltow was time-absorbing for a one-hour lesson and could not be properly reflected in the fee, though I was sure she'd have paid more if I'd asked for it. But I had a card in a stationery-shop window near Chlorodont Platz and had given out a few more to people holding jobs similar to Goldgruber's. With these efforts and some personal recommendation, I now had just about enough pupils, without Frau Mandelbaum, to break even financially so long as nothing unexpected cropped up.

I was spending the evening with Anna-Maria, but had to return some books to David before meeting her. He sympathised over the ending of the lessons at Teltow, but agreed that it was a long way to go to give one-hour lessons. "By the way," he said, "I've a change to report as well. Helga has left her job and gone elsewhere." He spoke in so level a tone that I felt for a moment that he must be almost indifferent about it. Then it struck me that he had been *too* casual. After all, we had been boys together in Fogston, so knew a lot about each other. While we both affected a coolness, even a slight cynicism, towards the opposite sex, each of us knew that this was a mere concealment for the fact that we could offer no firm basis for a happy future to any girl, for we had both been blasted and unmanned by the same economic storm.

But I knew there was no way to discuss or even mention any of this, so said simply: "Well, she did tell you. Which is something."

"Yes," he said, pausing, "she did do that. And I gather that it's part of the job to be at liberty to move to any part of the Reich without notice. They probably have a word of about eight syllables for it."

"Tough, though."

He smiled a little. "Yes, tough. But as the Germans also say: 'Life is real, life is earnest' — especially in the New Germany."

I wanted to ask more, but felt I had to respect his attitude, so kept silent. I must remember that this *was* Hitler Germany where all sorts of things contrary to the provisions of the Treaty of Versailles were manifestly going on, things that would cause echoes in many places.

When I next saw Anna-Maria and mentioned Helga's departure I thought I felt a sudden barrier go up. Yet she treated it lightly. "Yes, she just went — no notice, nothing. She's probably on emergency transfer somewhere. I'll tell you when she rings up from wherever she is, as she's sure to do."

"She didn't even hint she was going?"

"No. Probably hadn't time. Anyway, we've been on different shifts recently, so we haven't seen much of each other. Besides, we're only tiny wheels in a big machine, not even tiny wheels, really . . ."

"Well, just so long as they don't suddenly transfer you . . ."

"Oh, unlikely, I think. Berlin would fall down without me."

"My Berlin would."

"Silly, you shouldn't say such things."

Quite early next day I heard the firm thump of footsteps outside my door and a sharp rap on it. It was too early for Goldgruber to be on a rent round. Anyway, it was not the right day. I was apprehensive — and more so when I opened the door and saw standing there a tall young man in SS officer's uniform. On seeing me he bowed slightly, from the hips. There was no smile and no heel-click, but I'd been in Germany long enough to know that there would have been no bow, however slight, if there was anything to fear — and there would have been two of them, one to watch the other.

"Herr Yonson?"

"*Ja*."

"You teach English?" He spoke in German.

"Yes I do," I replied in the same tongue.

"Are you at liberty to teach me?"

"I should think so. Please come in." I stood aside and he walked past me to stand just inside the room. Rather to my surprise, he took off his uniform cap and tucked it under his arm with a single swift movement. Yet it was only later that I was able to get him to sit down, and when he did so, I realised that it was the first time I'd ever seen anybody sit down to attention.

It was impossible not to notice that he was a superb being. Even his hands were a perfect balance between beauty and strength and were spotlessly clean and manicured. Yet there was not a hint of homosexuality about him.

We made our way through the formalities of terms, where the instruction should take place, and so on, in a very short time. When I came to write down his name and particulars it emerged that he was Hermann von Steinfels. No sooner had he spoken the name than I said spontaneously: "Ah, I once nearly taught what I take to be a relative of yours — Fräulein Elfrida von Steinfels."

"Ours and the Berlin branch do not speak," he said icily, adding that he was resident in barracks, and was working to a tight schedule. "I shall require to know basic English in not more than three months," he said. "So I shall come as often as is suitable for that purpose, so far as my duties and your convenience allow."

I admired the precision, but couldn't help feeling that he talked a bit like a machine — a very good machine, in perfect repair. Well over six feet tall, he might have been Anna-Maria's brother, for he was fair-haired and had the same pale clear-blue eyes. He was, I supposed, Prussian Aryan Nazi man made manifest, and I had the distinct

46

impression that he felt he had a vocation for the role. Still, I'd no reason to think he'd bring his Nazi fervour into English lessons. In any case, I had too few pupils for luxuries of choice. So it was arranged for him to come for five hours' instruction per week "till further notice and so far as my duties allow." As he moved towards the door to go, he said: "I would like to concentrate the lessons on geographical matters, asking directions, giving orders, and that sort of thing. I assume you can do that?"

"Certainly, though I must warn you that I never was much good at geography."

"You will assuredly know enough for my purpose." He raised his right arm sharply from the elbow, the hand open. "Heil Hitler!" he barked.

I was astonished. I'd lost count of the number of times I'd seen Party members in newsreels giving the full-arm Nazi salute and bawling "Heil!" but I hadn't previously come across this domestic version with its ultimately absurd words. It seemed more silly than sinister and must surely be reserved for the most besotted Nazis.

"*Aufwiedersehen*, Herr Baron," I replied, neither knowing nor caring if he expected me to match his ridiculous farewell. But his face told me nothing.

When he'd gone, I sat down and tried to work out what he'd meant by his "geographical" reference, but couldn't make any sense of it. I was not impressed by his being a baron; Germany had no shortage of barons. But I did wonder how he had selected me for a teacher.

At the very first lesson, next day, the "geographical" problem was resolved. He wished to be familiar with British place-names in English. He was both intrigued and a little dashed to find that Edinburgh and Scarborough were not pronounced at all as he had expected. When I read them out as he pointed to them on a map he said: "*Ach, wie dumm*!" — "Oh, how stupid!" Then he apologised rather stiffly, as though he was doing it for the benefit of his soul, or his social place — for anything, in fact, but my feelings. This amused rather than annoyed me. The baron was going to be an interesting pupil.

Within a week his intention was crystal-clear. He wanted the facility with geographical terms in English for military reasons, and soon had me coaching him in such phrases as "Advance carefully up this hill, using the natural cover" despite the fact that the examples were well ahead of his stage of learning. But he was prepared to learn by rote and wait for understanding to come later, so we pressed on. It was funny, really, and I was tempted to teach him something absurd, but resisted this.

Happily, he did not persist with his "*Heil Hitler*" farewell salute, presumably having felt it necessary to use it on his first visit to establish his Nazi credentials. But the substitution of a stiff little bow and a snapped-out "*Aufwiedersehen!*" was only a moderate relaxation. In everything else he stayed quite formal and rather frighteningly systematic.

At his suggestion, we sat at opposite sides of the table, each with a piece of writing-paper laid on a large sheet of white blotting-paper that nearly covered the table top. He would say something in German, and simultaneously write it down in red ink on his piece of paper, giving it a number. I would provide the English version, which I wrote down in black ink, using the same number. When we reached the foot of the page, we exchanged papers and he started at the top, first reading out the English twice, and then trying to speak the phrase without looking at the paper though taking occasional promptings from me. For this rigmarole, which I had privately to admit worked well, he had provided all the necessary equipment including two small bottles of ink and steel-nibbed pens to match, one with a red stem and the other with a black one. Perhaps it was coincidence that, together with the paper, these were the three colours of the Nazi flag, now in effect the German flag. Perhaps not.

Before long I found myself taking a perverse pleasure in his company. He was the first "holy" Nazi I had met at close quarters, and the sheer simplicity of his approach to life was fascinating. For every problem in personal and national life there was an answer, and doubtless a few in reserve. The Jews were "vermin", and he did not waste sympathy — or much powder and shot — on vermin. The economic problems of Germany, and the world, were caused by wrong teaching, by Jews. Remove the Jews and the teaching and the problems would almost solve themselves, given a small push here and there from "clear-thinking, creative Aryans freed from their previous shackles and using constructive capital where Jews use parasitic capital."

Daft-simple as all this was, it was far too complex to be put into usable English for him, though he had a little fundamental knowledge of the language remaining from his school days. So he tended to rattle it out in German, asking only for selected gems to be translated. Then, when he was given the English version, he would slowly repeat it, like a padre intoning a prayer. So I found myself carefully working out politico-military mumbo jumbo that would not otherwise have engaged my attention.

Fortunately, he rarely sought my opinion on anything. He *knew*; I was merely the instrument of his knowledge. This I also found rather priest-like.

All the time, the military phrases kept cropping up, even more frequently than the Nazi gibberish, and had to be put into the English of military command. Anybody less naturally gifted for this than I was would have been hard to find, for my military knowledge was virtually nil. I had to dredge my memory for old soldiers' tales that included commands, and so make out as best I could. Quite early in our association he had discovered that there was no obligatory military service in Britain and I'd expected this to trigger off a certain amount of open scorn. But it didn't; it merely confirmed his already poor opinion of British decadence and low morale of all kinds. "England," he said — and it was always England — never Britain — "I think is a military joke."

"Do you want me to translate that into German?" I asked, showing no trace of emotion.

He permitted himself a small smile. "Not necessary. Not necessary."

If he had been more politically convincing he would have been more offensive — and unteachable. But he was as fascinating as a masterly clockwork doll, and he unwittingly taught me quite a lot about Nazi psychology.

He even asked me to put into English the slogan that appeared in massive letters on posters at sites where Hitler Youth activities took place. This was, "*Wir Sind Geboren für Deutschland zu Sterben*" — "We Are Born to Die for Germany." He found this truly inspiring, so much so, in fact, that he took it for granted that I also found it full of noble sentiment. Privately, I wondered if he would be faintly irritated to learn that the English translation was neater and briefer, as I'd often noticed translations of German into English were. But he was incapable of letting such a thought cross his mind.

Day after day, week after week, we gnawed our bilingual way across the map of Europe, always stopping for a particularly long spell at the Polish Corridor that cut Germany in two and ended at the North Sea in the ultra-German Danzig enclave. The Corridor was so deep an affront to the Baron that he could hardly bear to let the words "Polish Corridor" in either German or English pass his lips. Sometimes his indignation spurred him into working out other names for it, such as "the territory that criminally bisects Germany" or "that stolen part of present-day Poland that is really Germany." Far from apologising for these excursions into abuse, he merely explained them by saying that this "criminal absurdity" would shortly be redressed and the maps redrawn showing Germany in full possession of her historic inheritance. The German Army could "stamp through the so-called Polish Corridor as easily as I walk across the road." I feared precisely this, but gave no hint of any such thought.

Much to my amazement, one of my other pupils told me around this time that "certain unruly elements" of the SS were held in concentration camps. This information came as a great surprise to me, for I had thought the camps were only for Jews, Communists, active Socialists, certain churchmen, and a few non-denominational people who stood in the way of the Party. That some members of the SS could be in them — as prisoners — suggested a massive struggle behind the scenes.

I had confirmation of this as time went on and spring turned into early summer. Goldgruber said to me one day that before long leading Stormtroopers would take over "top positions" in the *Reichswehr*, the German Army. He did not tell me to inform me, but to boast. I knew that the *Reichswehr* was the last bastion not thoroughly penetrated by the Party and I expected it to prove even more difficult to penetrate than other key parts of the German Establishment had been. I felt, too, that the contempt the traditional Army leaders had for Hitler and his supporters would at least ensure a long struggle before any surrender took place. "You mark my words," said Goldgruber, ramming my rent money into his breeches pocket and pushing out his fleshy chest: "our *Sturm Abteilung* will shortly take its rightful place at the highest levels of *all* the important departments of the Reich. Most of the work needed to clean out the rotten elements in Germany has been done by us Storm Troops. And we are prepared to do the rest." And he banged off down the corridor, making the floor tremble as he went.

Although the tenants of Haus Odol tried to pretend that Goldgruber was really only a joke in very poor taste, we knew otherwise. Shortly after the takeover of power the previous year, I was told, two occupants of the best apartments in the house, on the ground floor, had been turned out by him without notice and offered violence when they protested. It seemed they were Jews. Even during my stay in the house, at least two other tenants were evicted who were not known to be Jewish or even partly so, but had Jewish friends or relatives. And these were tenants in the most modest rooms in the house, on the third floor. I knew they had gone because Goldgruber opened doors and windows and made a great fuss about "thoroughly cleaning" the rooms in question. He did not actually use the word "disinfecting" — that might have alarmed remaining tenants — but he left no doubt in anybody's mind that he was carrying out something equivalent.

Whether this struck the other tenants as it struck me, I didn't know, for it was unwise now to compare notes too closely on anything that touched Nazism. It was there, visibly growing in strength, and you endured it as best you could — or, like Goldgruber and von Steinfels, you rejoiced in it. I wasn't sure that Goldgruber was making an excessive fuss about the cleaning of the rooms in question, for I had to admit that he did keep the whole place very clean. But in this he was not exceptional. Germany — anyway, Berlin — was a very clean place, physically.

6

It was in Berlin — from Anna-Maria — that I'd first heard June described as "the month of roses", but as this June of 1934 progressed nobody seemed to be thinking of roses. The politics — and the weather — grew hotter and hotter. I knew that no thunderstorm was likely to cool the weather, and no release of political tension was in sight. Tempers got shorter, and even a political half-wit could feel the rivalry in the air. But the fight was no longer between the Nazis and the Communists. This time, it seemed to be within the Nazi Party itself.

I never encountered a mention of this in the press or on the radio, but everybody had some titbit of gossip about it except, of course, the po-faced Party purists. Although the newspapers were propaganda sheets, they had to print *some* news, and what they selected gave a hint of what they'd rejected. So I grew skilled at reading official denials in reverse and reading between the lines, along with most Berliners. And I developed a knack of interpreting the nods and winks of my bolder pupils.

Every time I bought a loaf or a stamp there were more Nazi uniforms on the streets, and more men — older men — wearing swastika lapel badges on ordinary suits. The Nazi creed must be sinking deeper into the population, I felt. A year ago, when I'd first arrived in Berlin, the Nazis were progressively closing down every child and youth organisation that wasn't putting out the Party line. Now they were in total control of everything that touched the young, who behaved as though they found it all a great adventure.

As I looked at my diary to make sure I had a lesson booked, I remembered that two days ago Goldgruber was stamping around the house in undisguised fury — and civilian clothes. It seemed that the entire mob of Stormtroopers, now variously estimated at two million to four million, had been given leave for the whole of July, officially because the Nazi Party was now so solidly in power that "the most faithful friends of all that is best in the New Germany are entitled in honour to a good rest." "Who the devil wants a rest?" he had demanded of anybody who would listen, "when there is still so much to be done. I certainly don't." Then he added hastily: "But I shall obey orders, of course. Orders are orders." While I looked sympathetic, I was thinking what a nice change it would be to see him in ordinary clothes for a whole month.

When the Baron arrived for his lesson, the bits of the political jigsaw began to fall into place, for the first thing he asked me when we resumed exercises was the English for "Arrest these men, they are trouble-makers." He repeated the phrase over and over again in English, and as he did so I felt he was unwittingly bringing into the lesson things that had recently preoccupied him in the SS. To the end of the lesson I fed him small phrases calculated to reveal more, and so gained a little further insight into his mind and his SS background.

I would have been thankful to put the Nazis and everything connected with them out of my mind for a while, but the moment the Baron appeared for his next lesson he made it clear that his fascination with every facet of Nazidom was as strong as ever.

"How do you say '*Sturm Abteilung*' in English?"

Surely not the bloody Brownshirts again? But he was serious, and I had to ponder.

"Storm Troops," I said.

"And SS? Which means *Schutz Staffel*, as you doubtless know."

But I didn't know the English, and had to consult a dictionary, which gave only a literal translation of each word. I hoped he wouldn't move on to Gestapo.

"SS means Security Section," I said.

"Ah, yes. I like that. It has the same initials. At which he repeated, over and over: "Security Section, Security Section . . ."

But he went through the entire rigmarole, including "Gestapo", which I had to translate as "Secret State Police", assuring him that this was not a biased but a literal translation of "*Geheime Staats Polizei*", which abbreviated into "Gestapo."

Next came "unauthorised departure from official orders," "disobedience of orders," "failure to conform to higher commands within the Army regulations" and "treason". I gathered from remarks on the way that the penalty for several of these, including of course the last one, was now death — even in peace-time. He wanted more Army expressions translated that were specifically SS expressions, and I wondered if he knew where the German Army stopped and the SS started; I certainly didn't. But I did know that Roehm, head of the Brownshirts, had visions of himself as Minister for War, and thereby in command of the Reichswehr together with all other German military power.

As the month of June proceeded, we laboriously did the round of these more-or-less fixed phrases. Then we would have a few days back on geographical phrases, though with military overtones, before we went back to the SS and the SA, with the Baron's contempt for the brown-shirted SA Storm Troops never disguised or abated.

Like many others in Germany, I suspected that the SS had been established above all to control the Brownshirts if it ever came to a showdown, and that one day, when the time was ripe, Hitler would make this clear. The Baron's impatience with the rather unclear status of the SS underlined this for me.

* * *

Nearer the month-end I found myself almost looking forward to some sort of a punch-up between the rival bodies, if they really were rival bodies. I was confused now about everything except the reality of the inner power struggle.

The occasional letter or bundle of newspapers from England seemed like a missive from Mars. I didn't expect the *Fogston Newt* to take much account of Germany, for that wasn't its function. But I certainly did expect more than rare down-page paragraphs about German events in copies of the national press I had from home now and again. And even these were strange. They reported Germany as though it was some curious never-never land that could in no conceivable circumstances ever have any serious impact on Britain. The liberal papers were irritated, even angry sometimes, at the total loss of personal liberty in Germany and the disappearance of both free speech and a free press. But they tended to show their objections in petulant phrases of the sort one would use about a person who had broken the rules of a good club. Meanwhile, the conservative press didn't trouble to hide its hope that Hitler would prove to be a useful bulwark against both Communism and Socialism. The popular newspapers I saw gave twenty times as much space to the time-killing japes of wealthy young socialites as they did to the whole of events in Germany. I found myself reading only the headlines and then turning back, with no enthusiasm, but with some sense of reality, to the wretched German press.

Three days before the month-end I had a letter with a familiar-looking handwriting on the cover. The stout envelope felt empty, but there was one of the Baron's visiting-cards inside. On the back he had written: ''Regret must suspend studies for a few days'' followed by the unintelligible squiggle that all Germans seemed to use for a signature.

Perhaps I did him an injustice, but I couldn't help feeling that he'd sent me the note more out of pride in his weird "correctness" than good manners and thought for me. Anyway, there was a much more material consideration. I took out my wallet and mentally subtracted the amount of the rent. I should just manage.

On Saturday, the last day of June, I woke in a sweat. But it was a sweat of heat, not of fear. The day was obviously going to be a blisterer.

I threw back the top sheet — I'd discarded the other bed coverings during the night — and switched on the radio. I was just in time for the weather forecast.

It was exactly what I expected: the day would be very hot, with clear skies and very little wind. Towards evening the temperature would fall "somewhat", and so on.

Lying there naked on top of the bed, I concentrated not on the message, but the manner of its delivery. The announcer was engaging to a ridiculous degree, as usual. I fumbled around in my drowsy mind for a word that would suitably describe his style. Avuncular? Paternal? Obsequious? Sugary? Hm, maybe something of them all; but none quite hit it. Ah, yes — unctuous. That was it. He was unctuous. And how, I went on to say to myself, do you say that in German? No idea. Ah, well, it was much too hot to think and, anyway, I didn't need to say it in German. Sod the Germans, all of them. And sod their rotten country. And above all, sod Haus Odol — Haus Odious would be a better name.

I looked carefully around the narrow limits of my room. Yes, that was the right phrase for it: narrow limits. A cliché, no doubt; but my whole bloody life was a cliché. What was I doing in Berlin, anyway? With all your struggling, I told myself, you haven't a spare Mark to scratch your arse with, as your Fogston friends would no doubt be quick to say if they knew your circumstances. Well, I would take pains that they never got the chance.

As I stood up I remembered the tensions in Germany, and, as a sort of gesture to public as opposed to personal life, looked out of the window. Would one pack of Nazi wolves fly at the throats of another pack with slightly different markings? I hoped so. Then honest men might come into their own.

But the nearest thing to strife in the streets was two dogs, both on leads held firmly by their owners, sniffing at each other. The larger dog growled and pawed the air. Its owner pulled a little more firmly on the lead and the dog swung round and dropped on to four legs. It saw a tree conveniently close and disdainfully sprayed it.

I turned back and began to wash my hands and face. Plenty of time for some breakfast and to stroll along to the Zoo station of the

Stadtbahn to meet Anna-Maria. Then, no doubt, we would go into the Tiergarten.

One of the nicer things about Berlin, I thought as I sorted out my clothes, was that the air was so clean that clothes stayed clean far longer than they did in Fogston. Strange, how I hadn't realised this until one day one of my pupils, when I had asked him to describe his idea of a typical Englishman, had said: "Well, first of all he is wearing a dirty raincoat . . ." My own formerly dirty raincoat was immediately behind him, hanging on the door. I had had it "chemically cleaned", as they said in Germany, on realising how out of place it looked. Now it was German-clean. Perhaps I would take it for us to sit on in the Tiergarten. Perhaps not. It was so hot and dry that there would be no need for it.

I set off in good time, for hurry was out of the question in such heat. Quite often we met in the Memorial Church but hadn't made it our rendezvous today for some reason I'd forgotten.

The first time I'd suggested meeting in the church, Anna-Maria was startled, if not shocked. She knew I was no more religious than she was, and I had to explain that I rather liked that pool of peace at the very heart of Berlin. A further point was that whoever got there first could sit down. More than once she had come across me there, not with my head bent and dozing in an attitude that might have been usefully mistaken for prayer, but staring at the ceiling mosaics of the kings and queens of Germany. These were carried out in such realistic detail that they looked like giant-sized coloured photographs. More to the point, for me anyway, was that they looked ludicrously like our own royalty, which was not surprising when one considered how many ancestors they had in common.

When I reached the telephone room at the Zoo station, there she was, just arriving, and wearing a cotton dress with a red-rose motif. From one wrist hung a small blue patent-leather case that served both as handbag and food-bag. I simply squeezed her free hand and said: "*Entzückend*!" If this had been England, and she English, I doubted if I would have said: "Bewitching!" But this was not England.

"Ah," she said, "quite the English gentleman!" But she spoke in German, only the word "gentleman" being in English because there was no German for it.

"Your English is marvellous today, Anna-Maria."

Her total ignorance of English was often a joke between us. She always said that speaking correct German was quite difficult enough for her, but I suspected she thought I had quite enough teaching of English to do already without adding a non-paying pupil.

We began to saunter off in the direction of the Tiergarten as she chattered away about her mother's attitude to housework and how important her mother thought it was for young girls to know how to do it. "Not my views at all," she said. "Anybody can do housework, but not many people are good at office work, which has to be learned." As she spoke, I realised how rarely she ever talked about her home or her work, and that I hardly knew anything about either. If it hadn't been for her young man in East Prussia, I'd probably have made an effort to get to know more about both. As it was, I couldn't seek to know more than she cared to tell me.

Although most people worked on Saturday morning, many did not, and they all seemed to have decided that the green shade of the Tiergarten was quite the best thing to seek out. So we soon found ourselves gently moving in that direction amidst a scattered crowd.

But once in the great green area, the crowd was quickly swallowed up. We went deeper and deeper into the trees and eventually settled down on the bank of a canal-like stream in the shade of a mature oak. Near us was a small barge piled high with hay. A man on the bank was passing more hay in great forkfuls to another on top of the load.

"Surprising they make hay in the Tiergarten, not to mention using a barge for a hay-cart," I said.

"But it's quite logical. If they didn't make hay it would be wasted. And one man can pull twice as much on a barge as a horse can pull on a cart. And they can pile it high because the water's as flat as a mirror."

It was the perfectly logical explanation of perfectly logical, perfectly German, conduct.

"But, of course, It's very German. I'll bet, too, that they have double-entry municipal book-keeping for it, and know to a pfennig what it's worth."

"Why not?" She was getting used to my little digs at German efficiency in unexpected places.

We ate the sandwiches, hard-boiled eggs and fruit that Anna-Maria had brought with her, and then wandered off into the woodland to an open-air café, built in the form of a peasant-style house with large balconies, where we drank pale, ice-cold Berlin beer "with a shot". Anna-Maria assured me that Berlin beer with a dash of raspberry juice was a long-standing local custom. The time passed imperceptibly away.

How far we sauntered among the trees I neither knew nor cared, though I was conscious that the green area was so big that the city of Berlin seemed to have disappeared completely.

We had unconsciously walked in a circle, for we came across the hay-barge again. As it was late in the day, the two men must be working overtime, I thought. But now, after a final patting and trimming of the load and making sure that the mooring-rope was secure, they shouldered their hay-forks and walked away. I had noticed that when the man on the load slid down he had used a rope to steady his descent, later concealing it under the hay. Then he had pushed the barge out into the middle of the canal, where its mooring-rope held it.

"Do you fancy a sail?" I said to Anna-Maria.

She thought the idea "very irregular". But we lay on the bank at the point where the barge was moored and I slowly pulled it in. There were few other people about by now and finally, when nobody was near, I uncovered the rope under the hay. After a momentary hesitation, Anna-Maria scrambled up the load, giving an enticing display of bare thighs and tiny knickers, before disappearing into the centre of the hay-pile. I quickly followed her. Soon the barge drifted out to the full extent of its mooring-rope again and ceased to rock. The evening sun shone brightly on us in our nest of hay, but we were completely private.

She wore virtually no clothes apart from the rose-speckled dress but was soon too hot even so and it was not difficult to persuade her to take everything off. I did the same. German-fashion, she had not removed the hair under her arms, and it was almost as fair as the hair on her head. So, too, was the hair on her pubis. The sun seemed to shine right through her breasts.

I caressed her body for a long time before we made love and the light had almost gone by the time I hauled on the mooring-rope, pulled the barge into the bank, and helped her down.

As I walked out of Zoo station I heard a distant clock chime midnight. Only then did I remember Berlin and Germany. So June was ended and the Nazi thugs had not flown at each other's throats after all. And June *had* been a month of roses for me and for Anna-Maria.

Next morning, as usual, I switched on the radio to hear the news while I shaved. The bulletin droned on through the normal collection of Nazi-favourable items of dubious news value. Then, without in any way modifying his oily tone, the announcer went on to say that here was a special announcement: The previous day there had been some minor disorders. General Goering stated that some small unruly elements in the SA had attempted to extend their operations beyond their proper sphere of duties and had been "dealt with" by the police, helped by a few personnel from the SS. The whole event was quickly over and now everything was back to normal. That was the end of the news. Light music would follow.

A few more driblets of information came out with the next bulletin. It had been necessary to "use some force" and there had been a few casualties among the Storm Troops. The chief centre of events had been Berlin, but there had been minor echoes in other parts of the Reich. In Munich there had also been "a few casualties". Order had been quickly restored throughout the Reich.

Towards noon I caught sight of Goldgruber on the stairs, in civilian clothes. He was positively grey, and said nothing, not even "Good day".

At lunchtime I was planning to have a frugal meal in my room, going through the entire routine of money and fuel saving down to the last detail of cooking a sausage in the kettle in residual heat. Although this was not strictly necessary, yet I often did it from habit.

But when twelve-thirty came I abandoned my plan and decided to walk round to David Whitaker's. There was no question of telephoning him. One simply didn't risk the telephone now for anything but routine. And I didn't even ring him to make sure that he would be in. To have done so would have obliterated what was left of my little exercise in economy and, anyway, I wanted to walk in the streets to see if I could pick up any clue there as to what was afoot.

When I reached the flat, having seen nothing unusual on the way, I paused at the door and listened carefully. If there was a murmur of voices it would mean he was giving a lesson and I would wait in the garden till it was over, though he didn't usually teach on Sunday.

As I could hear a slight buzz of talk, I went and sat down on the flags of the path in the shadow of the building. Even so, it was very hot and I slipped off my jacket. About ten minutes later a middle-aged man carrying a briefcase came out of David's flat, gave me a hard look — for Berliners did not normally relax to the extent of sitting on garden paths — and walked on.

When David saw me he switched on the radio and we stood silent a while until it warmed up and began to send out some sugary "*Unterhaltungsmusik*". "Well," I said, "what do you know? Has the balloon gone up?"

"There's been trouble, that's certain. But I haven't any information apart from the crap we've both heard on this thing." He nodded towards the radio. "How about you?"

"I know nothing, but suspect a lot."

"Your Baron ought to know something."

"He talks about nothing but orders — I mean military orders, such as 'Run up this cliff,' 'Keep off the skyline' and that sort of thing."

We spent a little more time putting together tiny bits of information, but made no useful progress, so agreed to keep in touch. He offered me some food but I refused it and made my way back.

Greatly to my surprise, I found the Baron there, waiting for me outside my room. He looked tired and drawn, but managed his usual bow. "Do I disturb you?" he asked.

"Not at all." I opened the door with my key and motioned to him to enter. He stepped inside.

"Are you free?" he went on. I nodded. He swept off his uniform cap and actually dropped it on the table. Then, without invitation, he suddenly sat down, saying: "*Gott sei Dank*."

Quite apart from the fact that members of the SS were supposed to be totally free from "religious superstition", to hear so unrelenting a person as the Baron give thanks to God was very strange, and in sharp contrast with the occasion when I had last heard the phrase, from Frau Mandelbaum. Clearly he was greatly upset.

"Did you want a lesson now?" He looked up, almost unhearing, as though his mind was elsewhere.

"A lesson?"

"Yes. I can give you till three — that's fifty minutes." In fact, I was likely to be able to give him longer, for my pupil due at three was not well and might not come.

"Oh, yes, I do. I've been up all night." He looked around the room, seeking something, but evidently not finding it. "You don't happen — I know it's a great liberty — to have something to drink?"

"As a matter of fact I do. You're welcome."

At Christmas Anna-Maria had given me a bottle of Danziger Goldwasser, an exotic spirit in which tiny fragments of gold leaf floated around, folding and unfolding, every time the bottle was touched. Most of it remained. I brought out the bottle and a tumbler. "Help yourself."

He poured half a tumbler — far more than a normal measure, but I knew that he needed it.

I couldn't imagine why, under such stress, he had chosen to have a lesson at all. Perhaps it was the totally innocuous nature of the exercise that attracted him. It was impossible to tell. I got out the two bottles of ink and the rest of our usual equipment for the lesson.

If I'd expected a departure from our usual style of a semi-military stroll through common phrases of command, I was mistaken. We went over phrases that we had used many times before, the Baron carefully writing them down and later repeating them with reasonable success. Then he looked at the bottle of spirits again, and I waved an inviting hand. He poured a second drink hardly smaller than the first, and drank it no less quickly.

I'd heard somewhere that part of the training of regular officers in the *Reichswehr* was in drinking, and that they had to drink a specified amount of alcohol while sitting on a straight-backed chair without its

60

notably affecting them. Perhaps they did something similar in the SS, though this seemed unlikely in a corps that was supposed to hold physical fitness and Aryan purity in far greater esteem than social pretensions. Yet the Baron showed no signs of intoxication.

Eventually his eye fell on the label of the bottle. "Danzig," he said. "Danzig." The word seemed to touch a trigger in his mind. "Danzig," he went on, "the most significant place in the world."

All I knew about it was that it was a wholly German city surrounded by the Polish Corridor and the sea.

He was speaking in German, and immediately asked for it to be put into English. As he wrote down the translation, I thought I saw some hesitation in his hand, but a quick glance at the handwriting showed no roughness. Certainly he was writing much more slowly than usual. The last item was numbered 5. As he penned the figure, he said: "That is absurd. Obviously it should be number one." Pedantically, I translated this into English, but he waved a slightly irritated hand. "No, that was not part of the lesson. Just a comment. But an important one."

He took up his pen again, ran a line through the last entry on the paper, and then laboriously rewrote it at the head, making it number one. Then he crossed out the previous first entry in that position and rewrote it as item five before surveying the paper as a whole. Now his sense of neatness was offended. "I shall start again," he said, and promptly did, with a new sheet of paper.

Time was going and he was not using it to much advantage. Still, that was his privilege. I watched without interest as he reconstructed the sheet. I knew it was his habit to file all the sheets and use them for revision. This was probably part of the reason why he didn't want to include a botched sheet.

He laboured on, getting slower all the time as the handwriting got slightly larger. Reaching the end of item five, he laid down his pen. "There," he said, like a child, "I've done it." Then he noticed that he had not put a full stop after the final entry, so reached to dip the pen into the bottle of ink again. The nib caught the edge of the neck and the bottle tipped over, spilling the red ink across the fingers of his right hand, his work, and the blotting-paper. He jumped to his feet and held his dripping hand so that a few red drops fell on to the blotting-paper where I noticed that the large ink-stain was heart-shaped.

"Oh, my God," he said, quite softly. "Oh, my God." His face was totally colourless.

Not a speck of ink had touched his uniform so far as I could tell, and the whole mess was neatly contained by the piece of writing-paper and the blotting-paper, except for the ink that still dripped from his hand.

"Don't worry," I said. "No harm done — apart from spoiling your sheet. Use the wash-basin." I pointed to the hand-basin in the corner.

He dabbed his finger-tips on the blotting-paper. His hand was now shaking, and he seemed to abandon any attempt to control the trembling. Then he crossed to the wash-basin and most carefully washed both hands, spending a long time with nail brush and soap scrubbing at his right hand. He came back to the table and sat down. For the first time his back drooped a little.

I'd replaced the stained papers and there was just enough red ink in the bottle when I turned it upright for us to carry on as before. The Baron laid his right hand on the white blotting-paper and we could both see that there was still a thin line of red ink under the nails of three fingers, including the index finger. "I must tell you," he said slowly, "what has happened." His voice had risen a whole tone.

Now I was really nervous. "There's no need; I quite understand that you have your duties to perform and that they can't always be pleasant."

"No," he went on, "I must tell you." He leapt up. "I must tell somebody. We shot them in droves."

"I assure you that you don't need to tell me. I understand. I can imagine what you had to do." I was not afraid of hearing, but of having the knowledge.

He had a wild look and the words began to burst from him. "Against the barrack wall at Lichterfelde Cadet School. In droves. All night. And the same thing was happening elsewhere in the Reich at the same time. In Munich the leader of the SA, Roehm, was arrested, put in prison, and given a pistol to shoot himself, but refused. So he was shot as well, today. Some of the Storm Troop leaders thought that we who arrested them had risen against Hitler and the Party. Some of them screamed 'Heil Hitler!' as we blasted them down.

"The important ones — such as the SA generals — we shot singly. The others in lines, their eyes unbandaged and staring straight down the barrels of the rifles of our firing-squads into the eyes of their fellow Germans. We used a searchlight pointed at the opposite wall to bounce back the light. It was like daylight — lighter. And the shooting was like target practice, except that it was impossible to miss. We ordered the men in the firing squads to fire at their hearts, and the bullets smashed right through them and into the wall behind them, cutting holes and channels into the surface, then filling and refilling the holes and channels with bone, blood and the dark flesh of hearts.

"When it was all over, our own Fire Brigade detachment hosed down the wall and the parade ground with water, and the gullies choked with human debris and blood. Then the bodies were immediately sent to be cremated, using every crematorium in Berlin for the purpose. The ashes are to be scattered on the parade ground so that we stamp on them as we drill. Those are the precise terms of *Hitler's* written orders.'' He almost spat the words.

He suddenly flopped back on to the chair. ''I have told you because I could not bear to carry the burden alone.''

I was quite terrified. At last, after a long pause, I said in almost incoherent German: ''I didn't really hear what you said — didn't understand it all, that is. My German is very faulty. I don't understand lots of things.'' But I convinced neither of us.

The Baron rose and made a visible effort at self-control, straightening. He opened the door, then turned in the doorway and seemed to look past me, or through me. ''Thank you,'' he said, then walked out, as erect and elegant as ever.

7

The speed and savagery of the events of the last forty-eight hours were such that I hardly knew what day or date it was, but went through my routine as well as I was able, with only part of my mind working. I was oppressively conscious that I could share knowledge of the Baron's terrible confession with nobody and would have to behave as though I had never heard of it.

I was particularly sorry that this put up a barrier between David Whitaker and me; I had few enough friends to be able to dilute friendship. I'd arranged to go round to David's flat later that day so that we could listen to Hitler's explanation on the radio of the events of June 30. If this had promised to be a routine Hitler speech we would not have treated it with such forethought, but we both felt that the clash with the SA was a watershed.

As the day went on, I tried to think of a few items of normality that I could mention to David, but could not bring any to mind that didn't sound too trivial to recall and this made me realise how abnormal daily life in Germany had become.

I noticed, as I turned into Meinecke Strasse, that the number of people on the streets had visibly fallen during the twenty minutes or so that it had taken me to walk from Haus Odol. Evidently we were not alone in our interest.

We'd expected the usual highly emotional tirade, but as soon as Hitler began it was clear that he had sensed a need for something more measured. Starting softly and in a low emotional key, he sketched a more or less historical outline of the way the Nazi hierarchy had been built up so that it could, at all times and in every possible way, best serve Germany. This was by relentlessly pursuing its ennoblng purpose of subjugating everything to a total rebuilding and revitalisation of the country while saving it from the horrors of rapacious Communism which, as everybody now knew, had come very close to enslaving the country for the benefit of an alien power.

The delivery was fluent and efficient, as usual, and I noticed that within seconds of beginning to speak, Hitler communicated in an uncanny way his sense of total self-confidence and dedication. For a fleeting moment I thought of the impossibility of even hinting at this in any translated report.

Inevitably, he went on, in this massive and unrelenting struggle there were different views of the correct division of responsibility within the Party. And since he was but one man, though a man who pondered night and day on nothing but his sacred duty to his country, he could not undertake every task and personally ensure that everything was done in strict conformity with the splendid vision of the Nazi ideal. Some delegation there had to be, and would always have to be.

Yet he took this opportunity to reaffirm that, in the last analysis, the rock on which Nazi Germany had been built was the rock of his personal responsibility for everything. Sometimes this terrible task almost overwhelmed him but he had not borne it so long, and through so many dark days, to shrink from it now.

For this reason, when it became clear to him that there had been some departures from the original and correct model of a National Socialist Germany, it became no less clear that he must personally take over responsibility for putting right what had gone wrong. This he had done without the least doubt or hesitation, applying his iron will to the unhappy duty.

It had been necessary for certain people to be removed and he had removed them. ''For a short time I had to constitute in myself the Supreme Tribunal of Germany.''

When he came to the passage where he spoke of old Party friends who had strayed from the proper path, his voice suddenly took on a lower, choking tone, as though he was only just able to master his emotions. He held this for quite some time, sounding like a deeply unhappy father who found himself honour-bound to condemn his own sons in public. Then, as he began to move towards his peroration, his tone rose a little, and gradually hardened, so that at last, when he had to tell how he had fearlessly and impartially wielded the sword of justice, his voice took on an immensely authoritative weight and power. His closing sentences sounded like the words not of a fallible man, but of a just and stern god.

As I listened I felt that if there had been anybody in Germany who had previously doubted where supreme power lay, his doubts must now be totally removed. This was the dictatorial national will made manifest.

I wondered if David had also expected the speech to end in the usual ranting frenzy and, like me, had not been prepared for this monumental authority. But, as the words ended and the valedictory music began, he simply switched off and said nothing. We sat there, silent with our

65

thoughts for quite some time. Then David looked up and said: "Shall we take a breather?" I nodded.

Once we were in the street, I said: "Well, did he convince you of his sincerity?"

"If you mean his sincerity as the blackest villain, the biggest liar and the most dangerous man in the world, yes he did. But I do believe as well that he's the most persuasive speaker in the world. Talk about charming birds out of trees . . ."

"My feelings precisely. Germany is doomed to some sort of horror, though it could be horribly successful."

"More to the point, are you and I doomed, Eric?"

"Not necessarily, though I can think of safer places to be in just this minute."

"Such as Fogston?"

I grinned wryly. "Safer, to be sure. But far less attractive. At least things are happening here. Nobody is dying in Germany from inertia, or sheer lack of use."

"No, they have other means."

"They certainly have." I made a noise vaguely like a machine-gun and a passing pedestrian walking a dachshund on a lead gave me a strange look.

"Don't frighten the Berliners any more than they're already frightened," said David.

"I don't know about the Berliners, I'm not feeling so secure myself just at the moment. And I haven't the least doubt that the Big Fellow and his gang of dedicated cut-throats can't wait to lay all England waste."

We walked on in silence, trying — at least as far as I was concerned — to tell from the attitude of the people in the street what they thought and felt of it all, for most of them must have heard the broadcast. Two drunks at a street corner near a hot-sausage stall both talked at the same time in raised voices about "getting rid of the old rubbish" of "a healthy house-cleaning" and what a good thing it was for Germany that now it had Adolf Hitler to put such matters right. Neither listened to a word the other was saying and all the pedestrians might have been equally stone deaf for the effect it had on them. Did they not feel involved? Or were they glad that the Nazis were stirring things up in such a way that Germany would benefit, and they with it, without their having to lift a finger? It was impossible to tell. Even when we stopped at the bar of a pavement-edge café and drank a cup of coffee each, we learned nothing useful from the crowd of Berliners all around us who must have heard the broadcast on the bar radio.

When we turned to go, David offered to walk back to my room with me. "I need some exercise," he said. "Teaching English to the sausage-eaters does nothing for the muscles." So we re-traced our steps down the bright street, heading for the "dentifrice area" as I used to call it sometimes.

"Have you thought of trying to write about it all?" asked David as we walked along.

"Write about it? How?"

"For the British press."

"I wouldn't know how to begin. Anyway, what British newspaper would publish the truth as I see it?"

"Oh, some might. They aren't all time-servers and puffers of the Establishment."

It was only when the conversation took this drift that I recalled that he had recommended to me before I came out to Berlin to describe myself on my passport as a freelance journalist as well as a language teacher. He had not said why at the time, but I realised now that a journalistic qualification might be a rather better basis of personal security than a teaching one. I had no real qualifications as either, but reasoned that since I had equally no particular qualifications for rotting among the unemployed in Fogston or for bringing on my unfortunate family the miseries and deprivations of the Means Test, I need not feel any pangs of conscience about a little fiction on my passport. So, on the strength of one half-baked poem in the school magazine years earlier and the pretence that I'd a string of would-be pupils waiting in Berlin for me to teach them English, I had persuaded a not very bright young clergyman to endorse my passport application form.

It would have been very useful to have been able now to earn a little money by writing. But I hadn't the least idea how to set about it. Neither had I a typewriter, as I now explained to David.

"Yes," he said, "That's a point. A typewriter."

"Do you do anything yourself in the way of writing now?"

"No, haven't time — or the outlet. I'm afraid I'm another imitation freelance journalist on my passport. I thought it might open doors."

"And has it?"

"No, but I still feel it's some form of protection."

"I hope you're right."

We walked on awhile in silence. I was thinking of Fogston and the bit of freelance writing that David had done there, reporting amateur football matches in the Fogston League for the *Fogston News & Intelligencer*. It was once seeing him walk straight past the ticket-gate with a nod to the man collecting the money that gave me my first glimpse of the privilege of the press.

"Heard from your family recently?"

67

"Seldom from my brothers; they've got writers' cramp. But my mother writes fairly often." He knew she sent me back issues of the *Fogston Newt* because I passed all these on to him.

"Give her my love when next you write to her. Tell her I could just eat one of her Yorkshire Puddings."

"I will. Pity they can't tin Yorkshire Pudding."

"They will."

We walked on in silence, looking at things in the shop windows that we couldn't afford and at handsome female Berliners we couldn't approach.

"Have you seen anything of your Aunt Hildegard lately?" I said.

"Yes, I saw her the other day, as it happens. But I see her less and less. All she cares about now is her bloody cat and Adolf Hitler."

"How did your uncle come to marry a German? She didn't live in the Fogston German colony, did she?"

"Well, she did in a way. She was staying with relatives there when she met him — she was on a teachers' exchange before the war. I feel sorry for her, really. Both my father and his brother — her husband — were killed in the same attack on Hill Sixty, but she stuck it out to the end of the war in England. Then, when it was over, I suppose it must have seemed a bit late to go back. Maybe teachers' pay was better in England — I don't know — and Fogston was the least anti-German place in England, mind you. Then, when she retired, she just went back to Germany."

"Well, let's hope she won't have to be here under British bombs, after all she's gone through."

"Not much danger, really. Our senior British statesmen — forgive me while I puke in the gutter — see Adolf as a splendid safeguard against Red Ruin. Wouldn't surprise me in the least if they weren't pumping him up a bit via a numbered Swiss bank account."

"I think that's putting it on a bit, David."

"Well, maybe. Perhaps they're not actively helping him — as I'm certain they're actively helping that Bullfrog of the Pontine Marshes in Italy. But you mark my words, my lad, they'll manage to be wonderfully philosophical in England about his latest bit of butchery. Anyway, I don't think my Aunt Hildegard need lose any sleep about British bombs falling on her, or her cat."

By now we had arrived at Haus Odol. He gave a cheery wave and left me.

I'd taken a post-card from my letter-box in the entrance as I went into the building. It was a view of Cologne Cathedral. I knew nobody in Cologne. Turning it over, I read the message. "Have been thinking about you recently. Would like to see you sometime if you get

68

anywhere near. Oh, the heat! R.M.'' There was no address. I could make no sense of it at all, until I deciphered the postmark — Teltow. Then ''R.M.'' must be Rebecca Mandelbaum. I re-read the message. Was ''Oh, the heat!'' a reference not to the weather but to the political situation? It seemed more than likely. As I tapped the card on the back of my left hand I tried to work out why she had sent it. Perhaps she reasoned that a post-card would attract no official interest and would in any case carry very few signs of identification. Evidently she didn't want to telephone me or, presumably, me to telephone her. I resolved to go at the first opportunity. Checking with my appointments book, I saw that I would be able to go towards the end of the afternoon on the following day.

From time to time I found myself wondering what Frau Mandelbaum had in mind. It seemed improbable that she would want English lessons again, but it was possible.

The Baron was due for his next lesson at nine-thirty the following morning. I very much doubted if he would come; it seemed more than likely that he would be disgusted with himself for having confided in me details of the terrible events that had involved him so closely. Perhaps I should never see him again. I was not sure whether I welcomed this or feared it. If I never did see him again, I would have no guide as to his later feelings, and that was a very uncomfortable thought. All that fancy prose inside my passport would be pretty thin gruel if the Gestapo decided that I was ''inconvenient'' to them.

At nine-thirty precisely there was a firm knock on my door. It was the Baron.

In appearance he was back to normal. So, too, was his manner. In reply to his stiff little half-bow I smiled a rather watery smile and motioned him to come in. He stepped into the room did a left wheel, and hung his cap behind the door. Then, after pivoting back, he stood motionless for a moment and I quickly waved him to sit down, which he did, again with the same splendid economy of motion.

On the table, everything was exactly as usual and he immediately reached out and took up the pen, unscrewed the cap from the bottle of red ink and said, in English: ''Very well, I'm ready. Where shall we start?''

''Is it raining?'' I answered, and he looked a little surprised, then realised that the lesson had begun on my side also.

''No,'' he snapped back, ''it is not raining. The weather is quite fine and the sun is shining. I like the sunshine . . .''

And so we went on, for an hour, both working to an unspoken ordinance that there should be no military phrases and that the emotional and political content of the exchange should be nil. It made

69

rather a poor lesson, but it was a considerable relief. Throughout the session I'd been at some pains not to look at his right hand, but I had noticed, all the same, when first he stretched it out to the ink bottle that there was no trace of red under the nails. He must have spent some time with the nail-brush.

The lesson ended as it began, without incident, and he left. He did not say as he went out of the door that he would attend as usual in future, but I felt reasonably confident now that he would. If he felt angry or ashamed of his outburst of weakness and guilt at the previous lesson, he had shown no sign of it.

Towards four o'clock I set out for Teltow, making a mental note to buy some methylated spirit while I was out, for I'd been unable to make a hot drink all day. I called in at the chemist's shop at ground level in Haus Odol and bought a half-litre bottle. To avoid having to climb back to my room, I thrust it into my raincoat pocket. Anyway, there was no time, for I hated to be late, and I had left myself just long enough for the journey.

Last time I called at the Mandelbaums's the disfiguring paint-daub on the door seemed to be fading, but this afternoon it was as hideously conspicuous as ever, and I was appalled to see that it had been repainted recently. I rang the bell and, after identifying me through the door, Frau Mandelbaum let me in.

We went upstairs to the flat where her husband was apparently waiting for us, sitting in a chair with the radio turned on. When we went in, he did not reduce the sound but I knew that this was not a discourtesy. We sat down together, our heads very close.

"My wife and I have decided," said Herr Mandelbaum, "that recent events indicate a new state of affairs in Germany." He was almost whispering, and I had to strain to catch what he said.

"Yes," said his wife, "we feel that things must now get worse, not better: perhaps they will never get better again for us Jews. I know this latest murderous thing had nothing to do with the anti-Jewish pogrom, but if the Nazis are prepared to slaughter their own, what possible value will they put on our lives?"

There was no need to answer, yet I did answer, saying: "I'm truly sorry, but I must in honesty agree. I'm just as pessimistic as you."

"No, young man," he said gently, "I'm not pessimistic — just realistic. Anyway, to come to details. We shall both leave Germany as soon as we can see a way to do it without ruining ourselves. These things are not easy. You know, of course, that they are quite happy for Jews to leave, so long as they can be thoroughly plundered before they go?" I nodded.

"But tell me, Herr Johnson, if you will forgive a personal question:

70

why do you, a free Englishman, stay in this pit of vipers?''

"I'm here because I've no choice," I said simply. "My job in England ended and the unemployment situation made it impossible to get another. I couldn't even consider living on my mother's tiny earnings — I've no father. But I'm glad I'm here, all the same. Whether we like it or not, Germany is now the centre of the world, and Berlin the centre of Germany. Not that you'd know this if you got your impressions from the popular British press, which refers to Berlin as though it were some village at the back of the moon.''

"Ah, the British press! My friends who know England well tell me that it is part of the entertainment industry. It seems hard to believe . . .''

"It's true — at least for the big-circulation papers.''

"Well, I'm sorry to hear it. We had high hopes of England, didn't we, Rebecca?'' She nodded agreement.

"Perhaps you will again. It takes a lot to stir up the English, but, once stirred, they're usually pretty effective.'' I hoped my lack of conviction didn't show.

"Ah, yes, I think England will intervene at some point. She *must*, or she will become a cipher. But let's not get too serious. We are happy with our own contact with England, with you. But do forgive me taking this personal line. My wife and I feel we can speak to you with some freedom and confidence. We like you — though it is no privilege, I'm afraid, to be liked by Jews in the Third Reich, is it Rebecca?''

"Alas, no.''

"I consider it a privilege," I said, and hoped it gave them some comfort.

"You are kind, Herr Johnson," said Herr Mandelbaum, "and I have asked you — or, rather, my wife has, to come here to do us another kindness if you will. Our plan is that my wife shall go to Switzerland to her sister's, by rail, with a return ticket. But she will not use the return half. I should — we should — esteem it greatly if you would go with her. I should feel much happier if I knew that she was travelling with a responsible foreigner — with an Englishman, with you. I feel that this is a sort of safeguard. You could do it over a weekend or, of course, take longer if you wished. Naturally, I should pay all your expenses and a fee. I do not think you would be exposed to any danger. My wife would not carry anything that was forbidden.''

There was no need for him to elaborate; I knew what he meant. If a Jew were caught exporting any sort of valuables, the least that could be expected would be confiscation. Other, unofficial, penalties would probably be far worse.

Apart from the drone of the radio, there was silence for a while as I thought the matter over. "There is no need to make a decision at once," interposed Frau Mandelbaum. "There is no hurry."

"When would you be ready to go?" I said.

"Anytime."

I'd been trying to make a gap in my programme of lessons so that I could take a week's holiday, though I couldn't really afford it. I'd hoped that I could match this week with a similar period to be taken by Anna-Maria, but had not got round to telling her before she told me that she was "forced to go" to Eastern Germany for two weeks for her summer holiday. There was no need for any explanation. Anyway, I could not bear to talk about it.

So now I would shortly have a week free from lessons, but free from income, too.

"Very well, Herr Mandelbaum. Please make the arrangements. I suggest the last weekend of this month if that is suitable, and that we both take short-period excursion tickets."

"Excellent!" he said, rising.

"I am very pleased," said his wife. "Would you be able to stay a little, then, at my sister's? Zürich is a very interesting city; I'm sure you would like it."

"If she would have me. For a week."

"Of course she would. Then it's settled." We made all the arrangements there and then and drank a quiet little toast in brandy to the enterprise.

As usual, I made my own way out, thinking about Switzerland and the Mandelbaums. I put my coat over my arm, closed the front door behind me, and stepped out of the house. I trod on a piece of gravel and stumbled. Putting out an arm instinctively, I brushed against the door with my raincoat. Too late, I snatched it away, but it had a red paint stain on it. Furious with myself for my carelessness, I took out a handkerchief and was about to wipe it off when I felt the bottle of spirit in the pocket. I took it out and dashed a generous amount on to the handkerchief. Resting the coat on one raised knee, I rubbed quickly at the stain. It spread. More annoyed, I took the bottle and shook some spirit straight on to the stain; a little splashed on to the door and made the paint run. I raised the bottle, deliberately splashed more on to the door, and made a brisk wipe with the handkerchief. In another minute I would probably have removed the whole disfigurement.

But that minute did not come. Suddenly, I felt myself seized from behind and I was conscious of two men, both a good deal taller than I was, holding me. Within seconds they had frog-marched me down the steps and the path. At the gate stood the old Opel car I had seen before. One opened the back door; the other flung me in.

72

8

When sheer terror had retreated enough to allow me to move, I pulled myself up and fell on to the seat. Beside me was a man in a long black leather coat and a soft hat; in other circumstances he would have looked almost smart. He was not even looking at me, but his right hand was ominously in his overcoat pocket. He seemed to be relaxed. He had apparently decided that I would not or could not offer any resistance worth his attention. Neither he nor the other man, who was now in the driving seat, had said a word from the moment of seizing me.

This did nothing to reassure me. Murder, torture, disappearance and imprisonment without trial were routine in the Third Reich and I did not doubt for an instant that I was in the hands of anything but the ultimate power in the land, the Gestapo.

The car moved off and was soon through Teltow and into Steglitz; it was obvious that we were headed for Berlin. For a moment I thought of snatching open a door and hurling myself out, perhaps at traffic lights. Then I saw that the inside door handles were missing.

I wondered desperately if it would be any use saying that I was British, but dismissed the idea. They would be likely to know, for the Gestapo seemed to know everything in present-day Germany. Without turning my head, I looked again at the profile of the man next to me. It was like a rock.

Once or twice we were held up in lines of traffic, but each time the car stopped the man simply turned his head slightly in my direction, almost as though he hoped that I would make some attempt to escape. Now I knew why he had not spoken. He had no need of speech.

The driver never once turned round. He too, apparently, was quite sure that everything was under control. The car rolled on, deeper into Berlin.

Then, after turning several corners in a part of the city I didn't know, we suddenly stopped outside a building of no particular character. The driver got out without haste, walked round the car, and pulled open the door nearest to me. His other hand was in his overcoat pocket. He, too, looked almost disappointed that I was unlikely to give any trouble.

The man next to me said one word: "*'Raus*". I got out, and he stepped out behind me. Then, like some nightmare ballet team, each of them seized one of my arms and projected me towards the entry of the building.

Just inside the door were two tall soldiers in black SS uniform and steel helmets, one on each side of the corridor that now faced us. They carried machine-pistols on leather shoulder-slings and, at our approach, spread their feet and automatically took up the firing grip.

There was a momentary pause for identification of the men at each side of me, then we passed along a wide corridor and through the double doors at the end into what looked like a general office. Men and women were busy at desks, some in SS uniform, some in civilian clothing. Nobody looked up at our passage, even when we stopped at a desk where there sat a senior-looking SS officer who had a scar from one eye to the corner of his mouth. He looked up and began a monosyllabic exchange with the man in the black leather coat. The officer glanced at a wall clock and made an entry in an open book in front of him before giving a slight inclination of his head towards a row of numbered doors in the wall behind him. "*Sieben*", he said.

We passed through door 7, which was stout and had a small double-glazed inset window. Immediately inside was a solid padded door standing open. There was no window in the cell-like room beyond. A stout sheet of metal filled the space in the wall facing the door where a window might once have been. In the centre of the concrete floor was a drainage gulley. There was a battered steel desk with a steel-frame chair behind it. Over the gulley stood a similar chair. The car-driver let go of me and the man in the leather coat flung me at this second chair as one might throw down a garment. Then he sat behind the desk. The other went to the double doors, closed them both and took up a position in front of them, legs apart and arms folded.

"Name and address," barked the man at the desk as he took out a pen from an inside pocket and opened a file before him.

"Eric Cosgrove Johnson," I said, "146 Ranbury Road, Fogston, Yorkshire, England."

I had hoped that this information would surprise him. But if it did, he failed to show it. He simply looked up and said, with deliberation, "In Germany."

So he knew I was not a passing tourist. This came as no surprise to me, but it did remove a slender thread of hope. I said: "Haus Roseneck, Europa Strasse, Wittenberg Platz, Berlin."

When he had written down this information, he said: "Right.

74

Everything in your pockets on the desk — and I mean everything.''

I put the contents of my pockets on the desk and, when I had done so, he looked up briefly from his writing and his eye rested on a packet of contraceptives of a popular brand. ''So part of your plan is to contaminate our German girls, is it? Perhaps you would give me the name, or names, of those upon whom you have been pleased to bestow your favours.''

''Only prostitutes,'' I lied.

As I said it, I wondered for a second if he was going to deny that there were prostitutes in Germany, which would have been ludicrous. But nothing was too ludicrous for the Gestapo if they chose to have it serve their turn. Then it suddenly struck me that his use of the word ''contaminate'' could mean that he thought I was a Jew. If he did, then my situation was even worse, for it was illegal for a Jew to have sexual relations with Aryans. At the same time, presumably because my eyes were getting used to the strange light, which came from a single powerful bulb inside a cage fastened to the ceiling, I saw that there were dry bloodstains on the floor. They constituted the only colour in the room.

But he did not pursue this line, merely making a further terse entry on the sheet of paper before him. ''Right,'' he snapped, ''all your clothes off.''

For a fleeting moment I toyed with the idea of trying to assert my right of access to the British Consul, and, as I hesitated, my inter-rogator looked up at me and said: ''Do I have to help you?'' I took all my clothes off, and put them on the desk, beside my possessions. Giving me hardly a glance, he stood up and carefully felt in all the pockets, then crumpled the lapels of the jacket, listening, apparently, for the crinkle of paper. He did the same with the trouser turn-ups. Then he threw all the clothes on the floor in front of me.

The inner padded door opened and in walked a man in SS officer's uniform. He stared straight at me, without the faintest movement of recognition. It was von Steinfels.

As the Baron had come in, the man at the desk had jumped to his feet and whipped off his hat. ''Well,'' said the Baron to him, ''what arch-criminal have we here?''

''An Englishman,'' said the other, ''apprehended in an act of sabotage and interference with the internal conduct of the Reich.''

''Details,'' said von Steinfels.

''I and my colleague caught him removing, with the aid of this bottle of paint-remover and a rag, an anti-Jewish inscription on a house door in Teltow. He is a regular caller at the house which is, of course, occupied by Jews. I have details here . . . ." He moved as though to bring something out of his inside pocket.

"Not necessary," rattled out the Baron, "I am not concerned with trifles." Then he did one of his smart half-turns to face me.

"And what is your version?" It was impossible for me to tell from his demeanour what he was thinking or to get the faintest hint of his intentions. I seemed to be on my own.

"He is mistaken," I lied, "and I can prove it. I brushed against the paint accidentally with my raincoat . . ." I gestured towards it where it lay on the floor, fortunately with the smudged paint-stain uppermost. "I happened to have the methylated spirit with me — I use it for a spirit stove for heating water — and tried to remove the stain on my coat with it, using my handkerchief. I had to splash the spirit quickly on to the coat for this purpose, for it is well known that a paint stain must be removed at once or it cannot be removed at all. In doing this, I accidentally splashed the spirit on the door, from which I immediately wiped it with my handkerchief — the one on the desk. While I was doing this, I was seized and brought here. That is all — apart from the fact that, as an English teacher, I give English lessons at the house in question."

He wheeled back towards the desk and picked up the bottle of spirit. A typical example of German thoroughness, it bore a clear label giving the name of the chemist in small print and the name of the contents in large print — "Bennsprit". Holding the bottle so that the other could read the label, he said: "Idiot — can't you read?"

"Yes, sir."

"Then read."

" 'Bennsprit' — sir."

"Not 'paint-remover'?"

"No, sir." The Baron pointed to the handkerchief.

"Is that a rag — or a handkerchief?"

"A handkerchief, sir."

"You are a blundering, ignorant fool," roared the Baron, "unable until you have your nose rubbed in them to tell methylated spirit from paint-remover and a handkerchief from a rag. You are also determined, it would appear, to turn an example of your own miserable incompetance into an international incident that could cause acute embarrassment to the Reich. Apologise immediately to this man and pick up his clothes."

Whatever the man in the leather coat had expected, it was clearly not this. He hardly knew how to frame the words of apology, yet struggled to do so, then rushed to pick up my clothes and shook them, I thought, not so much to remove the dust as to conceal his own trembling. He folded the clothes with elaborate care, placed them on the desk, and stood beside it to attention.

Turning to me, the Baron said: "Please be so good as to dress. There are officious incompetents in every country, I think. You had the misfortune to meet one in ours. I am extremely sorry." And he did the full German bow, complete with heel-click. Turning back to the desk, he took up the piece of paper on which my details were recorded, then said to me: "Do you wish this record to be kept? Do you intend to make representations?"

"As far as I'm concerned, the incident is closed."

The Baron, while continuing to look at me, then handed the paper to the other. "Destroy it, now," he said, "with fire."

The man whipped out a pocket lighter and clicked it into flame, which he immediately applied to the bottom corner of the paper. When it was fully burnt apart from the small portion by which he held it, he let it fall to the floor, where the last bit burned away. He wiped the ashes into the floor with his shoe and, at a further gesture from the Baron, scraped the resultant dust together and pushed it into the gulley. "'*Raus!*'" bawled the Baron, and the man almost ran from the room, followed by the other.

For the first time, I was seriously afraid that I was going to faint. I think the Baron knew it, too, for he said: "Take your time dressing. I shall return in a few minutes," and went out. He had spoken quite formally, and even now I was by no means sure that I was going to escape unscathed. I knew that the Germans were prone to elegancies of procedure that could be no less savage for being elegant. I hurried into my clothes, stuffed my possessions back into my pockets, and sat down before I fell down. The door opened and the Baron came back into the room. Without saying a word, he held out towards me a small silver pocket-flask, the top of which was already folded back. I took it and drank. It was brandy.

"Now," he said, "I want you to obey my instructions."

I returned the flask and stood up.

"Walk in front of me," he said, "to my instructions. It is a way we have here."

"I understand."

"Right. Go through this door. Turn right outside it and walk to the far side of the room, past the door marked number 1. Turn right again and go through the unnumbered door beyond it, straight across the room inside, and out through the door in the opposite wall. Ready?"

"Yes."

"Very well. Go."

I did exactly what he had told me to do. The officer at the desk outside the row of cells gave us only a glance, saying nothing. We walked past the numbered doors and I opened the door beyond number 1 and went inside, the Baron only a pace behind me.

I saw that we were now in a sort of telephone exchange, with desk-like switchboards dotted at regular intervals all over the floor. At each position sat a girl dressed in civilian clothing and wearing a telephone headset. The air was full of the sound of female voices speaking several languages and of the sound of plugs being pushed in and pulled out. I saw all this within a second or two but was more concerned to spot the door at the other side of the room.

It was there plain enough, and I walked as rapidly towards it as I could. Some of the girls looked up as we passed between them along a sort of alley-way between the switchboards. I'd hardly time to take in much more than this general impression before we were at the other side of the room, near the exit door. The girl at the position immediately on the right of this pushed in a plug and said in perfectly modulated English: "Hello, Stuttgart. Mr Watson? This is London. Your call to —" She broke off as we drew level with her and our eyes met for an instant.

I kept walking, pushing open the door while moving and not even looking round to see if the Baron caught it as I let it go on its spring. But the sound of his jackboots behind me did not break step. Now I was in a narrow, rather dark corridor. "Straight forward," said the Baron's voice behind me. I kept moving.

About twenty paces along the corridor was a large steel door set in the wall. It had two massive lever-like handles, from one of which dangled a padlock. "Stop," said the Baron. I stopped. He stepped in front of me and, with his customary precision of movement, opened the padlock. Then he weighed on the two handles and thrust at the door with his shoulder. It opened slowly. "Keep walking," he said, "until you come to an Underground station. Behave normally. Remain silent about today's events." His voice and manner were absolutely neutral and he looked beyond me as he spoke. I stepped past him and into the open air. The steel door closed silently behind me. I was in a narrow entry full of dustbins.

When I came out of the entry I found myself in a dreary side-street where the nondescript buildings were of the poorer apartment type. There was not a pedestrian in sight. One block I noticed, had a boarded-up shop at pavement level with a fading sign indicating that it had once been a laundry receiving office. I looked behind me but saw nobody. I walked on.

The street led to a slightly more important-looking one which also consisted largely of old apartment blocks. Some had open shops in them.

There was no sign of any Underground station. With another quick glance behind me that revealed nothing to suggest that I was being followed — for now there were quite a number of pedestrians about — I kept walking. My legs were beginning to function normally again and I set myself a pace that made good progress without suggesting haste.

About five minutes later I had reached a road of the kind that might appear on a large-scale street map, though I did not recognise it. About two hundred yards away I saw the big "U" of an Underground station. I was infinitely relieved to walk down the steps and melt into the anonymity of the stream of passengers. I bought a ticket with the first coin that came into my hand — a half-Mark piece — and got into the first train that pulled in. Three stations further on I'd worked out approximately where I was, and that I was going in the wrong direction. I got out and took a train going the other way. As I sat down I tried to get a glimpse of my reflection in the carriage window opposite, over the shoulder of a young woman with a large shopping-bag on her knee. My face looked very pale and my tie-knot off centre. The woman with the bag shuffled uncomfortably, thinking I was looking at her. No doubt I looked strange, and if I smiled at her to reassure her I would do just the opposite.

Shortly afterwards I got out at Wittenberg Platz and, as I walked out of the building under the Chlorodont Toothpaste sign, I could feel my legs beginning to tremble again. I felt desperately tired.

I was reasonably confident that noboby had followed me, and when I got back to Haus Odol there was nobody waiting for me. So I was free, at least for the present. Yet this hardly weighed with me. I threw myself down on the bed. All I could think about was the girl at the last switchboard position at the Gestapo office who had simulated a London operator with such perfect English. It was Anna-Maria.

9

I looked at my watch and saw that it was only half past seven. Not four hours had gone since I'd set out for Teltow, and I was back in my room not looking noticeably different. Yet everything was completely changed. I'd heard of the Gestapo using attractive girls to spy on foreigners in Germany, especially journalists, and how it was taken for granted that they could get the most useful information in bed. I'd said it was like something from a bad film; I'd even talked about being prepared to "suffer" such treatment. It had a very different aspect now.

Yet I could not, *would* not, believe that Anna-Maria was such a person, and with me as her victim and dupe. We had been too tender, too loving with each other. No, she *couldn't* have done it.

Or could she?

I looked up at the mirror on the wall above the wash-basin. Stuck in the frame was a tiny porcelain primrose that she had given me quite soon after our first meeting. Of no material value, it was the German equivalent of a paper flag and, coming from Anna-Maria, it had taken on a special significance. I got up and threw it into the waste-paper basket.

Looking around the room for other reminders of her, I realised that I'd never had a letter or a note — not even a card — from her. She had put nothing in writing. I opened the cupboard and saw the half-full bottle of Danziger Goldwasser that she had given to me at Christmas. I poured it away down thé wash-basin, then dropped the empty bottle into the waste-paper basket.

It was some time before I regained control of my emotions. Then I remembered with a jolt that I had arranged to meet her at the Memorial Church at eight. Though there wasn't the least hope of her being there, I'd just time to keep the appointment. I tidied myself up as well as I could and set out, compelled to taste the full bitterness.

As always, the arrangement had been that if the church was locked or a service was taking place we would meet at the main entrance.

But the church was not locked and I passed into the cool interior, grateful for the suddenly subdued light and the hushing of the sound of traffic. No service was in progress but a few pensive people were scattered among the seats. I sat down in the end seat of the back row, and waited.

She did not come. How could she? And what could we possibly have said to each other if she had? Yet I thrust this from my mind. All that I knew was that I felt a great void that she alone could fill.

Some of the people began to slip away, their feet making hardly any sound. The organ started to play, not in snatches as in organ practice but in a smooth, unhurried flow of beautiful music, which I recognised as Bach's "Sheep May Safely Graze." A priest wearing a long black gown and vividly white twin tabs at the throat began to walk slowly up the nave towards the doorway behind me. I felt guilty at using his church improperly. Yet was it so improper? Was I not there seeking some sort of solace? And was not a church — and a priest — supposed to give solace?

I thought of one German word for priest. Unlike so many dauntingly functional German words, it was poetic: *Der Geistlicher* — the Spiritual One. Could he give me some spiritual comfort? I felt sure that he would try if I asked him, and I could see now that he would pass so close to me that I should be able to reach out and touch him.

But as he drew level with me I knew that there was nothing I could say to him. Half a confession could lead only to half an appeal, and I could not tell him, or anybody else, even half the thoughts and fears that were tormenting me. He passed by, and the moment was gone.

I stayed so long in the church that I lost count of time. The organ had long since ceased to play and the day was almost spent before I rose, stiff and weary, and left the building.

I was glad to meet nobody on the stairs of Haus Odol, to be spared the need for small talk. I went into my room and, in the now fading light, looked around it as a stranger might have seen it. How could I have ever thought it pleasant, almost comfortable? It seemed impossible. It was a cell.

Tired as I was, I had little hope of sleep. Instead, I tried to marshal my thoughts logically, taking people's motives as a starting point. If Anna-Maria worked in that room at the heart of the Berlin Gestapo office, and had concealed from me all the time that she spoke fluent English, then she could only have done it to report on me. And the same must have been true of Helga and David. And why had Helga suddenly been transferred at the end of February?

But David might have first met Helga in normal social circumstances. Surely even Gestapo girls must be allowed some normal social life. But all my justifications couldn't obliterate the fact that I'd heard Anna-

Maria not only talking perfect English, but pretending to be a London switchboard operator. And I knew, if only from the example of the Baron, that to be employed at the centre of the Nazi establishment was automatically to be totally involved. And where did the Baron fit into this maze? And David?

Could it all be coincidence? That seemed the most unlikely explanation of all. If there was one thing that the Nazis did not rely on, it was coincidence; they were planners to the last dot.

But the Nazis couldn't remove coincidence from life in Germany. Perhaps I'd better start at the beginning again.

But what was the beginning? It was my going to Germany. No, it was David's going to Germany after his mother died, at the suggestion of his Berlin aunt. I'd followed later at David's suggestion and, I gathered later, at his aunt's. David's aunt was very pro-Nazi, yes, but so were millions of other women in Germany.

Yet she might have induced David to go to Germany for a purpose. But I just couldn't believe that she — or anybody else — had secretly recruited David to the Nazi cause. Anyway, she seemed a most improbable agent.

But the best agents *were* improbable, even drab. So I ought to know more about David's aunt, and I couldn't do that without David's help, which would mean confiding in him and so wrecking that line of approach. Better start again . . .

I *must* believe in David. And I must tell him about Anna-Maria working for the Gestapo. And I must do it for several reasons, one of them being that if I disappeared, it was important that somebody reliable should know the likely reason. Another was to put him on his guard for his own benefit. Although the Baron had ordered me, in fact, to remain silent about my being at the Gestapo office and how I had got out of it, did he know of my association with Anna-Maria? That seemed unlikely when he had led me past her.

So I could tell David about Anna-Maria — and Helga — without going against the Baron's order.

But was the Baron secure? And had he acted on his own initiative and authority? It looked like it. Burning the piece of paper bearing details of me was strange, in record-crazy Germany, but there was reassurance for me in the way it was done — and the fact that it was done. It showed me that he wanted me to be sure it was burned, and that he wanted the plain-clothes Gestapo agent to be equally sure.

I turned the same thoughts round and round in my brain, not making any progress, yet afraid to let them slip in case I forgot some detail that might prove later to be vital.

Was it possible that David was doing something that made him interesting to the Gestapo? I'd previously rejected this notion as too silly. But I must be prepared to contemplate such things.

Yet if David was engaged in something secretive, they would have arrested him, not me. Ah, no, they would not. At this stage they would have arrested neither of us. Was it not vastly more likely that I was arrested simply because I'd behaved with such incredible folly in Teltow? And that my arrest, if persisted in, would wreck any plan for keeping David under surveillance until such a time came as it was desirable or necessary to arrest him? That was a possible explanation, though a most unlikely one. My part was too much like being caught shop-lifting and allowed to put the goods back. But it would account for the Baron suddenly setting me at liberty with the warning to keep silent about being arrested and released. Could the Baron afford to risk it? *Would* he risk it? Had he any choice, considering what I knew about him? Were we now each other's prisoner, on parole?

Now I was in a worse mental tangle than before. I was beginning to invent phantoms and then clothe them with logic.

I tossed about on the mattress and tried to empty my mind of thought entirely, but could manage it only for a few seconds at the most before everything came flooding back.

Well, since sleep was to be denied me, I might as well try again. If only I could work out the Baron's motivation perhaps I would get somewhere. Why had he intervened at the Gestapo office? Evidently he must have been in the general office when the two low-ranking thugs frog-marched me through, and had not acted immediately so as to avoid drawing attention to himself. Yes, that made sense. Or he had waited awhile simply to sort out his own thoughts and projected actions. That also made sense. And he would be familiar with the routine there for dealing with newly arrested people, so probably knew to within a fairly narrow margin how long it would take for my interrogator to write down the bare details of my case. But this assumed that I would not be ill-treated first, which would take a little time. Well, he must have assumed that, or been prepared to risk it. Anyway, it would almost certainly be wrong to attribute to the Baron any comradely feelings towards me, for, having the rank he appeared to have, he would have intervened at an earlier stage in that case. To put it at the lowest, and most improbable, if he wished to keep me intact simply for his own convenience in the sense of not having his English instructor smashed up or expelled, then he might conceivably have done what he did.

But this was based on two large assumptions: that he carried enough rank to put the rigid Gestapo machine into reverse, and would be able to snuff out the charge against me. And, when he came into Room 7, he could not have known what that charge was.

Perhaps, then, he came into the room ready to take a line in either direction, and was prepared, if he found the situation irreversible, to do nothing. If only the man's face was not such a mask, or his voice carried some small instructive overtone! In fact, the more I thought about the Baron, the less progress I made. Anyway, within a few hours I might know a little something. He was due at nine-thirty for another lesson and it was already dawn. If he did not come and sent no message, then I had to try to accommodate myself to the possibility of his reversing his previous action in freeing me — and ordering my re-arrest.

In that case, it was important to get to David Whitaker in time, or to send him a message. Well, I couldn't get to him before nine-thirty and writing or telephoning was out of the question. No, I would just have to sweat it out.

I got out of bed and switched on the light, having decided to make a cup of tea, using for the purpose the remainder of the methylated spirit that had caused me so much anguish. Soon the blue flame was heating the little kettle and the very normality of the procedure — despite the Haus Odol rule against it — was a comfort. I took out an unopened packet of tea, and thought of my mother. Were they all safely asleep there in Fogston? No doubt they were, and even if their prospects when they awoke were dull, insecure and ill-paid, they were not perilous, as mine were. I envied them.

Yet, here I was at a place where I now felt the world's destiny was being decided. So far as I could tell from talking to the few British I knew in Berlin and from the British radio and press information that reached me, Britain was quite unaware of the seriousness of the German situation or simply did not wish to know. How did you set about warning a man of a danger he would rather not hear about? What could I do anyway?

Yet if I did nothing, as an insignificant victim who disappeared or as a mere observer, then I would be failing to use a chance given to very few. But some chances were too hot to handle, especially by English provincials with nothing in their favour and no notion anyway of what to do.

The water boiled and I poured it on the tea in the mug. The faint whiff of garlic came up to me as I put a piece of card over the mug to keep in the heat while the tea infused. The milk was condensed and sweetened, and in a tube like toothpaste. It irked me to buy it in this unappetising — and uneconomical — form, but I had to make some sacrifice to convenience. Five minutes later I stirred in the milk and took a cautious sip. It was delicious.

Now I allowed myself for the first time to give serious thought to the Mandelbaums. If I was in danger, then I was disqualified as an escort for Frau Mandelbuam, even if I was available. But if I had, in effect, got my clearance from the Gestapo, then I might be a better escort than before. If only I could discuss the matter with the Mandelbaums, the Baron, and David. In any case I must tell David the simple fact that I would be making a short visit to Switzerland with Frau Mandelbaum. I drank off the tea and climbed back into bed. But there was no hope of sleep. Every time I closed my eyes I saw Anna-Maria.

10

Promptly at nine-thirty there was a firm knock on my door. There was no need to speculate who was there. When I opened the door, the Baron gave me his customary half-bow and came straight in.

Not to be outdone in calm assurance — though I knew mine was bogus — I'd laid out the table with the usual equipment. Within seconds the lesson had begun.

The Baron set the tone, keeping matters on a purely civilian basis, for which I was thankful. This time it was all about traffic on English roads, in English. "Of course," he said, "you drive on the wrong side in England, don't you?"

"Of course," I said and, to my surprise, found I meant it.

Again we went through the routine of question and answer, with the Baron writing in red ink and me writing in black. As we exchanged papers, I remembered with an inward shudder the one he had held, dripping red ink, on the day after the massacre. He gave not the slightest sign that anything had ever interrupted the normality of the lessons. It was uncanny. There he was, saying out loud such things as "Where can I get some petrol?" and "I have a puncture, could you direct me to the nearest garage?" Yet we both knew that this was the same voice that had so recently given the commands that had snuffed out men's lives. Was it possible that he was still dreaming of marching with German troops across the face of the earth, shooting down anybody who offered the least resistance, and singing: "Today there belongs to us only Germany, tomorrow the total world"? His face and manner gave absolutely no clue.

The lesson proceeded — and ended — in just the same way. He gave me another of his half-bows, and was gone. I had learned nothing.

It was urgent that I see David as soon as possible, and I set out immediately, looking in my post-box as I passed through the entry. In it was a neat, stiff little envelope. I locked the box and left the building, opening the envelope as I walked. Inside was a piece of white die-stamped writing-paper. "Dear Mr Johnson," I read, "My husband and I would be happy if you would join us at the Vicarage for tea at four o'clock on Saturday, July 13th. We already know Mr Whitaker slightly, who is, I believe, a friend of yours, and he also has been invited. I do hope that you will both be able to come. We British in Berlin are so few, and perhaps getting fewer. Yours sincerely, Amanda Fitzherbert.'' And, in the bottom left-hand corner: "R S V P''. The address, I noted, was in fashionable Dahlem.

The utterly English normality of the thing delighted me, though I would perhaps have been derisive about it only a day ago. Certainly I would go to Mrs Fitzherbert's tea-party — assuming I was still at liberty. I'd be thankful to go. I sniffed at the paper and envelope, almost disappointed to find no trace of lavender.

By now my sense of near-panic was subsiding, though I knew that somehow I would still have to clarify things with David and the Mandelbaums without being completely frank.

The fact that the Baron had given me a plain warning not to tell anybody what had happened at the Gestapo office was not the only reason why I couldn't speak freely to David. I didn't want to involve him. Yet something must be said to warn him.

I think he must have picked up some of my anxiety in advance, for the moment I sat down he turned up the volume of his radio and said: "Well, spit it out, Eric. What's eating you?"

But this was no occasion for a few warning words spoken softly to background music. "Let's stretch our legs, David," I said, and he knew that it was more than exercise I had in mind.

Out in the streets, I came straight to my point. "David, you'll just have to trust me about certain things I'm not able to tell you, but what I must tell you is that I *know* that Anna-Maria works for . . . for State Security. And if she does, then Helga does, too." I just couldn't say "Gestapo."

He gave me a hard look, and kept on walking. "I know, Eric. I've known it since February."

"Then why on earth!" — I began; but he stopped me.

"There were at least two reasons for not telling you, much as I wanted to. In the first place, you were crazy about Anna-Maria. And I just didn't know how you'd react. And it was possible that she was seeing you quite outside her Gestapo duties. And even if she wasn't, I knew you'd nothing to hide. So, after a long think, I decided to say nothing. I may have been wrong — but I don't think I was. And I'm sorry now, in a way that you've found out. After all, you are in love with her, aren't you?"

"Yes. But I don't suppose I'll see her again. You see, she knows I know." There was a silence of a full minute. Then David suddenly said,

87

"Helga hasn't been posted somewhere else. She's gone underground — politically, I mean — and we're married."

"Married!"

"We loved each other and had to do something about it. Helga confessed about her Gestapo job and we decided that she must find some way to leave it and then we'd get married."

"But if they find her —"

"I know. Nobody just leaves the Gestapo. But we planned it down to the smallest detail — Helga knew the office routine for falsifying papers. So she introduced a set of false papers into the system for herself, giving herself a new name and occupation. They included a passport and she stuck on her own photograph late one night. Then, when she'd got all the papers in order, she destroyed the official request notice asking for them to be made. This making of false documents is routine in the Third Reich. Dr Goebbels has even been known to boast about it, in public. They forge banknotes, as well.

"Anyway, Helga called herself Lilli Schultheiss, night-club hostess. Why she picked on Schultheiss as a name, I don't know, except that there are advertisements all over the place, as you know, for Schultheiss Beer, so it's a common name that would attract no particular attention. And she made herself a night-club hostess for the same reason. It's the sort of job that a person of no significance would be likely to have. In the particulars, she made herself an orphan, with no living relatives.

"Then, when everything was ready, she left a suicide note at the office saying that she just couldn't stand the whole wretched life of deception that her duties now involved her in. That was true, anyway. A lot of people joined the Nazi movement thinking that they would be working for a reborn Germany without knowing what would be involved. It said in the note that they'd find her body in the River Spree where it runs through Berlin."

He shook his head.

"Poor Helga. She thought a long time about that. She knew it meant that she'd never be able to make contact with her parents in Frankfurt again — at least not so long as she was in Germany. But if it prevented the Gestapo searching for her, she thought it was worth it. She was terrified, too, that the Gestapo might put the bite on her parents to see if she'd tipped them off that she was still alive and in hiding. She still has nightmares about it."

"But, David, this country's document daft. The Gestapo must know that she'd spent some time with you, and you're registered as resident in Berlin —"

"Which is why we got married in romantic, relatively inefficient

Vienna. I know Austria's infiltrated with Nazis, but I can't see any record of our marriage there being sent back here. And there's another good reason for our getting married, you know. I mean another one besides wanting to. It makes her a British subject, and that ought to be some sort of protection.''

We turned and began to walk towards the flat. I wanted to ask a string of questions but I asked only one.

"Is there anything I can do?''

"Well, there might be, though it's a very long shot. When you go to Switzerland, I'd be glad if you'd look into the chances of teaching English there. Our only hope of a normal life is to get out of Germany.''

"Of course I will.''

"Thank you. And there's something you could do. Helga's lonely. I'll tell her that I've told you about us and ask her if she wants you to visit her. I think she'll jump at the chance to speak freely to a friend.''

"I'd be glad to go. Give her my love.''

"Could you call and see me tomorrow about the same time? And if you can, would you have at least two hours free?'' I agreed.

He must have been very curious to know how I had found out about both girls working at the Gestapo office, but I was grateful that he respected the proviso I'd made. Now my revelation looked unimportant beside his. I'd gone to speak to him full of anguish on my own account; now I felt desperately anxious for him and Helga.

But when I called the following afternoon, David's door was locked and the splendid Turkey-red carpet had gone from the marble stairs. I knocked on his door and rang his bell again, without effect. With a growing sense of alarm, I was just about to search out the caretaker when I heard David's voice behind me: "Sorry about that, Eric, we're in some disorder here, as you see. All this morning workmen have been busy taking up the stair-carpet. It occupied them most of the morning. They swept underneath it and removed all the screws. Then they took it away in a van. This afternoon we learned that they're thieves and that this is the latest 'fashionable' crime in Berlin. But come in.'' He opened his door and we went in. But we stayed only a minute or two, and then set out.

"Where are we going? I asked as we made for the nearest Underground station.

"A place called Wedding, a few miles across Berlin. Funny name, isn't it?''

"They seem to like funny names in Berlin, such as 'Am Knie' and 'Wedding.' Imagine a part of London called 'At the Knee'.''

"Well, there is the Elephant and Castle . . .''

But the joking ended there. First, he told me Helga's address, and made me repeat it carefully. Then he told me just how to get to it, but asked me to give him at least ten minutes start, so that we didn't get the same train and didn't arrive together. I was to give just two knocks on the door, three seconds apart. Once more, we went over the instructions and the route, then he left me.

I found Wedding infinitely shabbier and more workaday than the West End, but wasted no time gazing around. Soon I located the forbidding-looking apartment block, and went in. The flat, he'd said, was on the top floor — the fifth — and there was no lift.

The entry was unprepossessing, and each flight of stairs was meaner than its predecessor. All were uncarpeted, and gloomy. Eventually, I arrived before door 20, and knocked as arranged. David opened the door at once and I stepped quickly in.

I was in a bleak one-room bed-sitter. Lying on a hard-looking settee that was too small for comfort, was Helga, now with blond hair. She was clearly pregnant. A radio set was playing the inescapable "*Unterhaltungsmusik.*" She gave me a wan but cheerful smile and held out a hand towards me, over the back of the settee. I took it in both mine. "Meet Lilli," said David. "Lilli Schultheiss. Speak English if you want. She's fluent in it."

"I'll talk whichever language you want, Lilli," I said, in English. "Though I'm afraid I haven't a lot of news."

"Doesn't matter, Eric. It's wonderful to see you." It was strange to hear her speak English.

"Perhaps I ought to explain a few things before we go any further," said David. "This girl seems to have as many names as a cat has lives. Here in the block she's 'Frau Mann' — and I'm 'David Mann.' That's to look ordinary and to avoid the name 'Whitaker' which she has on her marriage certificate. And the name 'Mann' is both German and English — and, as a sort of bonus, it means 'husband' in German, as you know." We all laughed at this, though I felt far from laughter.

"He's always joking," said Lilli. "But it's true."

It struck me as a terrible risk for her to be in Berlin at all. But then, the Gestapo were all over Germany, and there were four million people in Berlin to hide among. If she and David had to be in Germany, maybe Berlin was as good a place as any. But how bitter to have to be in Germany at all. The moralists were always saying what money couldn't buy. For these two even as little as £50 might be able to buy life itself.

Turning to David, Lilli said: "Did you get some potatoes?"

He grinned. "She dreams about spuds does this girl." Then,

turning to her. "Yes, Darling, I did, and I shall now perform on them. Eric, keep Lilli entertained."

"I'm terribly sorry about you and Anna-Maria," said Lilli when I sat down again beside the settee. "You must be very upset about it. She, too, maybe. But, believe me, Eric, she hasn't any choice — any more than I had."

"What does she plan to do?"

"I don't know. Go to East Prussia and marry her soldier eventually, I suppose."

She hauled herself off the settee and, opening a cupboard, took down a tin box. On the table were three cups and saucers. "David's making some tea," she said over her shoulder, and he came in at that moment with a teapot. Opening the tin, she took out half a sweetcake of the sort that could be bought at any corner shop in Europe. "Eric must have some Wedding cake," she said, smiling at David, who must have heard the joke before.

As we drank the tea and ate the dreary cake, David produced the invitation. "I suppose you've had one of these," he said, "I don't want to go but Lilli insists that I should."

"It's important for him to behave normally," Lilli said. "Anyway, Mrs Fitzherbert's cake will be much better than this one."

"Not for me it won't," I said.

11

Early in the afternoon of Saturday the 13th I looked at my small collection of clothes, not to pick out the most suitable for the vicarage tea-party, but to select the least unsuitable. As I took my well-worn flannel trousers from under the mattress, I reflected bitterly on Oscar Wilde's comment that we are all "branded in the mouth"; some of us were branded in the breeches as well.

But I wasn't going to allow any such corroding thoughts to mar this day. At least I knew my shortcomings, or most of them, and had come to terms with them. Although I wouldn't claim to be socially secure, I was reasonably confident of the soundness of my peculiar education: grammar school, night school and massive midnight reading. And I knew I spoke grammatically, even though my teaching English sometimes made me sound pedantic. I gave my shoes a particularly thorough polishing, put on a clean white shirt and the silk foulard tie I kept for such rare occasions. If the promise of heat was fulfilled, I would be able to carry my jacket. David looked cheerful when he arrived.

"Well, you look reasonably optimistic, David, anyway."

"Yes, I haven't listened to the news yet. Have you?"

"I'm afraid so. I'm a news addict."

"Don't tell me what it said. I prefer to keep my illusions — for half a day, anyway."

"What time are we due at Barchester Towers?"

"Four — they'll just be cutting the cucumber sandwiches."

"I fancy a bun."

"Even that, my son, shall be granted unto you, for in the house of the Lord all things are possible."

"Well, just let me gird up me loins, then, and we'll be off."

I knew we were less light-hearted than we pretended to be, but we set off for Dahlem in reasonably good spirits.

We both fell silent, watching the animated Berlin scene around us as the bus moved steadily on. Apart from noting the inescapable Nazi flags and other Nazi Party insignia, a visitor might think that everything was normal. But I, like everybody who lived in Germany, knew

92

that certain foodstuffs were beginning to be scarce. Butter and eggs, in particular, tended to come and go from the shops in little surges. Anyway, that was unlikely to trouble them at the Vicarage . . .

We got off and walked into an even more treed and pleasant road than the one in which the bus had set us down. "What's the name of this street, then?" I asked.

"I'm not sure, but I believe it's not even a street: could be the Linden Allee."

"Ah, Lime-tree Way; I like that. And there really are lime trees."

"And weeping willows in the gardens. Few sights in Berlin are prettier than a good-looking German girl stepping out from under a weeping willow, as you will shortly see, all being well."

"Will there be Germans there, then?"

"Oh, I should think so. Certainly some half-Germans. Mainly British, of course. But one or two full Germans have been known to penetrate the portals. Even our dear Amanda Fitzherbert has to face the fact occasionally that she is in Germany, and that there are Germans in Germany."

"Bloody foreigners, you mean."

"That's right. Bloody foreigners. Rumour has it that Amanda — who is reputed to be stinking rich, by the way — doesn't speak a word of German, though I suspect she can say rudimentary things such as 'Come in' and 'Put it down there' in the local patois."

"And how about the Reverend himself?"

"Oh, he tangles with the alien tongue sometimes on an '*ou est la plume de ma tante*' level, though he doesn't use a word of it in his services, of course."

"Naturally, God wouldn't understand what the hell he was talking about, would he?"

We were now among detached houses of considerable size and solidity, all with well-kept gardens, though there were curiously few people in the gardens. Finally, we rounded a bend and saw one garden dotted with people, the girls in gaily printed cotton dresses looking like giant blooms. A buzz of talk — English talk — came from them.

"Here we are," said David.

We walked through the open gates and crunched up the drive, nobody apparently seeing us. Yet we had not gone more than twenty paces before a slim, handsome woman of about forty-five wearing a Paisley-pattern silk dress stepped off the biggest of the lawns and faced us: "David Whitaker and friend, I presume," she said, smiling pleasantly.

"Hello, Mrs Fitzherbert," said David. "Yes, you're right. Meet my friend Eric Johnson."

"How do you do, Mrs Fitzherbert. It was kind of you to invite me, for I'm a bit of a fraud really, at a vicarage tea-party. I don't go to church, I'm afraid."

"Come, Mr Johnson, that can't be true," she laughed. "If you were afraid, you'd go!"

She led us at once towards the scattered groups standing around the lawns. The guests, I saw, were of all ages but were mainly under 30. I'd thought she would take us straight to her husband, whose sombre clerical clothes and dog-collar singled him out. But she didn't. She pushed her way into a little group of young people of both sexes and, with an ease that I envied, introduced us both.

I found that I was standing next to a girl with dark hair and clear fair skin of the kind that is quite common in England but much less so in Continental Europe. She was wearing a little upside-down watch pinned over her breast. Well, I had to start somewhere. "I suppose there's no shortage of sick people in Berlin?" I said.

"Ah," she said, turning and smiling, "Sherlock Holmes. No, there's no shortage. And all the nationalities look remarkably similar lying down ill in bed."

"I'll bet they do. And if things go on as they are, there'll be more of them."

No sooner had I said it than I regretted it. This was, after all, a party, not a political meeting. I saw her face cloud. "I was thinking of winter," I lied.

"Is everybody here English?" she asked.

"Well, I've only been here a few minutes, but I've heard nothing but English spoken — that is English English. By the way, in case you didn't hear, I'm Eric Johnson. And I'm English, too, I'm afraid."

"I'm glad," she said. "And I'm Mercia Adam. Also born in England." She held out a hand.

"Do not trust him, gentle maiden," said a voice behind me. "I'm Robin Greene-Dunkett, and vastly more English than this chap."

I released her hand and he as quickly took it.

I was not annoyed that he had taken the social initiative from me: only irritated that it was so easy. Yet, on quick reflection, I was almost glad. And I was certainly glad that for once in a Berlin group there was no truly blonde girl to remind me unbearably of Anna-Maria. I heard Mercia Adam say that she worked at the Achenbacher Krankenhaus and that it was a municipal general hospital in Achenbacher Strasse. I had seen the street sign; it was fairly near to Meinecke Strasse. Why couldn't I extract such information so easily? I drifted away to pay my respects to the host.

The Reverend W.R.P.J. Fitzherbert looked fully twenty years older

94

than his wife. He was in a comfortable canvas-seated chair, spectacle case resting on one of the wooden arms. I judged him to be no taller than I. He was dressed in charcoal grey worsted, his only concession to the heat being a silver-grey double-breasted waistcoat made of some lighter material. His general appearance was undistinguished, yet he had that mysterious social ease that only a good education and a secure place in a stable society can give. I was quite sure that I never would have it. But if I could, I was going to manufacture a sort of self-assurance that would be a good second-best.

I eased my way gently through the scattered group around him and, waiting for a brief pause in the desultory conversation, stepped in front of him and held out my hand. "How do you do, Mr Fitzherbert," I said. "I'm Eric Johnson. It was kind of you to invite me."

He looked up in a slightly bewildered way, for the sun was behind me. Without rising, he took my hand briefly, and limply. "Oh," he said in a milk-and-water voice, "how do you do. Have you had some tea? Er, um, no, you won't have, on reflection. It hasn't been served yet, I believe. And are you resident in Berlin, then?"

"Well, I suppose I am." I knew this was his delicate upper-middle class way of asking what I was doing in Berlin. I remembered that when you are asked a question that's not easy to answer or you don't want to answer, you should ask one back.

"Have you and your wife been here long, then?" I asked.

"Oh, I suppose we have: a good few years, anyway. At least we remember the old Berlin." I knew what he meant, as did all his hearers. I knew, too, that he was too shrewd to elaborate the remark, however much of a duffer he might be, or choose to appear. Even the Reverend Fitzherberts on the German scene were now well aware of which side their bread was buttered.

"I've been admiring your lawn," I said. "I hadn't imagined it possible to get so English-looking a lawn in Berlin." He glanced down at it.

"Oh, you're too kind. I doubt if it is as robust as it looks, even though the man has orders to water it daily in summer, and twice a day in heat waves. It is a false deceiver of a lawn, really. Amanda keeps threatening to play croquet on it, but I tell her that it would probably fail to stand up to such violence."

"A pity," I said, smiling dutifully.

"Do you play croquet then, Mr Johnson?" he asked, his voice having just a trace of the liturgical sing-song of the Anglican service. I felt he might as easily have said: "Do you believe in the transsubstantiation, Mr Johnson?"

"It's a favourite game of mine — after tennis."

"Oh, you do surprise me. I thought nobody played croquet these days. I used to play myself many years ago, before I joined the Church. Yes, the opposite of the commonly held parsonical convention. But I don't play now. I suppose I'm a tiny bit afraid of looking like a living music-hall joke, since the idea of chaps in dog-collars playing croquet is generally supposed to have rich overtones of humour, I believe."

"Well, I mustn't monopolise you," I said. "Most kind of you to spend so much time with me." He returned my thin smile and I slipped away.

Without quite noticing it, I found myself close to a very different group a few seconds later. They were under one of the beautiful weeping willows that David had mentioned, and I was able to see only their legs and feet as I approached. Three were evidently men, as their expensive worsted trouser-legs and hand-made shoes announced. The other was a girl, with golden, down-dusted legs and black-and-white doeskin shoes. I parted the long frond-like branches with my hands and stepped into their midst. The talk instantly ceased and they all looked coolly at me.

"Have you had tea yet?" I said to nobody in particular. The men were all about my own age, though a good deal taller than I. The girl was disturbingly blonde and beautiful. She looked straight at me, full face. If she had not done this, I think I should have retreated in disorder. As it was, I was confident that she must be English. German girls did not look strangers straight in the eye. Even so, her beauty and her boldness momentarily upset me and instantly removed what bit of self-assurance I had brought.

One of the young men standing next to her had a half-smile on his lips. He tapped the ash off his cigarette, and said to me in response to my enquiry about tea: "No, we haven't. I thought you must be bringing it."

Was it deliberately offensive? Or was it my imagination? Or had he carefully chosen his words so that they could be either offensive or facetiously suited to the occasion? I saw them all watching me, waiting to see how I would reply.

I returned the girl's cool stare, hoping without much conviction that I was matching it. She was smiling, but only in a patronising way, as one smiles at children.

The other two men were not even pretending to smile, though they also were looking directly at me. I was sure that they were all indicating by their attitude that I was intruding.

How long this social impasse would have gone on I'd no idea. Already an eternity seemed to have passed. There was a swish of silk behind me and Amanda Fitzherbert's voice saying, greatly to my relief: "Let me introduce you." As she spoke, she took hold, very lightly, of the upper part of my arm. Turning first to the girl, she said: "Elspeth, this is Eric Johnson. Elspeth Tremayne." The girl gave the merest trace of a nod. I tried to do exactly the same. Then, turning to each of the men, my hostess repeated my name and theirs. Their nods were hardly perceptible. Even von Steinfels did better than this. I noticed that the one who had made the patronising reply about the tea was called Kevin St. John Malplas. He bloody well would be, I thought as I wondered if I would ever be able to bring myself to say "Sinjin." But then, if the present situation was any guide, I would probably never need to.

Mrs Fitzherbert did not wait to see if they would absorb me into their circle. Her intuition had evidently told her that they would not, for no sooner had she made the last introduction than she whisked me out from under the tree. "Come on," she said, "you must meet William. That's my husband." When I'd introduced myself to him a few minutes earlier, I'd clearly seen her over his shoulder and thought she saw me — unless, of course, she was short-sighted.

"I've already met him. I introduced myself a few moments ago."

"Good, that's what parties are for, though I'm not sure that the Embassy people always grasp this. But I'm rushing on. The young men you've just met are at the Embassy. I believe the girl has something to do with air travel. I know it's something overhead, anyway. And I don't think she's a tightrope-walker. No, I'd have remembered that. Did you notice that we grow hollyhocks in our garden?" She pointed to some which were growing tall against the side of the house. "They didn't care for Berlin at *all* in the beginning. Took them ages to acclimatise themselves. But they've finally deigned to breathe the alien air and bloom, though I'm sure they disapprove of the neighbours."

"They're very pretty," I said. "And as English as you are." At least I had taken care to find out from David before we set off that she *was* English and not Welsh, Scottish or Irish — or, of course, German.

She liked the compliment, for she took a discreet grip of my upper arm again, and pressed it gently, once. We were walking away from the willow as we talked and we saw two maids come out of the house carrying a large silver urn between them. They took it to a table in the middle of the largest of the lawns, where they set it down on the white tablecloth next to the cups and saucers already there.

"Ah, tea!" said Mrs Fitzherbert. "Let me give you some. But I'm being remiss. I must show you where the 'usual offices' are in the house. I think that's always a good start. Anyway, there's lots of time for the tea." She moved quickly towards the door from which the maids had just emerged and I noticed that it was very fine and of a very heavy hardwood like mahogany. It was only when I looked at it from close quarters that I saw that the pieces of wood in it discreetly formed a Star of David. Instantly, all the anguish of the Jews in Germany and of the Mandelbaums in particular struck me like a blow in the face. Fearing that my expression may have betrayed something of my feelings, I said: "What a splendid door."

"Yes," she said, "it *is* rather splendid, though the Star of David is a dubious distinction in the New Germany. I believe the house was built by Jewish bankers. We've lived here, of course, since long before the Nazis came into power."

I helped her to push open the door and we passed into the cool interior, where matching elegance was on every hand. We were standing in a wide parquet-covered corridor. Indicating a door on her right, she said: "The 'usual offices'. By all means leave your jacket there if you wish. It really is terribly hot outside." She turned and went back to her guests.

The cloakroom in which I found myself was about three times the size of my bedroom at Haus Odol. There were a few raincoats and two alpaca jackets on hooks, all evidently belonging to the Reverend Fitzherbert. But two other jackets, rather smaller and of a tweed far too bold for a cleric, were also evident. After transferring my wallet to my trousers, I slipped off my own jacket and hung it beside them. It made such an unfavourable contrast that I wondered if Mrs Fitzherbert had suggested I hang it in the cloakroom because it was so shabby. Then I felt ashamed for having entertained such a thought. I left it hanging and walked back to the garden.

The guests were still chatting in rather self-conscious groups and I saw that the exclusive little club under the willow had not increased its membership. Mrs Fitzherbert, standing in the middle of the large lawn, clapped her hands above her head and cried: "Tea, everybody! *Do* help yourselves. William does very well with a chalice but he's hopeless with an urn."

As her husband slowly rose from his chair, he said with the crystal-clear articulation of his kind: "Oh, I don't know, Amanda. Given the circumstances, I think I might do reasonably well at urn burial."

"He won the poetry prize at Kings," said his wife to me in something like a private aside and I warmed to her, not because she had said it, but because she had said it to me. Clearly the Fitzherberts shared an unusual sense of humour — and a curiously buttoned-up company of friends and acquaintances, for nobody had moved to take tea.

98

I stepped forward, picked up a cup and saucer which I noticed were made of thinnest bone china, and filled the cup from the urn. Then I gave it to my hostess, adding milk from a Georgian silver milk jug, and being guided in the amount by the look in her eyes. I may not have made a hit with the Embassy crowd, but I was doing a good deal better than I had expected with Amanda Fitzherbert. Or was it that she, being rich and perfectly at ease, was taking pity on an obviously under-privileged young man from the depths of the English provinces?

Guests, including David, were now serving themselves with tea and cakes. I was tempted to serve a few bystanders myself, but crushed the impulse, and poured only my own cup of tea. David, as usual, was thoroughly at ease and, as I passed him, I heard him speaking with a lightness of heart he couldn't be feeling. I moved over to the table spread with a rich selection of cakes and sandwiches. Little flags stuck in the sandwiches indicated contents, which I'd expected to be in German, though they were, naturally, in English. I stood for a moment reading them, seeking the most nourishing. I picked a chicken sandwich before eating my way through the meats to the cucumber, then turned to look at the sweets. An unmistakably clerical voice at my elbow said: "I can recommend them all, dear boy, but especially the queen buns. Amanda is a dab hand at queen buns. The others are entirely edible, but are, I believe, from the *Konditorei*." It was the first word of German I had heard that afternoon.

I turned and looked at the Vicar. I longed to say to him: "The world is going mad all around us. People are being tortured and terrified and here we are sipping tea and nibbling cucumber sandwiches." But all I said was "Thank you," and took a queen bun.

I drank the tea and ate the bun without the least pleasure, but felt annoyed with myself for being so graceless. The day was now very hot, and people were seeking shade under trees and in a summer-house made of oiled cedar-wood.

The house door stood open. More than once I had heard Mrs Fitzherbert say to the company at large that if anybody wished to retreat from the heat, she hoped they would feel free to use the house, so I made my way there now. I passed along the parquet corridor and into a spacious study at the far end, where the garden scene could be clearly observed through small-paned windows outlined by Virginia Creeper. It was a long time since I'd seen so many books in one room. New copies of *The Times*, *The Spectator*, *The Times Literary Supplement* and *Punch* lay on a leather-topped table. I slipped into a chair beside them and picked up the first that came to hand. It was *The Times*.

The leading article was about Germany, but it was a Germany of which I knew nothing, since it was described in terms of a bulwark against radical terrors from beyond the Balkans that, unstemmed, might overwhelm all Europe. It did not quite *say* this, but the implications were inescapable. Could it, I wondered, be right? Was such a balance of power necessary, and life even cruder and more dangerous than I had thought? And would Hitler Germany, now that the Communist threat was overcome and clearly seen to be overcome, settle down to a sort of brisk authoritarian liberalism with strong military overtones? That seemed to be the hope, and possibly the expectation, of the writer of the editorial, and he must, after all, have vast reserves of knowledge and information to draw upon. Was I just a provincial ignoramus looking at Germany through the keyhole of my paltry room in Haus Odol, and frightening myself with swastika-bedaubed hobgoblins? A bumble-bee blundered in and out of the hollyhocks and then into the window panes. I put down the paper, lay back in the chair, and closed my eyes.

Perhaps I ought to be glad, really, that the vicar's tea-party was giving me such mixed emotions. If it had turned out to be a tiny island of the best, the warmest sort of Englishness it might easily have made me unbearably homesick. Even now, when I opened my eyes and caught a glimpse of the unlikely green of the Reverend Fitzherbert's lawns, I felt a pang of longing for the deeper, more durable green grass of the hills all around Fogston. The English journals and newspapers — even those I never normally read — intensified the feeling.

But this was idiotic. What had England ever done for me but reject me? The green grass around Fogston was something I saw only fuzzily, in the distance, behind the mill chimneys, and felt under my feet on rare occasions, when I was trespassing. If I sat down on it, a light film of soot soiled my clothes. If I was ever to do anything useful or interesting anywhere, I must first face reality.

I must have fallen asleep briefly, for I woke to the sound of male, self-confident voices behind me. "But surely, Kevin, you can't *like* living in Berlin — leaving aside the political dangers for a moment?"

"Oh, I don't know," said another. "One isn't likely to be here for too long. And it has its compensations — such as Elspeth here."

"But I'm not German!" said the girl, half diffidently, but flattered.

"You will be if you marry one of the sons of the New Germany," said the other.

"I can assure you, Kevin, that I have no intention of becoming a Hausfrau."

"You mean: one comes; one looks; one might even be a little amused. But one does not stay to marry?"

"You make it sound like a peep-show."

100

"Well, isn't it? And don't you peep down at it from your high perch almost every day?"

"I suppose so — if you put it like that."

"Well, I do."

"But should one not be worried just a teeny bit, Kevin — politically, and all that, I mean?" The first young man was speaking again. "After all, I should have thought it was fairly clear that the Hun was cooking something rather horrid for somebody."

"My dear chap, well, of course he is. He always was. It's his beastly nature. One simply accepts it — and uses it. There may be a bit of a twitter going on in England in certain quarters now about the dangers of newly arisen Germany, but I can assure you, my dear chap, that there is no twittering at the Embassy — at least no more twittering than usual about such vital matters as the right colour for H E's socks. No doubt it will be necessary to make reassuring public noises at home reflecting political anxiety about Germany from time to time — and I grant that their top political brass might get a bit too uppity occasionally — but I can assure you that the really experienced people at the F O are not unhappy about the situation. This is, after all, a typical *Realpolitik* confrontation that some of us actually rather enjoy. And even those who don't share our tastes have to admit that the New Germany is the perfect offset for the New Russia — well, fairly new Russia."

"But if the pot boils quite over, might we British not be scalded?"

"Oh, no danger. No danger at all. I know that the Leader and his friends say a lot of rude things about our decadence and all that. But they envy us, really. Scratch your average German — and certainly your average upstart political German — and what do you find underneath? You find a would-be English gentleman. For all their fine talk about the munificent generosity of the Almighty in making them holy Germans, you could bait a trap with a British passport and they'd trample on each other to grab it."

Had they seen me? Probably not. Or had they seen me and decided to pretend I wasn't there? Anyway, what was I supposed to do now?

I shook myself, opened my eyes, picked up *The Times*, looked at the title, and flung the paper down before walking out.

12

I knew that I'd been dodging a decision about taking Frau Mandelbaum
to Switzerland for quite a time, though she, poor woman, had no
reason to think that there was any threat to the plan that I should go
there with her around the end of July. For that was all arranged before
the Gestapo had seized me, and I had funked a re-examination of the
plan ever since.

Yet I knew I would have to come to a decision, and soon, if I was
not to let her down too late for her to make other plans. If only there
was some way I could tell if I was now a marked man with the Gestapo
. . . And even if I had been truly cleared by the Baron's extraordinary
action, and he really had destroyed all record of my arrest, would I be
risking a reversal of this attitude if I took Frau Mandelbaum to
Switzerland?

Half the trouble was the man's incredibly buttoned-up condition.
When he had ordered me to keep my mouth shut about the incident,
was it a condition of release without repercussions, or just a piece of
advice? I could have asked him later, I supposed; but I had the feeling,
and I had it strongly, that he just didn't want any further reference to
the whole affair. What I did know for sure was that if I disregarded the
Baron's command enough to confide in the Mandelbaums that I'd
been in the Gestapo's hands it would greatly upset them.

So there were three options, all unpleasant. I could say nothing and
make the journey, only that would be both taking and imposing a risk,
and I was supposed to be helping Frau Mandelbaum, not running her
into danger. Or I could confide the barest minimum in Herr Mandelbaum alone and then continue only if he thought I could still be a
useful escort. The third choice was frankly cowardly; that I should
invent an excuse — illness, a sudden urgent journey — and
ignominiously dodge the whole affair.

I did not pretend to myself that I was brave. Anyway, this might be
a case more for discretion than bravery. But I knew, too, that I simply
could not make myself walk out of the whole matter; I'd taken a

resolve, no less binding because it was to myself, that I would oppose the entire Nazi concept.

These thoughts ran through my head as I lay in bed at Haus Odol a day or two after the Vicar's tea-party, which had ended — for me, anyway — in anticlimax. I could see now that I'd made no social progress there, apart from a very minor and wholly unexpected success with Mrs Fitzherbert. I'd spoken to one or two people at the party, but their talk had been full of impudent interrogatives, and I hadn't gone all the way to Berlin to submit to that. I supposed that I'd attended the party to wallow in a bit of Englishry, and it had served me right that I'd found the experience disappointing. Well, I'd had my sniff of imported English air. Now I was back strictly to the German kind.

I threw back the bedclothes, got up, and set about washing and shaving before sitting down to my usual austere breakfast. First pupil at ten. Well, that left a bit of time to whip my thoughts into better shape and come to terms with reality.

Shortly after nine there was a knock on my door. It was Goldgruber: not the nicest apparition for first thing in a morning. But he was in civilian clothes and seemed to have his best civilian manners in operation, too, for he actually smiled as he held out a letter bearing a British stamp. "Post, Herr Yonson. I was coming up anyway, to clean the corridors."

As he handed over the letter he nodded towards the British stamp and said, not offensively: "England. Perhaps from your gracious lady mother."

"It's possible," I said, taking it, and putting it, unopened, into my pocket. I had a Thermos flask full of tea and, since the bottom drawer was shut, Goldgruber was not to know it had been made in the room. "Would you care for a cup of tea?" I asked him, I could not imagine why.

"Ah, you're very kind, Herr Yonson. Very kind. It's always tea with the English! Very nice. Very distinguished. But, alas, it does not suit me. Irritates the stomach nerves and stops me sleeping. But many thanks, all the same. Some other time, perhaps." And away he went, his ego nourished.

Curious how the Germans below a certain level in society were convinced that tea irritated the nerves of the stomach and banished sleep. And, I supposed, if they thought it did, then it did.

I could hear him now outside my room, busy with his cleaning routine. Apparently it was to be an "intermediate" rather than a "thorough" clean. How like the Germans even to have clear names and routines for cleaning the corridors of a third-rate rent block!

As I tried to make up my mind whether I liked the German

approach or hated it, I found myself listening to the sounds of Goldgruber's progress. First there was a quick circuit with a moist mop; followed by a waiting period to allow the linoleum to dry before he polished it with a felt pad attached to a heavy iron weight on a long handle. Why the woman of Germany had not rebelled ages ago against this laborious system of floor-polishing I would never know. In Haus Odol it was done by the male caretaker rather than his wife because Goldgruber said it was good exercise for his Stormtrooper duties, which doubtless it was, since these included a lot of marching and banner-carrying punctuated by street fighting with anybody even vaguely "red" and, latterly I supposed, terrorising Jews and smashing up their houses and shops.

That reminded me of the Mandelbaums. Well, Baron or no Baron, I would resolve it if I could by trying to see Herr Mandelbaum at his furniture factory in Teltow. As soon as I was free long enough, I would telephone him there and ask if I could come out and see him. Ah, no; his telephone line might be tapped. I would simply go there and risk his being out.

Shortly after two, I took the Stadtbahn en route for Teltow, after first looking out the address of the factory in the telephone book.

After a brief enquiry at the outer office, I was taken through to the private office where Herr Mandelbaum was alone. He seemed quietly pleased to see me, though naturally a little curious. I had assumed — rightly, I now suspected — that neither he nor his wife had seen the Gestapo pick me up at his door. After all, there had been no reason for them to watch me go.

Now that I saw his relative composure, I realised that I might be able to keep from him the fact that I'd been arrested in connection with the anti-Jewish slogan on his door.

"You have come to make the arrangements?" he said, after he had given me a chair.

"Well, yes, I hope so. But there is . . ." I sought my mind, and my knowledge of German, for a suitable word ". . . a complication. By a misunderstanding a few days ago I was arrested by the Gestapo and held briefly at their Berlin central office." His face clouded and he rose.

"My dear boy, how on earth — ?"

"Oh, it really was a misunderstanding; they thought I made a gesture against the regime. But it was all quickly over and they released me — and destroyed the record, binding me to silence about the matter. I only mention it now, in strictest confidence, because it could touch you, and Frau Mandelbaum." I looked around the room, not for the first time, wondering if it was wise to speak so freely. Yet I felt sure that he would have given me a sign if he had feared a concealed microphone. Anyway, the buzz and rumble of the wood-working machinery made a background noise that would probably drown the conversation for an eavesdropper. "I mention the event only because I feel that you have a right to know about it and judge if you still think I have any value now as a companion to Frau Mandelbaum for the journey."

He sat down again and for quite some time remained silent, thinking. Then, finally, he said: "I think you will be more, not less valuable. After all, you have been . . ." he hesitated, not wishing to be precise and clearly loathing to pronounce the word "Gestapo", ". . . in certain hands, cleared and released. Moreover it is likely to be known that you have Jewish pupils. Certain people would be quite glad to see us leave Germany, you know. And if the learning of English, or any other language, speeds our departure . . ." Here he shrugged his shoulders in an eloquent gesture, and then pulled his chair closer to mine. "But there is something else," he went on. "I had intended in any case to seek a private little talk with you. It falls out well that you should come now for such a purpose. Herr Johnson, the last thing I want to do is burden you with troubles that should not concern you." He looked hard at me for an instant, as though seeking agreement that he should go on.

"I do not see it as a trouble, Herr Mandelbaum."

"You are kind, young man, very kind. Very well, then, I shall tell you. My wife will leave the country permanently towards the month-end. She thinks I will follow her into exile. But, alas, I cannot. But neither can I tell her that nor the reason for it. If I did, she would not go. And I want her to go. It is her only hope: the only hope of all people of our race. You know I have been in concentration camp?"

"Yes, I do."

"Well, there I suffered from some kidney injury from beatings from rubber truncheons, and the resultant kidney failure is progressive. I shall not live long after she has gone. No, don't say anything; it is quite a common occurrence now. Perhaps I have a month, perhaps two — half a year at the very most. If I were to try to leave with her, I fear I might be detained again, that both of us might. After all, it would look suspiciously as though we were emigrating if we both went without having previously sold out everything at a sacrificial price to some Nazi. This is, of course, what they want, and they would be sure that we had made a secret private arrangement with somebody about the business, and they would take steps to extract the information. No, it is not to be contemplated. Actually, I am leaving the business to my workpeople. This will secretly infuriate the Nazis, but I doubt if they will be able to upset it. And by the time it happens, my dear wife will be in Switzerland, with some provision, too, thank God. Frau Mandelbaum, Rebecca, and I are unusual for Jews in having no children and few relatives. This makes us perhaps even more attached to each other than most old couples . . .''

I was deeply overcome but could say nothing that would even remotely meet the need of the moment.

"No doubt, Herr Johnson, you are thinking that Frau Mandelbaum will want to return for the funeral, and so put herself again in the danger from which I wish so much to remove her. Do not fear. It is Jewish custom only for men to attend such funerals. She would not attend it anyway. And when I do go, she will be told quite specifically that it was my last wish that she should *not* return to this country on any account. She will respect it, I know. We have always respected each other's wishes.''

Still I couldn't find words, and he began speaking again to bridge the gap. He seemed to be more concerned that what he had told me might upset me than by the circumstance itself. "We Jews,'' he went on, "have not always been wise. We have not all been wise in Germany. I am a German-born Jew of a family that has been here so long that I cannot trace the record. Like thousands of other German Jews, I fought in the last war and have the Kaiser's decoration to prove it. But others are more recent arrivals. And quite a lot came here during the inflation period when the German Government let the value of the currency go to nothing to get rid of old war debts. This massive inflation was widely exploited by newly arrived Eastern Jews to get hold of valuable properties, and this was much resented.

"Try not to judge us too harshly in this, Herr Johnson. We, too, are the victims of history. Perhaps also we work too hard, for the stranger within the gate has to be more effective. He also has to *prove* himself *more* successful to feel *as* successful as the native. This is foolish, but it is widespread — and not confined to Jews. Anyway, I am not a stranger here. Neither is my wife. We have been made into strangers. But I must not lecture you of all people. Do forgive me. I am very glad you came. I shall now go ahead with the arrangements.''

As I rode back to the West End of Berlin in the train I thought of many things and tried to foresee what the next few weeks would bring. My hand, fumbling in my pocket, came across the letter that Goldgruber had given me that morning. It was strange that I'd forgotten it, for I was always glad to hear from home.

I took the letter out, and for the first time noticed that it was in an unfamiliar handwriting that looked like my mother's but was not hers. Quickly I tore open the envelope and looked at the foot of the single

106

sheet of paper inside. It was from my brother Fred, who had never written to me before.

"Dear Brother," he wrote. "Our mother has been ill for over a week but is better now. Anyway, she's back at work and managing fairly well, though it does mean that yours truly is having to be something of a dab hand with the frying pan. She says you're not to worry because you'll have enough troubles of your own among all those Huns. Hope they don't have censors, by the way, because they might not like being called what I've just called them. No offence. Just English humour. By the way, if you get any good German stamps, please send them to me because the ones you send on your letters are always the same. Your ever-loving brother, Fred."

Only now did it strike me what a joyless life my mother led. She was really quite a nice looking woman, though I doubted if she ever thought of herself in such terms. She was still young enough to have the right to expect more from life than the long hard slog to earn a bare living and bring up a family without help. What she needed was the sort of man my father had never been. I was her eldest son and wasn't the least use to her; I had had such great plans but they'd disintegrated into a daily fight for survival.

I looked out of the train window at the alien scene. Surely there must be more to life than this miserable struggle just to keep alive. There was again talk of the Great Depression perhaps being near its end. Well, there had been similar talk ever since it started, five years ago. So why should it end now? It was clear that all the most learned politicians and economists in the world hadn't the faintest notion of how to deal with it. Perhaps it would go on forever, or at least for the rest of my life — which amounted to the same thing as far as I was concerned. Here in Germany, Hitler made bold claims about having taken "radical and positive steps" to provide work for the rotting millions. And in a way, he had done something. But everything that he'd done had a military motivation. Even the many thousands now shovelling earth all over the New Germany were helping to build strategic roads and dual-purpose airfields. But it looked good in the newspapers and the newsreels, and it nourished hope.

In Haus Odol, next to the chemist's shop, was a florist's, and I remembered that it had on its glass entrance door a sort of winged Mercury figure and the word "Interflora." Surely this meant that I could send some flowers to my mother. I'd never sent a bunch of flowers to anybody in my life, and could ill afford to do so now, but it seemed a good time to start.

The woman in the shop was the essence of helpfulness and seemed to know that I'd little money, for she immediately mentioned the lowest sum for which flowers could be sent. I paid it and gave my mother's name and address. "And the greeting?" said the woman.

I stared, uncomprehending for an instant. "Oh, yes. The greeting." I knew that in Germany one always said "*Gute Besserung*" — "good recovery," but the English was stiff and unfamiliar. "Can it be in English?" I asked.

"Why, certainly, sir. In any European language — without surcharge. It is part of the service. Wait, I will give you a card to write on."

She did so, and I wrote: "With all my love, Eric. Hope you soon feel well again."

By the time I got to my room I'd turned it over in my mind several times and felt that it was completely inadequate. I didn't know what else to say. I'd have to hope that my mother would understand. After all, she was northcountry as well. She knew we weren't able to say much, no matter what we felt.

13

A few days later there came to me through the post in an open envelope a travel agency folder giving details of excursions to Switzerland. There was nothing to indicate who had sent the folder, but I knew that it came from Herr Mandelbaum, for lightly underlined in pencil was a departure date near the end of the month. The excursion marked was ideally suited to our purpose, being for seven days and relating only to the railway journey.

So the die was cast. We had agreed to reduce to the absolute minimum any communication between us and to confine it to strictly impersonal things, such as the folder. So I was not surprised when, three days later, the post brought me two return tickets for the trip, together with full printed details and a compliments slip from the travel agency.

The weather continued uncomfortably hot, but the Berliners seemed to take it in their stride. Whenever I walked about the town I was still haunted by near-glimpses of girls whom I thought to be Anna-Maria. I tried to bring some sort of detachment to this emotional torture by wondering how long it could possibly go on. Surely it must fade eventually; yet I had no sense of any fall in its intensity. I cursed myself for a sentimental fool, unable to face the world as it was rather than as I wanted it to be. It made not the least difference. The next time I caught some fleeting sight of a fair-haired girl disappearing into a shop or down the steps of the Underground, I was instantly reduced to the same despair. Well, in a few days I would be out of Berlin and out of Germany.

Arranging lessons so as to leave me with a full week free — without losing my pupils — had not been easy. But the pupils were co-operative, especially when they knew I was going to German-speaking Switzerland. To them it was apparently a sort of joke country where the natives were friendly and keen on making money, but so stupid that they were not very good at it. ''You, with your High German, will find their Swiss German hard to understand,'' said one, but smiled as he said it. ''They speak a vile sort of squashed and distorted German a bit like Viennese German, only worse," he added cheerfully. "I suppose it's all right for the hotel trade, or the wood-carving and cuckoo-clock industry." I thought this a curious sort of snobbery, but said nothing. After all, I hadn't been to Switzerland, so couldn't judge.

Next day I had a post-card. It bore the Teltow post-mark and said in German: "If you're in the area any time in the near future, perhaps you'd pop in and discuss English lessons. Greetings from R.M." It bore no marks of origin, but needed none, for it was the pre-arranged signal to call and finalise details of the journey.

I called two days later, and felt physically sick as I passed the now doubly odious daub on the front door. As I climbed the stairs I commanded myself to show no signs of my reaction.

If the Mandelbaums saw anything unusual in my appearance, they did not show it. Frau Mandelbaum motioned me to a chair and put a light to the spirit stove under the decorative pivoted kettle on the table between us.

After we had settled the particulars of the excursion, she said, "Today we shall drink English tea and think about that wonderfully calm country where everybody is happy." I assumed she meant England. I said nothing. We all needed dreams. I did my best to enter into the spirit of the occasion, so we drank the English tea and made a disproportionate fuss about whether to eat pink English-looking wafer biscuits or brown ones, while the radio played tinkling "*Unter-haltungsmusic*". I thought once that Herr Mandelbaum glanced with quiet despair at a dish of small cakes that might over-try his failing digestive system, but he smiled and took one.

"Will you pack your embroidery?" he said to his wife, looking at a half-completed chair-cover on a frame beside him.

"To be sure," she said. "Though I'll be far too busy to do any till you join me." The moment passed and we went on to talk of brightly superficial matters. But it was like a dialogue in a grave, and I was glad when it was over and I was on my way back.

Apart from the small items I'd eaten at the Mandelbaums' I'd had nothing all that day and now felt a little faint with hunger, and perhaps with suppressed emotion. So I got out near Quick, the coin-in-the-slot café, where I bought a sandwich and a paper cup of coffee. But my mind began to play tricks with the phrase "the quick and the dead," so I soon resumed my journey.

Reaching Haus Odol some time before I was due to give a lesson there, I walked on past the building in an unfamiliar direction, trying to sort out my plans.

Had I been right to come to Berlin at all? Certainly I ought to be in Fogston now, but simply hadn't the fare.

I reached the street corner and my reflections were rudely ended by the sight of a huge aerial bomb set in concrete in the pavement. It was painted a vivid yellow and on it in bold black lettering were the words: *"Niemals vergessen!"* — "Never forget!" How ironic, I thought, especially as Goering, as chief of the German Air Force, was so fond of solemnly beating his huge breast and assuring the whole nation that "in no circumstances will any enemy aircraft even be allowed to penetrate the German air-space." I waited for the traffic lights and crossed the street.

At the corner opposite was one of the increasingly numerous showcases advertising *"Der Stürmer"*. I would have scorned to stop and read either the specimen copies or the propaganda posters displayed, and I felt glad as I walked past that I'd never once seen a Berliner stop to examine such a showcase, either. Yet it was impossible to avoid noticing as I passed that it contained Julius Streicher's favourite anti-Jewish poster which showed the ritual slaughtering of a Christian baby by a hideous old Jew holding a long curved knife — presumably the circumcision knife — dripping with blood.

Everybody knew that Hitler had employed a sort of spoils incentive system during the long years of struggle for power, promising his favourite cronies whole vast areas of administration. To Streicher he had tossed the Jews as one tosses raw meat to a dog. I walked on.

The street in which I now found myself was much like the others in the Wittenberg Platz area, being composed mainly of apartment blocks, all about four stories high, some with integral lifts, some with lifts ingeniously built on afterwards in a sort of vertical steel tunnel fastened to the outside of the building. But most were like Haus Odol, with no lift, and built of brick around an unseen court in the middle of the block. It suddenly occurred to me that if there was one place in the world that should not be pugnacious about aerial bombing, it was Berlin, for most of it would fall like houses of cards if anything much bigger than hand grenades were ever to fall on it.

Perhaps it was a realisation of this that had made Goering give his preposterous reassurance. Or had he some secret — and reliable — system of aerial defence? After all, he was a First World War flying ace, with an impressive list of "kills." Reliable rumour had it too that he was a drug addict, and this was sure to be known by potential enemy countries. It seemed appalling that such an unbalanced man should be in charge of so deadly an instrument as an air force. And just how unbalanced he was, I recalled, had been shown to the world when he attended the Reichstag Fire trial as a witness and had stormed, there and then, in the court, that no matter what verdict the court might reach, he, Goering, would deal with the accused if necessary outside the court.

As I passed one of the dwelling blocks, the front door opened and two young fair-haired children came out. Their mother, wearing a decorative apron over her pretty cotton-print dress, followed them. All three were beautifully neat and clean. The woman looked both ways up and down the street, a lightly restraining hand on the boy's shoulder. Having re-assured herself that all was normal and peaceful, she gave him a gentle push, saying: "Right then; off you go. No loitering — and look after your sister, especially at the cross-roads. Keep tight hold of her hand!" Both children looked briefly at her and smiled before setting off down the pavement.

The utter normality of the incident made me feel that all the daily talk of war and the danger of war in Germany must be quite unfounded, and purposely hatched up by the Nazis so that people would turn to them for protection. I looked at my watch. There was just time to get back for the lesson if I hurried.

I reached my room a few minutes before the Baron did. It would have been a moral defeat — as well as a discourtesy — to have arrived after him. This would be the last lesson but one before I went to Switzerland and I'd made no attempt to hide the fact from him that I was going there for a short trip. I saw it as essential to treat the matter as absolutely normal and without significance. For this reason I had even let it drop to him that I was going with "an elderly Jewish woman pupil" — a detail that he had studiously ignored, though I had noticed that fully an hour later he had managed to bring it into the practice conversation that there was some anti-Jewish feeling in Switzerland. He had done this in rather a cunning way, referring to "anti-Jewish feeling in all parts of the European Continent". I had taken this to refer only to the mainland, but it did cross my mind that he might have meant Britain to be included as well.

As I prepared the equipment for the lesson, I was thinking about von Steinfels. In all the many lessons, he had revealed the man behind the proud presence only once, and even now I was still without any indication of why he had stuck so firmly to his resolve to get some sort of grasp of English. For I had to admit to myself that he was not a very good pupil. And I was probably not a very good teacher. I heard his precisely measured rap on the door, and let him in.

He gave his stiff little bow and said, in English: "Good afternoon."

"Good afternoon, Baron," I replied. "Do come in." And so we went through the familiar routine. It was fiendishly hot, but I knew

112

that it would be both useless and tactless to ask him if he wished to take off his uniform jacket, or even unbutton it.

Despite the heat, I kept him sternly to the task for, in his military way,he seemed almost to take a pleasure in submitting to difficult discipline. But precisely five minutes before the scheduled time for the lesson to end he asked, still in English — for we were using the direct method — if he might lapse briefly into German.

"Why, certainly," I said, in German, my curiosity aroused.

"Perhaps you have wondered sometimes why I have come to you, and not, for example, to the Berlitz School for my English lessons, yes?"

"Well, the thought has sometimes crossed my mind. But why should I question an arrangement that is to my advantage?"

"Why indeed. Well, I will tell you. I have come to you because I wanted to have contact with just one typical English person, over a considerable period of time, to try to learn something — forgive me for being candid — of the nation we may have to fight." He stopped and looked very hard at me.

I was careful to show no reaction — except to smile a little. I saw myself as something less than typical, but this was no time to say so. "The famous German thoroughness, I suppose."

"If you like. But the unpleasant possibility has to be faced."

I nodded. "Yes, I know. The armed forces of every big country have to take account of every military possibility, I believe. And may I ask if you feel you've learned anything — of England, I mean?"

Now it was his turn to smile slightly. "I have learned," he said, picking his words, "that the British are a very un-military nation."

I knew he thought this deplorable, and probably expected me to feel the same. "Quite right," I said. "We are civilians by nature and soldiers only if we have to be."

"Precisely the opposite of us Germans." There followed a short silence, then he added: "I was afraid my remark might be offensive, but I see that it isn't."

"On the contrary, it's a compliment."

Clearly he thought me idiotic, but seemed pleased to find me so in this particular. "Perhaps, now that we of the Waffen SS are no longer secret, you would like to see us do a little drilling sometime?"

"But, surely . . .?"

"You would, of course, have to stand some distance away and I would, naturally, be unable to recognise you."

"Naturally."

And so, to my astonishment, it was arranged for two days hence, at a precise time, in a precise place "regardless of the weather". I was to stand strictly on a specific public road, within five metres of a numbered street lamp, watch for precisely the duration of the drill, and then walk on.

When he had gone I called myself all kinds of an idiot for agreeing. I should have made an excuse. What could be the Baron's motive? Was he boasting? Did he hope to overawe me? And what if it was a trap — a way to charge me with spying? All this public road business only *seemed* reassuring. In Nazi Germany if they wanted to charge anybody with spying or with anything else, they just charged them, and that was that. I found myself sweating as I recalled the popular joke currently circulating in Germany about two old male Jews walking in the street. One bought a paper, read a short news item, folded it up and said he was going back home. The other asked why. ''Well, I've just read in the paper that a fierce tiger has escaped from a circus in Frankfurt and that they're out with guns and nets seeking it.'' To which the other replied: ''Well this isn't Frankfurt and you aren't a tiger.'' ''I know,'' said the first, ''but can I prove it?''

On the principle of the condemned man eating a hearty breakfast, I decided to go out and buy some better, tastier food than usual, and take it back to my room to eat.

I was fascinated by the wide choice of food at the nearby delicatessen shop, but went there rarely in case I was tempted beyond my means. I was afraid, too, that I might see something utterly English, though this had become less likely of late.

When I got in the shop my mouth went dry. The lush variety of food and the wonderfully wholesome aroma of new bread and smoked meats hit me like a wave. I saw no butter or eggs on display, but there were stacked masses of everything else, from tinned oysters to boxes of Bismarck herrings, grape-encrusted cheeses to stuffed olives. At least a hundred different sausages were on show. Right in front of me was a huge basket of straight-stemmed local asparagus. Next to it was an equally big basket of twisty asparagus, just as good in quality but less pretty, and probably awkward to cook. Even the better quality was vastly cheaper than asparagus ever was in England, where I believed it was eaten only by the upper classes and fashionable whores. ''I'll take half a kilo of the best asparagus,'' I said recklessly.

''H'm, very refined,'' said a mock-sarcastic voice behind me in English. ''None of your crooked asparagus for him!''

I turned round instantly. It was Mercia Adam.

''Hello,'' I said, astonished to see her in my local delicatessen. ''Have you seen David recently?'' I asked, simply because the last time I'd seen her she was with him at the Vicar's tea-party.

''David? Oh, David Whitaker. No, I haven't.''

114

"Do you shop here regularly, then?"

"No, I just happen to be in this area today."

"But the hospital's in the Achenbacher Strasse, isn't it?"

"Ah, what a memory. You'll be claiming next to remember my name. She grinned and went on: "And they do feed us, quite well, too. But not much on delicatessen — and certainly not on straight asparagus. Too suggestive, I suppose."

"In that case," I said, paying for my purchases and feeling I was halfway to ruin as I stuffed a tin of anchovies into my pocket, "they'd better be careful not to let the nurses eat Jelly Babies." I saw no reason why she should be the only one who could have a Berlin-style sense of humour. "*Aufwiedersehen*, Miss Adam."

"So you *do* remember my name! If you like to wait a minute perhaps we could walk part of the way together. I go through Chlorodont Platz on my way back. You did say that you lived near there, didn't you?"

"Probably. The Chlorodont Platz joke is useful at parties. And, yes, of course, I'd be happy to walk with you."

She turned and, reading from a piece of paper, bought a large variety of delicatessen. She must have seen some sign of curiosity on my face, for she said as she crossed off the last item with a stubby pencil: "One of our nurses is going back home to get married, so we're having a farewell party."

"Sort of delicatessen and indelicate thoughts?" I said. She laughed.

"Oh, no doubt there'll be a certain amount of fairly fundamental talk. But there are few surprises in marriage for nurses, you know. They see too much of the consequences of marriage at their work for that."

"Good as well as bad, I hope?"

"Oh, yes, both."

We chattered on, as she packed her purchases carefully into a large shopping bag, but not before marking each package with the price. I noticed, too, that she put the solid purchases at the bottom of the bag, grading them upwards in fragility as she filled it. Perhaps this care was a reflection of her nurse's training, I thought; but I wondered, all the same, if she would have done it if she had been a nurse in England.

When the bag was full, I took it and we left the shop.

We walked on to a point where our paths diverged. She was wearing a pale pink cotton summer dress and her lithe body showed through at every step. "Well," she said, "here we part," and took her shopping bag.

I wanted to make some farewell remark that would be interesting, not at all banal, and hinting somehow at a future meeting: an English equivalent, in fact, of "*Auf Wiedersehen*." But all I managed to say was: "Well, goodbye."

But she walked only three steps, then half turned, and said over her shoulder: "Come to the farewell party this evening if you want. It's mixed. Eight o'clock, at the nurses' home, Room 42. Goodbye." And she was gone, not even waiting for my reply. But at eight o'clock I had to give a lesson in my room to a fat, middle-aged German matron who thought that some knowledge of English was genteel — though she was beginning to wonder if, in the New Germany, it was also wise.

. Although the asparagus should go well with the fresh bread and butter and smoked ham, I decided first to eat the anchovies. When the tin was open, they looked surprisingly small for what they had cost, and I was hungry. I was amazed to find them so powerful in flavour that I had to eat plenty of bread and butter with them. So when the asparagus was ready, I lacked appetite and sense of taste for it. Well, that would teach me to splurge on fancy, unfamiliar food.

I found I had the bottom few inches of a bottle of wine, but had kept it so long that when I sipped it on top of the rich food, it tasted awful. I poured it down the wash-basin, and prepared a pot of proletarian tea. That, at least, was right.

Eight o'clock came, and went. At half-past, there was a familiar knock on my door, and Goldgruber handed me a delicate little envelope which was faintly perfumed. Was it possible that Mercia Adam had sent me a written invitation, by hand? I slit it open at once. "Dear Herr Johnson," it began depressingly, in German. "I am afraid I shall not be able to attend for my lesson this evening or, alas, in future. My son has come home on leave and I am now too busy. Thank you all the same. Goodbye. Elfriede Hummel." The "Goodbye" was in English. Well, she had learned one useful word.

I looked in the envelope again in case she had slipped in a banknote to compensate for the lack of notice. But it was empty. Fortunately, I'd made it a rule, on David Whitaker's advice, always to be paid slightly in advance. Screwing up the envelope and the letter, I set off at once for Achenbacher Strasse.

I had no difficulty in locating the nurses' home and I was rather surprised on going inside not to be challenged by some daunting female dragon. I walked straight up the stairs.

Another little surprise met me at Room 42. The doorway was festooned with roses and pinned to the door itself was a silver-paper cut-out of wedding bells. From inside came the faint but unmistakable sound of Marlene Dietrich singing in German on a gramophone record "Falling in Love Again".

Well, I told myself, I ought to have expected it, for I'd seen before how cheerfully and gaily the Germans could throw themselves into any sort of celebration, free as they presumably were from any backwash of Puritanism or other form of cold-comfort Christianity. I knocked on the door. Nothing happened. I knocked again, with no more effect. So I opened the door, and found myself confronted by another — a padded one — immediately behind it, which reminded me that nurses on night duty needed quiet rooms for sleep during daytime. It made a happy contrast with the last padded door I'd seen.

The cheerful noise of a party reached me through the second door, on which it wasn't possible to knock. I pushed it open, and the sounds of music, talk, laughter and the chink of glasses surged out. Before me were about thirty handsome young girls and men. Among the men was the usual scattering of Nazi uniforms and about half the girls were in nursing uniform. The other girls, presumably taking full advantage of being off duty, were dressed in their prettiest gowns.

"Do come in, Eric!" shouted Mercia, putting what I took to be a glass of schnapps into my hand. I turned round and made sure that both doors were firmly closed before walking in.

117

14

When my alarm clock woke me at five o'clock on the morning of the Waffen SS exercise, I had a total lack of enthusiasm for the event. It was scheduled for 6.45, some distance away, so I had to allow plenty of time for the journey.

Well before six o'clock, I was rumbling along in the Underground towards the other side of Berlin in a carriage full of workmen who must have been carrying food in their various boxes and satchels, for there was a whiff of garlic sausage in the air. I could take both tobacco smoke and garlic later in the day, but the combination was a trace nauseating so early in the morning.

A few of the men in the carriage were reading newspapers, but seemed to find little of interest in them. I had the *Voelkischer Beobachter*. As I scanned its great areas of unrelieved bombast and propaganda, I could see why it continued to be called "Hitler's own paper."

When I walked up the steps of the station into the street near my destination, I was a little taken aback by the sharp contrast with the West End. There was no sign of a tree and all the gloomy industrial buildings were unrelentingly functional. I thought the Berliners there were less attractive, too; they seemed somehow stumpier and tended to walk as though they were locked in their own depressing ruminations. No doubt they looked very much like me.

There was nothing even hinting at a military occasion, but I didn't expect there to be. Using a street map and a slip of paper bearing the address and time, I soon found the street where the exercise was to take place. It was no different from other streets in the area.

After walking a short way along it, I found myself near to a group of squat buildings set around what I took to be a courtyard. It looked like a school, but I could see no detail because a high brick boundary wall separated the buildings from the pavement on which I stood.

I walked on a little and came to a stout ironwork gate, which was closed. Behind it stood two steel-helmeted SS guards, looking straight forward through the bars and holding their machine-pistols at the port. Their legs were slightly apart in what I had come to recognise as the SS stance. Beyond a doubt, I was at the right place. I retraced my footsteps and stopped at the position I had been told to take.

As I had gone along the street I had been conscious of a steady stream of workmen, some walking, some on cycles, also moving along the road, all in the same direction. I saw now that they seemed to be heading for a large complex of drab looking buildings about a quarter of a mile away from which came reddish smoke of the sort common in steel-producing areas. I looked at my watch. Five minutes to go. I pretended to read my paper.

Precisely at the stated time, a siren sounded. After about half a minute it stopped and a distant voice shouted a command, which was at once followed by the low chomping sound of steel-shod boots moving over a hard surface. Still nothing was visible, but to the sound of boots was added the rumble of something like steel girders being manoeuvred. Meanwhile, the gates were being swung back by the two guards and, as soon as they were open, a squad of eight similar figures followed by a single figure marched smartly out and into the middle of the road. The officer in charge shouted a few terse words and the squad divided into two groups of four men each, standing back to back. At another command, they marched about twenty paces ahead, machine-pistols gripped at the ready, stopping all traffic on the road and pavements and causing it to retreat a little. The soldiers did not even look at the pedestrians and cyclists whom they were controlling, but everybody seemed to realise that the slightest show of reluctance in moving back would be instantly and severely dealt with.

The officer in charge remained smartly erect at the point where the two squads had separated, turning his head first to watch one of them, then the other, then coming back to the straight-ahead position. He must have been counting the steps they took, for, as he gave the command to halt, he looked at neither squad. When they did halt, the soldiers were evenly spaced out across the road, each squad at an exactly equal distance of about thirty paces from the officer. When they stopped, their machine-pistols were pointing just over the heads of the small group of workmen, who now stood quite still.

A minute later, the ends of two lengths of heavy steel trunking two or three yards apart appeared above the wall, pointing skyward. Then, under perfect control, they were extended and lowered into a level position, about a yard above the top of the wall, before sinking gently until they rested on the pavement. I could hear the sound of a diesel engine, and there was a faint squeal of rubber on steel. The muzzle of a field gun showed above the wall, between the two bridge-like structures formed by the trunking, which I now noticed had regular bars across the upper surface like tank tracks.

119

The engine roared, and the rest of the gun, clearly self-propelled on huge rubber-tyred wheels, slowly climbed up the trunking, paused a moment when it reached the level portion, then slowly descended the second slope, checked a moment on reaching the pavement, then gently rolled forward off the trunking and into the roadway where it came to rest, its barrel level, beside the officer.

Out of the gate there now marched another squad of men, about twelve in number and carrying no visible arms. Behind them and marching with them was another officer. It was von Steinfels.

As they were marching out under his shouted orders, I was able to notice that the bars on the trunking exactly matched the rubber bars on the tyres of the self-propelled gun. So this was why it had climbed and descended the little bridge with such precision and control.

Von Steinfels eventually reached a position facing the other officer on the roadway. The second squad of men now dispersed around the gun, with one of them giving something like secondary orders in a rather quieter voice than that of the Baron. The muzzle of the gun began to swing upwards and eventually stopped when it was very close to the vertical. The man controlling it made a few quick movements, then the soldier giving the secondary orders said to von Steinfels: ''Fertig!'' A split second later, the gun fired. Although it was obviously a blank shot, the ground and the watchers trembled. I noticed, though, that the recoil was taken up with remarkably little movement communicated to the wheels and framework of the gun, which I was beginning to examine in greater detail. Much to my surprise, I saw that it was a most crudely constructed affair, like something put together in a weekend's welding by a blacksmith. Even the breach-block was welded.

Then the significance of this suddenly struck me. If the Germans could make such obviously effective guns by welding — with such a range of traverse that they could presumably be field guns, anti-tank or anti-aircraft guns — then they could re-arm in a fraction of the time needed for traditional gun-making methods. No wonder the Baron was so arrogantly confident! ·

I had brought with me my English cotton gabardine raincoat and had slipped this on when I had seen what an industrial area I was in, hoping its neutral look would make me inconspicuous. When the gun fired, I was glad I had done this, for I instantly felt around me in the group of a hundred or more workmen a surge of something like Germanic intoxication. Their eyes had a faraway look I'd never previously seen and their few tiny movements were Robot-like. Then, before the puff of smoke began to disperse on the light morning breeze, they cheered madly and began, slowly at first, then with a mounting frenzy, to shout: "*Sieg Heil! Sieg Heil! Sieg Heil!*" as they gave the full-arm Nazi salute. I felt acutely embarrassed, for clearly I couldn't join their frenzy. But I also sensed real danger. They would feel that anybody who was not with them was against them. In a humiliating compromise, I began to open and shut my mouth in time with the shouting, though I could not bring myself, for all my terror, to raise my arm in the salute. Fortunately, a few of them were not giving it, though everybody was shouting.

The gun muzzle was lowered and the gun rolled to the side of the road. The crowd, now in a flush of patriotic joy, surged forward so enthusiasticially that they briefly surrounded the gun. Carried along with them, I was thankful for anonymity. Suddenly I realised that I must fix in my mind as much detail of the gun as I possibly could, for I had a strong feeling that it was a secret prototype. If only I could estimate the length of the barrel and the calibre — as well as the rough basis of the welded construction — it might be priceless information.

I could only guess the barrel length in paces. But, as the crowd hurled me forward, I thought that if I could manage to be pressed for an instant against the end of the lowered muzzle, I might get an imprint of the calibre on my raincoat. I had to wriggle fiercely in the crush to do this, but eventually I did it, pressing my chest strongly for a moment against the muzzle. A second later I looked down and was horrified to see that I had succeeded only too well. There was a clear circular imprint over my left breast. My God, it could kill me!

At this moment, von Steinfels must have judged the conduct of the onlookers too disorderly, for he bawled a command and all the soldiers present immediately threw themselves at the crowd, waving the butts of their machine-pistols like clubs and clearly not worried in the least if they made contact with skulls or shoulders. Immediately, the crowd stumbled back, me with them. As we retreated, I slipped off my raincoat and gripped it firmly to my body, folding it over my left arm when the chance came.

Less than a minute later, the gun had climbed the bridge again and disappeared behind the barrack wall without leaving a sign of having been in the road. The two squads now combined, and the first officer to appear took over again. At a few barked commands the soldiers marched back towards the gate, in perfect formation, now doing the goose step.

As they fell into this extraordinary stride, I felt something like a votive, almost religious, mood spread among the watchers. It was as though they had never expected to see anything so confidently, boastfully German ever again. This time they did not cheer. Tears ran down one or two faces. They looked transported. *"Der Tag"* was clearly not far away.

When the gates clanged together, the crowd of watchers began to move off towards their workplace in a near trance, and I was thankful to move with them, walking straight on, not daring to retrace my steps, which would have taken me against the stream and made me conspicuous. First, I must survive. I walked on and on, deeper and deeper into industrial Berlin and was soon quite lost. As I walked, I carefully shredded the slip of paper bearing details of the time and place of the event I had just seen, and dropped the bits at intervals.

* * *

I was by now in no doubt about Germany's intentions, but was still deeply mystified by the Baron's attitude towards me. Why had he sprung me from Gestapo Headquarters? And why had he taken care that I should be a witness of the little exercise with the remarkable gun? And, question of questions, was I supposed to recognise it as remarkable? I couldn't ask him, and I certainly couldn't ask anybody else. As the time drew near for his last lesson before I went to Switzerland, I tried to recall every detail of his conduct that might throw any light on what he was about.

Shortly after the organised murder of the 30th June, I had suspected briefly that he'd suffered a change of heart. Certainly he was emotionally shattered by the experience of having to order the slaughter of his fellow Nazis — and rumour now put the number killed at nearly a thousand. Yet I had the feeling that in less than a month his Nazi confidence had returned almost to full fervour. Somehow, like many more, he seemed to have reconciled it with his conscience that appalling things would have to be done, and tolerated, if the Nazi dream was to be realised.

Yet as I sat waiting for him to come, I could also see that if he had decided that the whole thing was going to be too dreadful and too bloody to be borne, he had no way of retreat. Obviously, men did not resign from the inner core of the SS. Their utter dedication was Hitler's constant boast. So, to stay alive in the Baron's situation a man would have to simulate enthusiasm even if he felt none. And if he felt positive revulsion, the need to conceal it would be still greater. Was von Steinfels caught in such a trap? It was just possible.

Perhaps I was grossly over-complicating it all. Perhaps, with true Germanic thoroughness, he had decided — even been ordered — to make fairly close and constant contact with some handy Englishman to observe and report on the effect of the growing Nazi strength on that man, for it was quite certain that the Nazis were almost obsessively concerned with British reaction. Over and over again since I'd been in Germany, I'd felt this mingled admiration and contempt for Britain — for England, as they called it. And this was true of many Germans who weren't Nazis. They seemed to feel that Britain, like some once marvellously virile animal now old and decayed, might still strike out with a flash of the old force that had brought it as near to being master of the world as any nation was ever likely to be — except, given the realisation of the Nazi dream, Germany. And all the time, too, there was a general fear of the Americans, who also spoke English, in spite of their successful rebellion.

Perhaps it was precisely because I was so very ordinary that my reaction to German aspirations might be considered to have value as being typical. It was a ridiculous thought, but it had about it a touch of the extraordinary German logic that made them so formidable. In a way, I wished the Baron would open up; but I was glad, too, that he probably never would. Some things in the New Germany were too dangerous for daylight.

I took my raincoat down from behind the door and, laying it on the table, unfolded it so that the imprint from the gun was uppermost. My own guilty feelings made the mark look terribly significant, yet I supposed, really, that it looked little different from the sort of smutch that anybody might pick up. From a drawer in the table I took out a steel metric rule and measured the ring. Being a bit blurred, it could not be precisely measured, but at the widest seemed to be ninety millimetres and at the narrowest eighty-eight millimetres. I made no written note of the measurement, but returned the rule to the drawer and, using some of the spirit intended for my little stove and a plug of cotton wool, removed most of the remaining outline of the ring and hung the coat back on the door.

As I did so, there came a sharp rap from the other side and I jumped like a frightened girl. It was the Baron, and I let him in with as much of a show of normality as I could manage.

Just as I expected, his attitude was precisely as before, and we were soon swapping banalities in English about writing and posting a letter, and how the letters in England were collected from the post-box. ". . . Then the postman opens the post-box with his key," I said, "and scrapes out the letters with one hand while holding a sack with the other, in this way stuffing the letters into the sack. Now repeat."

Von Steinfels, instead of repeating, showed some puzzlement. "What is *scrape*?" I made a scraping motion, but this seemed to mystify him all the more. "*Kratzen?*" he said, incredulously. "Does the English postman *scratch* the letters out? It is not possible." At which I had to explain that, unlike German post-boxes, which hung on the wall and at collection times had a bag attached to them into which the letters dropped when a lever was pulled, English post-boxes had a sort of chute arrangement but needed the letters to be scraped out of them manually. The Baron was far too polite to show any contempt for such a blundering system, but the effort of not showing contempt was quite as plain as the contempt itself would have been. Bungling English again, I could see him thinking. How on earth did they ever manage to get into the world-significant position they are in? I judged it wise to move on to mentioning how the bag full of letters could be fastened to a frame and picked up by a moving train, even at speed . . .

Just before the time came for the lesson to end, he said, in German: "Did you see the little exercise?"

"I did," I replied in the same language. "It was very impressive, *very* impressive."

"You noticed, then, that there was not so much as a boot-scrape on the wall or a mark on the road when it was finished?"

In point of fact, I had noticed this, but, just in time, decided not to reveal that I had been such a close observer.

"Really?" I said. "I'm afraid I couldn't see such details, but I certainly saw the speed and efficiency of the drill."

"They can do it in their sleep . . ."

"But they don't — do it in their sleep, I mean?" He shot me a hard look. Was this another bit of the strange English sense of humour?

"No," he said, "they do not. But it is possible that one day they will do it in other people's sleep." And he permitted himself a grim little smile.

124

15

To keep the trip to Switzerland as ordinary looking as possible, Frau Mandelbaum and I had arranged to meet at the railway station. Fortunately, she was not nearly so obviously Jewish looking as her husband, but I made sure, all the same, that she didn't arrive before I did, and so run the risk of some lout in or out of Nazi uniform insulting her. With "Jews Unwanted" signs going up every day in Germany — and getting plenty of publicity — I judged this to be a real danger.

So I'd been at Lehrter Bahnhof nearly twenty minutes when she arrived. If she'd taken a taxi, there was no sign of it. I knew that Jews couldn't afford to show the smallest sign of ostentation, but surely they could still use taxis? If not, then I had failed as a courier before the journey had begun. Anyway, there she was, rather sombrely dressed and carrying only a single piece of luggage — a weekend suitcase not unlike mine. Exchanging no more than a smile of greeting and "*Guten Tag*," I quickly took it from her and we moved off towards the train.

Fortunately, we were still early, which was as well, for there was no question of our travelling by anything but the cheapest class, which was likely to be crowded.

I put our cases on the rack and we sat down. There were three people in the compartment already, and I was relieved when they took no notice of us. Frau Mandelbaum opened her handbag, took out a newspaper, and began to read it. I saw that it was, of all things, the *Voelkischer Beobachter*. I was sure every line of it was loathsome to her, but her face showed no sign of it. In turn, I unfolded a copy of the *Berliner Illustrierte*. To the other passengers we must have looked absolutely normal.

Several more people came in and the train started. Frau Mandelbaum did not even look up although she knew, as I did, that she would never see Berlin again. I could make only the vaguest guess at her thoughts and feelings, and marvel at her composure.

Quite soon we had cleared the city, but I had no sense of relief. In the hundreds of miles that lay between us and the Swiss border there was time — and opportunity — for anything to happen. I particularly dreaded the border, where Frau Mandelbaum would have to show her passport, overstamped, no doubt, with a big "J" for "Jew". But all I said to her was: "You have all your papers?"

"Yes. And you have yours?" I took them out of my inside pocket for at least the fifth time and made sure they were all present. I could afford no mistakes any more than she could.

As we moved steadily across the landscape, I realised how little of any countryside I'd seen for a long time and what beauty and seeming-peacefulness I'd missed. The West End of Berlin was a handsome and pleasant enough place to live in — when one could pay the rent and eat regularly — but lacked what this vista so generously offered.

I didn't altogether trust what I saw. Instinctively, I couldn't associate these sunburnt peaceful-looking landworkers in their long, straight fields with any taint of the Nazi power that now held the towns in more or less open terror. Yet I knew this was an illusion: that the entire country, on both sides of the Polish Corridor, had been systematically organised down to the last furrow to serve the Nazi aim. In fact, the Nazi terror machine was probably more effective in the countryside, where everybody knew everybody else, than it was in the towns, where at least a trace of anonymity remained.

After no more than about two hours, there was a great shuffling of bags and opening of paper parcels in the compartment and the air was filled with the smell of salami, smoked ham, Knackwurst, Bockwurst and Leberwurst. All these delicatessen, or nearly all of them, had pig meat as their foundation, and I felt for Frau Mandelbaum. But she showed not the least sign of discomfort, even when one ample-hipped Hausfrau sitting opposite offered her a smoked-ham sandwich. "I'm sorry," she said. "It looks delicious. But I had a huge meal just before the train started." Well, at least one German had not spotted that she was Jewish. On we rumbled, across the great German plain.

Frau Mandelbaum's reply obviously ruled out any eating for her for some time. She turned to me and said: "Don't let me stop you, Eric. I know that young men have far better appetites than old ladies!" She had always called me "Herr Johnson" or "Mr Johnson" before; evidently she thought it wiser now to suggest some closer relationship. Aunt and nephew? Grandmother and grandson? Impossible to say. But all I could tactfully do was smile, for most of my own ill-considered provisions for the journey were also based on the much-loved German pig. Well, it would serve me right to go hungry awhile. Perhaps it would teach me a little tact as well, for only now did I remember that the Nazis, with their sure touch for the common taste and total lack of a sense of humour, had given a lot of support for a recent "poem" in praise of the pig as the best, the most *German* of animals.

I'd looked forward to the detour through the Rhineland, for it was a legend even in smoky Fogston. I remembered reading in the school primer that the stretch between Bonn and Bingen was held to be the most handsome of all. And, like quite a number of schoolmates, I'd managed to learn by heart the German poem about the Rhine Maiden, sitting on her riverside rock and combing her golden hair with a golden comb. But I daren't mention the poem now, for I had a feeling that it had been written by Heine, a Jewish poet.

But I did take a long look at the Lorelei Rock when the train passed it, and even smiled inwardly to myself for half-expecting to see the maiden of the legend sitting calmly on top of it, combing her golden hair with the golden comb. Everybody in the compartment apparently did the same, for they all stared at the great column of rock — including Frau Mandelbaum, who was presumably going over in her mind the forbidden poem. I knew that the Germans were prone to burst into song on such folk-occasions, and wondered what would happen if some amateur heroic tenor among us should start up: "*Ich weiss nicht was soll es bedeuten . . .*"

The eating never stopped for long, and I was now a good deal hungrier than I'd have cared to admit. "You should eat, Eric," said Frau Mandelbaum, which gave me a jolt. "Young men have good appetites. You have brought some food with you?" she added with sudden solicitude.

"Yes. And you too?"

"Of course." So we both fumbled through our belongings and took out more or less anonymous sandwiches. I was dreading this moment, for courtesy demanded that I offer her some of mine, yet it was impossible for me to say it at the time that they were not Kosher, for the word would have positively exploded in the carriage.

But she was not a shrewd old lady for nothing. "Oh," she said, unwrapping a large packet, "I always over-provide for such occasions. I am relying on your help with eating this lot and on no account will I eat any of yours . . ." So the moment passed, and my slight sweat with it.

It was still a long journey to Basel and sanctuary, and I felt sure that neither she nor I would really believe that we would ever get there until we felt the hard reality of Switzerland under our feet.

At last we saw Basel in the near distance. It couldn't be long now. The train drew to a halt and the passengers began to shuffle about, getting out money, passport and tickets, though the tickets had been dealt with already.

The passport official entered our compartment. "Your passports, please," he said, and began to check them with typical German efficiency. Mine was the only non-German one, but, to my relief, it caused him to hesitate only momentarily before he stamped it with his little portable stamp and handed it back to me. "Pleasant journey," he said, in English, and smiled. I thought the other people in the carriage gave me a careful look at this, for my companion and I had spoken nothing but German.

As ill-luck would have it, the last passport was Frau Mandelbaum's. He took it and checked it without the least hint of reaction, looking first at the document, then at Frau Mandelbaum, presumably making sure that the photograph matched. Then, without stamping it, he said in cold German: "Come with me."

"She is with me," I said, also in German.

"Then both come with me," he answered. "And bring your baggage."

It was a moment of silent terror for both of us. I simply dare not look at her. We gathered together our possessions as quickly as our trembling hands would let us. For a terrifying moment I wondered if the Baron had set up the whole situation to destroy me.

As we stepped down from the carriage, I needed all my resolution — first to help Frau Mandelbaum down, and then to take her suitcase. The official watched us impassively, then said: "You will each carry your own baggage." It sounded like a death-knell.

A burly woman dressed in something like civilian uniform walked up to the passport official and they exchanged a few mumbled words, the man looking once towards Frau Mandelbaum and the woman almost imperceptibly nodding. Then the woman approached Frau Mandelbaum and said: "Come with me." As they walked away together, I tried to take some comfort from the fact that the woman official did not take hold of Frau Mandelbaum's free arm in a motion of arrest. Then I realised that no comfort was to be had from this. Frau Mandelbaum was Jewish, therefore vermin, and one does not handle vermin from choice.

The passport official turned to me. "Your passport, please," he said in German. Evidently both the "pleasant journey" and the English were finished. I gave it to him and he put it in his side pocket. "Follow me." For a desperate moment, I considered trying to run away down the platform to Switzerland, now only a few paces away. But he seemed to apprehend the thought. "You will be aware," he said, "that we are still in Germany?"

"I have official permission to be in Germany."

"No doubt. No doubt."

"And I am registered with the Police as resident in Berlin, who have been informed officially that I am going to Switzerland for a week's holiday and have agreed. My papers are absolutely in order."

"We shall see."

The official opened the glass-panelled door of an office beside the track and nodded for me to precede him. I walked in, my suitcase banging against the door, which was on a spring. Two more customs officials were in the little room, one seated at a desk. My papers were laid before him and he gave them an almost perfunctory examination before nodding his head to indicate a door behind him. "Through there," said the first official, walking over to the door and opening it. I went through.

The room behind was another office, with filing cabinets, telephones, a desk, chairs, and another official, also in uniform — but this time police uniform. The windows were set so high in the wall that nobody could see either in or out.

The policeman remained standing while the passport official sat down at the desk, from which he fired the first question: "Why are you leaving Germany in the company of a German Jewess?"

"For a holiday, as I said." I put down my case beside me.

"And why the Jewess?"

"She is a pupil of mine. I teach English."

"Is she paying your fare?" Instantly I realised that this was a trap question. If I said she was not, then it suggested that I'd more money than, in fact, I had — and more than they knew I had, for I did not doubt that Goldgruber would as a matter of routine have informed officialdom of every detail of me he'd gleaned. But if I said she was paying my fare, then I laid myself open to the charge of being in the pay of Jewry. Why had I not thought of this before I set out? If I invented another source — say, my mother — then I had to remember that Frau Mandèlbaum was being interrogated at the same time, and that any discrepancy in our stories would instantly be taken as evidence of a guilty plot.

"Well?" rapped the official. "Make up your mind young man."

"She is paying my fare in return for my services as both a teacher of English and a courier; the journey to Switzerland allows me to be both."

"And a lackey of Jewry into the bargain." It was hard to tell whether this was comment or question. I decided to treat it as a question.

"I do not see it like that."

"Ha. No doubt you don't; but we Germans do. We have much experience of these matters." He sat back in his chair and began to

129

polish the nails of one hand on the palm of the other. Then he took off his uniform cap and put it on the desk. German officials did not do such things unless they had plenty of time at their disposal. Throughout the interrogation I had been unconsciously listening to the rhythmic pant of the engine of the train; it was broken now by a sharp explosion of steam.

"The train! I shall miss my train," I urged.

The passport official turned to the policeman and said in mock concern, "Our young friend is afraid he will miss his train. Can't we do something about it?"

"The train," said the other in a voice completely devoid of any human inflection, "will leave shortly. You will not be on it."

I wondered if it would do any good at this stage to demand to see the British Consul.

"Put the contents of your pockets on the desk," ordered the passport official.

In a nightmare way, I supposed, I had anticipated this possibility when I was planning the journey yet I realised now that so deep is the basic optimism of all human beings that when they take such possibilities into account, they do so only with the upper part of their minds. My raincoat was my starting point. I emptied every last trifle out of all my pockets, knowing that if I overlooked anything I'd be technically guilty of hindering officials of the Reich in the execution of their duty. This time there were no French letters; at least I'd learned that lesson. When the little pile of possessions was before him, the official looked at it, then said to me: "You are sure that's everything?"

"Yes, quite sure."

"Right, then take off your outer clothes, shirt included." I took them off, piling them on a chair at my side of the desk. The policeman stepped forward and began to examine them with professional thoroughness, not merely turning all the pockets inside out, but running his fingers along each seam, bending, probing and listening. He found nothing.

At the bottom of the pile was my raincoat, and he gave this particular attention. Again he found nothing. Then he examined the outer surface of it, inch by inch. Made of cheap putty-coloured gabardine — it had cost me 30 shillings at Dales Menswear in Fogston — the coat had taken on a sort of map-like look, recording the passage of everything that could possibly leave a stain or mark, and the fact that it had been cleaned once since I came to Germany only seemed to have made it more receptive to later staining.

Eventually he came to the remaining traces of the imprint of the gun barrel.

At this moment, the starting-bells clanged and the engine began to puff. I was thankful for the diversion of attention.

The policeman stared at the faint, rough circle. If he had the special knowledge that would enable him to recognise the zigzag of gun rifling, I was doomed. After a second or two, he put the coat down on top of the pile, then moved to me and felt over my underpants, making me stand with my legs apart so that he could pay special attention to the area of the crotch. "Take off your socks." I did so, and he examined them just as painstakingly, finally dropping them on the pile also. Then he opened my suitcase and examined everything in it, even squeezing out a little toothpaste.

"Right," said the passport official. "You may dress — and wait." I dressed, and he went out of the room, leaving the policeman there, still standing. Once dressed, I subsided into the chair. "Stand up!" barked the policeman. I stood.

How long I remained standing I'd no idea. It seemed an eternity. Eventually the passport official came back into the room. "Follow me," he said, "with suitcase." To follow was progress of a sort. We went through the outer office and back on to the platform. There was no sign of Frau Mandelbaum.

Suddenly, I realised I was alone, and presumably free. I looked around. There were a few passengers of both sexes standing about, apparently waiting for the next train. They looked typically German in their neat, unstylish clothes. The passport official had disappeared.

Again I looked around me, and again saw nothing odd. I took a few paces, first towards Germany, then towards Switzerland, and keeping all the time in Germany. As I turned, I noticed an old hag leaning against the wall for support. Dressed in rags and with stockings in coils around her ankles, she had a festoon of grey, rat-tailed hair hanging down to her shoulders obscuring her face. Beside her was a suitcase from which trailed other rags and ends of garments. It seemed strange that the order-loving Germans should allow such a person on the platform.

She turned her head and looked towards me, parting her hair before her eyes. It was Frau Mandelbaum.

I hurried over to her. "My God, what have they done to you?"

She was very pale and seemed hardly to be breathing. Yet she turned and looked straight into my eyes, and smiled. "Only interrogation and search." I glanced down at her tattered clothing, every seam of which must have been ripped open with a razor at points where it could conceal anything bigger than a postage stamp.

"Would you like to go to the Women's Room and change into some of your other clothes?"

131

"They're all the same."

I cast a quick look at Switzerland, now so near.

"I could carry you there. They might allow that."

But this raised a problem. Try as I would, I could not carry two suitcases in one hand. But Frau Mandelbaum solved it. "Don't worry. I shall walk, and I shall carry my suitcase." She pushed herself off the wall and swayed a little, then steadied. I took her arm, handed her suitcase to her and picked up my own.

The Swiss customs officials must have known something of what had been going on, for two of them had walked to the precise point on the platform where Switzerland met Germany, and were staring in our direction.

Moving very slowly, we crept forward, taking perhaps forty or more steps to cover the twenty paces, and so shuffled into Switzerland. Unbidden, the Swiss customs officials each took and carried a suitcase.

16

I was sure that every detail of our passage into Switzerland would be burned into my mind: the desperate sense of relief, the kindly fuss of the Swiss railway officials making our tickets valid for a different train, and the embarrassment of the other passengers at having to travel with so rough-looking a person as Frau Mandelbaum. But within two days it was already beginning to be dream-like.

We had telephoned her sister as soon as we were safely in the country and had been met at the main railway station in Zürich and whisked out to the house overlooking the lake almost as originally planned. Even so, it was going to take Frau Mandelbaum the best part of a week, I thought, to recover some strength and feel that she really was in Switzerland.

I walked over to the window of my bedroom, coffee cup in hand, and watched the little boats crawl across the luminous blue of the lake in the summer sunshine. From the high setting of the house, it was possible to see most of the town, marching garden-like and full of trees, down to a point where the huge lake ended in a small river. The air was clear over the whole town, so that even the older buildings crowding each bank near the town centre were so clean that they looked like paper models in a three-dimensional plan. So this was the biggest commercial town in Switzerland, not much smaller than Leeds, yet so incredibly different from Leeds. I strained to look as far as possible in both directions, seeking some area of dirt or disorder, but saw none.

Frau Professor Dengler and her Swiss husband lived in some style in what appeared to be the best part of the town. Frau Mandelbaum had told me that the Professor was head of his faculty at Zürich University, and that they were childless. Clearly they took a pride in their home, but I had a feeling that they rarely entertained and that this was the first time for quite a period that all their bedrooms had been occupied.

I was surprised that the Professor and his wife spoke a strange Swiss-German dialect with each other, but switched into High German for my benefit when I joined them. Frau Dengler laughingly explained:

"We are German-speaking Swiss, but that means Swiss, not German — even though I was born in Germany. So, like everybody else, we speak the dialect. Do they not speak dialects in England also?"

"Yes, when they can't help it." My reply totally mystified them.

For the first day after our arrival, Frau Mandelbaum had kept to her room, but now she appeared at the lunch table, dressed, I imagined, in some of her sister's clothes. She looked remarkably calm. "Well," she said to us all, "It's a little late in life to learn new ways, but I am now learning, if not to be Swiss, then to be good imitation Swiss — and already my clothes are Swiss." She held out an arm. "It must be a good omen." With a sob of both joy and sorrow, her sister went to her and embraced her.

"Dear, dear Rebecca. It's wonderful that you are free, and soon, God willing, Jacob will be free as well, and here with you. Then we shall truly be able to rejoice."

The whole room was decorated with flowers, as was the lounge. The dining table held a special display of roses, the centrepiece of which spelt out in tiny rosebuds "Heartfelt Welcome Rebecca."

Although they were at pains to make me welcome, too, I felt that I was something of an intruder into what was essentially a family occasion. So I took the first discreet opportunity to tell my hosts that I had quite a lot to do in the week at my disposal. This was true. I had to get the information about the gun to a responsible representative of Britain and find out if there was any chance of work in Switzerland.

The second of these I was able to mention to the Professor. His reaction was gloomy. "I'm afraid the chances are very slight," he said, shaking his head. "We have the Depression here too, and this makes the Swiss authorities very unwilling to grant work permits to foreigners."

"Even for teaching English?"

"Yes, even that, I'm afraid. We tend to see England only as a source of touristic income. The officials in charge of work permits may not put it so bluntly, but I can assure you — unfortunately — that such is the official attitude. Anyway, you will certainly have quite a lot of running around to do if you have to make that sort of inquiry. Do you, by any chance, happen to have an international driving licence? If you have, I will lend you a car."

"I'm afraid not."

"Ah, well. Never mind. Use taxis, then — and take this towards your costs." He held out two 100-franc notes. "If you need more, just speak. Go on, take it," he grinned. "Young men are always broke anyway." I took the notes.

"Most kind. Many thanks."

"Not at all. I can't put into words the relief my wife feels at getting her sister out of that unspeakable country . . ."

"What is the attitude of German-speaking Switzerland towards Hitler Germany, Professor?"

"Total contempt. Perhaps you've already noticed a certain reserve when you speak to any Swiss in High German?"

"So that's what it is. Yes, I had noticed it. But I'm afraid I'll have to risk it," I smiled, "for I haven't a hope of picking up any Swiss German within a week."

"Ah, well, you never know. Fate might ordain it that you spend more than a week in Switzerland."

After an over-emotional lunchtime in which every reference to Herr Mandelbaum's anticipated arrival in Switzerland was privately agonising to me, I left the house and went down into the centre of the town to investigate work permits.

At first the Aliens Police simply gave me the appropriate form to fill in, and even that grudgingly. I knew that it would take weeks for such an application even to be considered. "But what I'm seeking is some guidance."

"What guidance? The form is quite straightforward."

"No, not on filling the form, but on how the application is likely to be considered."

The official at the other side of the desk gave me a hard look. "Nobody can anticipate the decision."

"No, not the decision, but the general likelihood . . ." And so it went on.

I was handed from official to official, being quietly stone-walled by each. One even went so far as to say that it seemed that only the Minister for Foreign Affairs would be able to answer my question "and I can assure you that he won't." By the end of the afternoon I'd got nowhere.

Next day I tried again, and this time the sight of me at the same places making the same enquiries apparently caused them to realise that I was serious and to fear that I might pester them indefinitely. So I did finally get an interview with an official of some sort of standing. I told him that I was enquiring on behalf of a friend at present teaching English in Berlin.

"Oh, so he's got a job already?"

"Yes, but he finds the political atmosphere stifling." I had to risk it.

"So your friend has rather a delicate nose for politics, eh?"

I was tempted by this deliberately provocative remark to reply with more heat than caution, but managed just in time to check myself.

Already I might have said too much and done David a disservice. After all, this was German-speaking Switzerland, and while the general attitude was clearly anti-Nazi, why should I assume that there were no Nazi sympathisers in the country? Not five minutes earlier, as I was walking down the main street of the city, the Bahnhofstrasse, I had seen a poster advertising a folk festival in which a symbolic Swiss man dressed in traditional costume held one hand to his mouth as though shouting across a mountain valley. Somebody had written beside his mouth "*Juden heraus!*" — "Jews out!"

"My friend isn't political," I hurried to say. "But politics impose themselves on everybody in Germany now."

"Well, he can fill in the forms . . ." He began to shuffle papers on his desk.

"But what chance will he have?"

"You are asking me to prejudice his application?"

"No, just to give me some idea of the circumstances in which it will be judged."

"Switzerland is a very small country, with no natural resources. It, too, has an unemployment problem. Industrial activity is at a low level and the tourist trade is very bad."

"But, surely, for example, the people in your hotel trade want to learn English —"

"So they do. And they do learn English — either here, from Swiss who have lived and worked in England or America; or they go to England or America and learn it there."

I was much tempted to say, "While working there, too," but saw no profit in such a remark.

"So what you are really saying is that his chance of a work permit is very small?"

"That would be *your* deduction, but I see no reason to quarrel with it."

When I got back to the house, I told the Professor that preliminary enquiries were not very promising, but that I hoped to make some more.

I went to my room and laid my raincoat on the bed, with the fuzzy imprint of the gun barrel uppermost, then took paper and pencil and began to draw a sketch of the gun. Having no skill in drawing, I seemed able to draw only toy guns, and had to tear up several sketches in irritation. But eventually some of the details began to come back to me and I finally made what I hoped was a useful sketch of the gun and, on a second piece of paper, a sketch of the bridging device that had enabled it to surmount the wall so easily. Against the drawing of the gun I wrote the calibre of the bore and estimates of the length of

136

the barrel and of the gun overall. I put both sketches in my wallet, went to the kitchen, and asked the cook to open the fire-door of her stove, where I burned the torn-up fragments of paper.

My attempt to reach an informative official in the Swiss Aliens Police began to look like an easy assignment when I tried to reach a British official to whom I could usefully pass on details of the gun. I was not helped by the fact that I could do little more than hint at the object of my visit, and before long I found myself going backwards and forwards across the city — by tram and bus to minimise the cost — and getting nowhere. Eventually I was told that I would have to go right outside Zürich, to an address jotted on a piece of paper. I looked at the address; it was much too far away to be reached that day even by taxi. After enquiring about train times, I went back to the house, resolved to make an early start next day.

The following day I arrived at my destination well before noon, but it was towards five o'clock before I managed at last to get into the presence of a British official who might have some power to deal with the matter. His office was spacious and handsomely furnished and the fact that he was seated behind a large desk, and remained seated when I went in, suggested that he knew very well that I'd refused to be side-tracked by his underlings. Though seated, he was very erect. I'd time to take in that he was about forty-five and had the sort of "exploding grenade" type of moustache favoured by Guards officers before he said: "Yes?"

By now, I was far too weary to be delicate. Taking out the sketch of the gun, I said: "I have here a sketch of a new German field gun which I was able to see in Germany by a fortunate circumstance. It's an unusual gun, made by revolutionary methods that will allow the Germans to rearm in a fraction of the time needed by traditional methods."

If I'd brought out a pistol and taken a pot shot at him he couldn't have acted with more indignation. He sprang to his feet, which took him to a height considerably taller than my own, and I couldn't help noticing, even though events had taken such an unfortunate turn, that he looked like a fashion plate.

"Good God, man," he snapped, "you walk in here off the street, claiming to be a British subject, totally violate protocol, and then attempt without so much as by-your-leave to compromise me quite gratuitously by offering me details of something which in no conceivable circumstances could possible concern you legitimately —"

I thought for a moment that he was going to stop talking, for he checked momentarily, clearly irritated with himself for ever having started. But his face now had a slight flush and his annoyance was too deep to be cut off easily. "By what right do you assume that His Majesty's Government is uninformed of what is going on in Germany or, if informed, is incapable of appraising its significance in general and for Britain in particular? Your assumptions are as offensive as they are gratuitous and I totally reject them. I would have you know that there is one powerful country and only one in the world that is dangerously expansionist, and that country is most certainly not Germany. Indeed, Germany constitutes a bulwark of immeasurable value against that country, however objectionable some superficial consideration of the National Socialist regime may be. But I can't imagine why I am telling you all this." He stopped, possibly more angry with himself now than with me.

But if he was angry, so was I. "You are telling me," I said, "because it's the official line. You and your Establishment pals think you will be able to use Hitler as a pawn in your own game. Well, you won't. He's promised a thousand times to tear up the Treaty of Versailles, and the only way to do it is to smash the Polish, French and British armies, in that order. What's to stop him? Certainly not you and your complacent friends. And if you do eventually get the score, far too late, you'll find that you are making one gun to every ten he's making. *This* sort of gun." I waved the piece of paper. "I got these details in a way that makes sure that they're important. And I doubt if any other non-German has them. Now do you or don't you want the sketch?"

To my surprise, he hesitated. "If you wish to leave it, I am unable to prevent you."

I banged it down on the desk, turned round, and walked out.

But as I was leaving the building, I realised that I still had the sketch of the bridging mechanism. Well, I certainly wasn't going to jump through hoops again to see him. I walked back down the corridor and knocked firmly on the door. "Come in," he called.

He was sitting at his desk and looked up at me with a totally blank face. Manifestly I was the last person he expected to see. "I forgot to leave details of the bridging mechanism that allows the gun to cross obstacles." As I pulled out the second sketch, I saw the first one lying in his waste-paper basket. I snatched it out and thrust both sketches into my pocket, turned and went out, leaving the door open.

At the first public lavatory I came across, I tore both sketches into tiny bits and flushed them away. As the last fragment disappeared, I realised that this was exactly what he would want me to do.

* * *

In a way, I was glad when the week in Switzerland was over, if only to be able to stop having to pretend that Jacob Mandelbaum would shortly be there, too. Although he and his wife had given long thought and care to their flight — and I could only hope for his sake that they had done this before he knew he was dying — Frau Mandelbaum had remembered many unresolved details when she reached Switzerland. "Remind him, please, to bring his English winter underwear and socks; they are much the best . . ." And so on.

I had managed in my journeying to see quite a lot of Zürich, and the more I saw, the more I liked the town. Much of it was hilly, like Fogston — in fact, hilliness was all they had in common — and this meant that I kept getting sudden views across town and lake. I liked the tramcars, too, which also reminded me of Fogston. So I tended to walk down into the town and ride back in a tram, the weather generally being too hot for uphill walking. I was amused to see the Zürichers opened the tram windows to get some air into the car, but always left the door behind the driver shut, although opening it would have ventilated the car much better. But on the door was a little notice: "This door must be kept shut." Such dedication to rules was positively German, I thought. "Ah, yes, we are a bit formal," said the Professor when I mentioned it to him. "But we are also very democratic. We take so many plebiscites that I sometimes think we'll take one to find out what day it is! And I don't mean plebiscites like that one they took in Germany to see if everybody loved Hitler. We do not even pretend to love the Government here; but we respect it."

It was the Professor who took me to the station when I left.

"Come again, Herr Yonson," he said, holding out his hand. "You will be welcome."

When he had gone and the train was moving towards Germany, I realised that I did not know if he was Jew or Gentile. It was of no importance.

I would have preferred to go back by a more direct route, not only to see something of Austria, but to avoid having to pass through the station at Basel. But my ticket said "via Basel" so via Basel it had to be.

When the train drew in to Basel it was on a different line, supervised by different officials, and this was a relief to me. I was a bit surprised, all the same, when the German passport official stamped my passport, smiled, and said in English: "Pleasant stay in the Reich." Could it possibly be sarcasm? It was very unlikely. Anyway, whatever it was, I was now back in Germany, back in the Third Reich.

139

17

Once back in Germany with the border and Basel behind me, I slept. But each time the train stopped, I woke enough to get some vague impression of the stopping-place without any of the detail.

As it was an excursion train, it made no great speed and halted at several small Black Forest townships amid mountains, streams and trees that made them look more like romantic story settings than places where people lived and worked. At one of these, I was vaguely conscious that the empty seat opposite me was being taken by two young people, a man and a girl, who spoke softly and gently to each other. Their backs were to me as they put their luggage on the rack and I saw only the lower half of them under my drooping eyelids. Then they turned and sat down, and came fully into my vision. The girl was beautiful and so startlingly like Lilli that I was immediately awake.

She was brunette, wore no make-up and needed none. Her skin was darker than an English girl of her hair colouring would have had, but was in perfect harmony with the rest of her appearance, and her face was oval with long lashes that often rested on her cheeks. No sooner had they sat down, than they held hands and turned slightly towards each other so that they could talk in near-whispers. I could just recognise the High German of Prussia.

The man was tall and fair in the Prussian tradition of physical beauty combined with masculinity, and I noticed from his few movements that he had the grace that so often went with these characteristics. I saw now that they were both wearing new wedding rings and new clothes, and that their new luggage on the rack above them bore new labels.

How utterly different, I thought, from David and Lilli, surprised into marriage and even more surprised into parenthood in their appalling little flat in Wedding.

I rarely thought of myself and marriage, being financially disqualified, though I'd known the torment of longing to be married to Anna-Maria.

Outside the train, the Rhineland was slowly unrolling, and was just as attractive as the travel posters showed it. But I would not be in the Rhineland, gliding along the river in one of those spotlessly white streamers, drinking Rhine wine and eating Rhine salmon. I would be grubbing away in Haus Odol, drinking illegally imported Maypole tea and eating whatever came to hand, so long as it was cheap and convenient. And my pupils would be stumbling hopelessly as ever over "th" sounds and saying it was impossible for the German mouth to cope with such an English absurdity. Once, in a misbegotten attempt to make a joke of this, I'd asked one of them to practice by saying the name "Muriel Thistlethwaite." But she gained no skill and I lost a pupil.

Well, I was still alive, and free, and young enough to do anything. For the rest of the journey I'd concentrate on all the nice aspects of Germany, and slowly eat the delightful food that the Denglers had given me for the journey.

I unwrapped the parcel and took out a sandwich of crisp new bread, thickly spread with butter and well filled with air-dried beef. Delicious! Perhaps tomorrow Hitler would fall down the monumental steps of the Reich's Chancellory and break his bloody neck, and the whole Nazi nightmare would stop. Goering would go on the stage as a fat comedian telling vulgar jokes such as his favourite "We're not shitters, but shooters." Goebbels would teach elocution to door-to-door salesmen. Himmler would be promoted to Inspector of Sewers. Streicher would become a street newspaper seller. Goldgruber would revert to being nothing but a lowly, even obsequious, caretaker. And the Berliners would positively queue up to take English lessons from me so that they could get a breath of unfamiliar liberty in foreign parts, speaking *"Englisch, die Weltsprache"* — "English, the world language."

But when the reality of Berlin was under my feet again I didn't feel so jokey. I realised that Hitler and the Nazi Party had put their stamp on the city in some ways that had not been so obvious to me when I was in the midst of it. Bronze heads of Hitler abounded, some incorporated in the massive stonework of building façades, with laurel-wreathed swastikas cut deep into the masonry. Every time Hitler opened his mouth these days, he seemed to talk about "the Thousand-year Reich," and these monuments certainly underlined his words and made a Nazi millennium feel more likely.

When I got to Haus Odol, there was Goldgruber in his Storm-trooper uniform as well.

"Good evening, Herr Yonson," he said. "So you did go away." I'd told him I might, but his comment somehow made the trip feel like something improper.

141

"Good evening. You're very perceptive, Herr Goldgruber. But this could be a suitcase full of washing."

"That's true, it could."

But there was no point in fencing. I knew he was official nosey-parker for the block both for the landlord and the Party. "No, you're right. I have been away — to Switzerland, the German-speaking part."

"Ah, the mountainland. Very nice. Wonderful landscape; terrible German."

"I was in the lowland."

"Not quite so nice — but still terrible German."

"Yes, terrible German." There was nothing to be gained by crossing him, and it helped my credit for him to know that I'd been able to go on holiday. It would have helped it even more if I'd been able to tell him that I'd made a month's rent out of the trip.

My room looked exactly as I'd left it, which was reassuring to some extent. But not much. Ever since I'd arrived in Germany, forewarned by David Whitaker, I'd never left anything in my room that I didn't want to be seen during my absence. Searching the private effects of foreigners was absolute routine, according to David.

I wasn't afraid of being challenged about the spirit stove, for to mention it Goldgruber would have had to reveal that he'd searched my room. And he was unlikely to show his hand for so small a matter, not least because having a spirit stove was not the same thing as using one.

Thinking about the stove increased my longing for a cup of tea. But Goldgruber had just seen me come in, and if he made an excuse to knock on my door within a few minutes and found me drinking tea, he'd know I hadn't prepared it in the basement cooking cabin. That was the sort of petty calculation he loved.

But there was another way. I could make it in my vacuum flask. Then if he found me drinking it, he was not to know that I hadn't brought it in with me from the journey.

Here I was, not back in Berlin more than a few minutes, and already reduced to such humiliating calculations. Damn Goldgruber and all his sordid friends!

But I made the tea in the vacuum flask, all the same. And he *did* hatch an excuse to knock on my door just when it was nicely infused.

"Come in."

"Excuse me. Herr Vitaker was here. Yesterday." This news was not reassuring.

"Did he leave a message?" I unscrewed the top of the vacuum flask, squeezed some "toothpaste" condensed milk into a mug and poured some of the tea on to it.

"No, no message. He said you would be seeing him, no doubt."

"Thank you. Will you take some tea?" Much as I was concerned about David, I was careful not to show it.

He grinned. "Too late in the day, thankyou. Makes the heart thump."

The idea of a cup of tea making his heart thump was so ludicrous that I enjoyed it. "Ah, yes. We musn't do that. Not when you have to run up and down all those steps and, er, do other things no doubt just as strenuous."

"Yes, indeed. Tonight I carry a banner in a torchlight procession, in Moabit. So no tea, not only to spare the heart, but to avoid wanting to piss. No pissing when marching, eh?"

"Indeed not." I had often wondered about that.

"One can step out of line. But it is a black mark. Spoils the dignity."

"So does pissing oneself, I should imagine."

"Never happened to me, yet, God be thanked. My water department is strong."

I didn't doubt it, though I couldn't help reflecting that some poor devils who'd been through his hands or those of his Brownshirt cronies wouldn't be able to make the same boast.

I'd rung David Whitaker's number as soon as I got off the train, but there was no reply. Immediately after I finished my meal, I walked to Zoo station and tried again from one of the kiosks there. Again there was no reply. Although I was on my way to Herr Mandelbaum, I did not ring Teltow in advance, for security reasons, so I stepped out of the kiosk and into the train. If I'd managed to speak to David, however briefly, we'd have been able to exchange some sort of information — even if we'd been forced to use North of England dialect — without giving anything away to anybody who might be listening. But I had no hope of doing that in a telephone conversion with Herr Mandelbaum either in English or German.

When I rang the bell at his flat, he called through the door: "*Wer ist da?*"

"Eric Johnson." He seemed not to trust the reply, for he didn't open the door. "I've just come back today, with a message," I said, in English. I heard the bolt drawn at this, but he still examined me through the crack of the door, held on the safety chain. Satisfied, he let me in, and locked the door behind me. He looked awful.

"Go in, Herr Johnson. I'm alone, as you see." I went forward into the lounge, where the radio was playing softly. He followed me in and turned up the volume. At a motion from him, we sat close together.

"She's perfectly all right," I said, "and with her sister as planned. She was made very welcome."

"*Gott sei Dank.*"

"The journey out was not pleasant. There was interrogation and search at the border — this side of the border, of course." He gave me an anguished, questioning look, so much as to say: Was there brutality? I shook my head slowly in what I hoped was reassurance.

"And for you?"

"Only formal search — and, of course, nothing found for there was nothing to find."

"I am sorry you had to experience that."

"It didn't matter; it was a formality; it happens all the time." I felt that my remarks didn't deceive him, though he said nothing.

Without making it obvious, I glanced around the room. There was something a little strange about it, though I couldn't quite tell what it was. Perhaps it was caused by the absence of a caring woman. As Herr Mandelbaum put a rug across his knees, I looked at him too. His eyes seemed to protrude more, and he was more yellow, and looked infinitely older. It was as though he had held together only until his wife had gone.

"Anyway, Rebecca is out of it. That's what matters. Did she . . . did she speak of me much — about my following on . . .?"

"I'm afraid she did. She was full of instructions for me to remind you what to take with you — things like your English underwear." I wondered if I ought to be telling him, if it was cruel. But it seemed to give him comfort.

"She has no idea?"

"No, none." We fell silent. Could I possibly ask him how he was? His next remark removed some of my dilemma.

"Nothing is different with me."

Although we had taken the usual precautions not to be overhead, we were automatically phrasing our conversation so that it would have given very little away to an eavesdropper. "Do you have . . . some sort of help?"

"I have a doctor — a Jewish doctor. He does what he can." He took a little bottle holding about fifty green pills from his pocket.

"One of these per day kills the pain. They must be very strong because two is maximum dose. I am grateful for the help they give me."

There was nothing more to say, but I didn't want to show anxiety to leave. "Can I do anything? Make you something to eat, for instance." He appeared to ponder the suggestion.

"To eat?" It seemed to be an effort to think about it. "Me? Oh, no, thankyou. I eat very little. But you, will you eat something? There is some food here.''

"No, thankyou. I ate before I set off.'' How much ought I to ask about his arrangements? Had he any help with the housekeeping? How much would it be right to ask? We sat without speaking, listening with half an ear to the pleasant rattle of the radio music and the sugary interventions of the announcer. Heard outside Germany, it must make Germany sound very friendly, even charming. Was Herr Mandelbaum still capable of playing the cello? Could I ask him? If he had to say no it would be very painful. I looked towards the corner of the room where the instrument stood. He followed my gaze: "Here is the news bulletin,'' said the announcer. "Unemployment in the Reich has shown a significant reduction. Since the National Socialist Government took office, it has fallen from over six million to just over four million.''

Herr Mandelbaum reached out and switched it off. "Not that I disbelieve it . . .'' he said, shrugging his shoulders in an eloquent gesture. "I am sure there is more of a sort of work.''

Unwittingly, I looked again at the cello, and again he watched me. "Would you care to play a little something with me?'' he asked.

"If you feel you could, yes, I'd like to.''

He nodded, and I went and took the instrument out of its case and lightly plucked the strings to see if it was in tune with the piano. It was not. "Shall I try to tune it?''

"Please.''

I had no confidence in being able to do this, but did what I could, and then looked towards him, plucking each string gently, and playing the equivalent note on the piano. He made gestures up and down with a slightly trembling hand as I turned the pegs; and so we tuned it. For once in my life I really yearned to be able to do something well — to play the piano as well as he played the cello. But when we began to play he gave no hint of suffering from my shortcomings, though I noticed that he chose simple music, starting with Schumann's "Traumerei". Then we played some of Mendelssohn's "Songs Without Words'' though not before he had asked me to make sure that the window was firmly shut. He played where he sat, near the radio, away from the piano and, unlike me, needed no music.

We played for quite half an hour, much to my surprise, for I'd thought him incapable of the physical effort. But the playing seemed to give him strength rather than take it away, and we played nothing that called for special effort.

I felt, all the same, that he had exerted himself enough, so I stood up and straightened the sheets of music lying on top of the piano.

There was quite a pile and it included, unexpectedly, Bloch's "Schelomo". I glanced at this, and put it with the rest. "Do you think," said Herr Mandelbaum, "that you could manage a few bars of that?"

I hadn't realised that he was watching me. Quickly, I opened it again. As a sight-reading task it was formidable and quite beyond my powers. "I'm afraid it's too difficult for me."

"Try a little of it, please, and leave out the harder parts where it's too difficult."

Very diffidently, I put the music on the stand and made a tentative effort, going back to the start several times and getting slightly better each time. At about the fourth attempt, he joined in with the cello, playing it beautifully. As I feared, I had to skip quite large passages. But he played on, right across all my gaps, before he was beaten by weakness. Yet he seemed happy to have attempted any of it. I took the cello from him, put it back in its case and returned it to the corner.

"I'll come again to see you if I may."

"I'd greatly value it." He seemed to reflect, as though regretting what he'd said, and obviously thinking about it only from my point of view. "It won't be for long," he added.

"Are you sure there is nothing I can do now?"

He gave a painful but slightly amused smile: "I could use a nurse — but what old man couldn't? No, my friend, you have already been wonderfully helpful and I'm most grateful."

I slipped out, leaving him sitting there, the rug still across his knees although it was almost uncomfortably warm. It was not far from midnight when I got back to Haus Odol. I was very tired, but I thought I'd try again to reach David via the entry telephone. To my relief and surprise, I heard the coin drop and David's voice on the line: "David Whitaker."

"It's Eric. Caught you at last. Shall I walk round?"

"Yes, I'd be glad if you would."

A few minutes later we were walking along Meinecke Strasse. "Goldgruber said you'd been seeking me. Nothing wrong, I hope — nothing more, that is."

"Well, Lilli's fainted twice for no obvious reason, and it has me worried."

I thought about all those stairs. "Has she seen a doctor?"

"She's afraid to seek normal medical help, the suspense of sitting about in waiting-rooms or clinics . . . I've tried to persuade her, and assure her that with her new papers no one would question . . ." He shrugged. "But she is so nervous in case she bumps into someone who might recognise her. She's been pretending she's Christian Scientist to

146

allay suspicion in the block. They're all very kind to her there. One woman in particular who lost her own child, is very helpful. That's Frau Brandt, in flat 23. But how are things with you? How did the trip go?"

"Not too bad, all things considered. But I'm afraid Switzerland's a dead duck as far as a job goes. I took some pains to look into it. Apparently, the Swiss don't issue work permits for such an unreasonable purpose as an Englishman teaching English."

"Well, I can't say I'm surprised. Thanks for taking so much trouble." But I could see that he was disappointed. I had to leave him at this and go back; I was desperately tired.

Next morning three pupils turned up on time, an hour apart, and I took it as a good omen that I wasn't going to lose as many pupils in the holiday period of 1934 as I'd lost in 1933. This was soon confirmed, and while I welcomed being kept reasonably busy, I realised that it would make it harder to visit the dying Mandelbaum.

When I went again, I found that his flat was in some disorder, and while he wouldn't admit that he had any less help with it, I suspected that this was so. I didn't doubt that there were even some Aryan women in Teltow who would be glad to take his money for cleaning the place, though few who would dare to be seen taking it. But this was now secondary. I could see that what he urgently needed was not a housekeeper but a nurse.

I wondered if it would do any good to approach Mercia Adam. As there was no time to lose, I telephoned the nurses' home and was lucky enough to catch her off duty and free.

I put it to her fairly plainly over a hurried cup of coffee in Café Trumpf. "He's old, Jewish and dying. His kidneys have failed. He's in a flat in Teltow — with a slightly fading anti-Jewish daub on the door. He can afford help and he needs it badly. Do you think anybody at the Achenbacher, or anybody else you know, would take him on?"

"Let me think about it." The next day she telephoned me and asked if I would take her to see him. I took her the same day, for I now had two keys for the flat and was in a position to settle the matter there and then if she would accept the task.

I'd been afraid that she would never pass the outer door, but she'd hardly given it a glance. Evidently she was made of tougher stuff than I'd imagined.

As we walked back towards Teltow station she said: "If I can manage things, I'll do it myself. Judging from what I've seen, it won't be for long, and I need the money for a trip to England to see some of my relatives."

Two days later she had managed to get her holiday period brought forward and, to my great sense of relief, promised to be on duty either later that day or early the next.

The following day her Teltow time-table was dropped into my letter-box. This, she explained in a little note, was so that I could visit the Teltow flat at times when I knew she would be there, and so would be able to learn from her the condition of her patient. I felt grateful for her consideration and her efficiency.

"How long?" I asked at my next visit.

"It's hard to say, but I should think no more than a fortnight. There are some terminal signs."

"Does he complain?" I was wondering if he had given her any indication of why his kidneys had failed; I'd given none.

"No, he seems resigned."

I walked into the lounge and was glad to notice that she'd cleaned the place up, helped no doubt by the fact that her patient was now totally bedfast. I was amazed how quickly and firmly she had apparently taken charge of everything. Apart from a collection of bottles and medical supplies on the lounge window sill, the room looked much as it did when I'd seen it the first time, though a neat little label was stuck to the corner of the mirror listing doctor, lawyer and undertaker, with day and night telephone numbers. Among the bottles I saw the small one of the green, pain-killing pills was now about three-quarters full. So efficiency was tempered with mercy.

I knocked lightly on the bedroom door and went in without waiting for a reply, for I knew that Herr Mandelbaum was unable to make any. He lay quite still in the big bed. His body was grotesquely distended and his eyes were closed. As I approached the bed, he opened them, and a flicker of a smile passed across his face. I touched his hand where it lay on the counterpane. The time for talk was past.

It was two days before I could call again at a time when Mercia Adam would be there.

I put the key in the lock and opened the door. The flat was silent. The bedroom door was closed, so I tapped softly on it and went in. The bed was unoccupied with the mattress rolled up. On trestles, beside it, was a closed coffin.

My feelings overwhelmed me. Although I'd been mentally prepared for this for a long time, I found now that I was not ready for it. And Mercia had thought about a fortnight, but less than a week had gone.

I went back into the lounge. The funeral arrangements must be already made or there would be no coffin. I knew, from frequently passing a Grüneisen funeral shop near Haus Odol, that German coffins were square-cornered and standard-sized, so would probably arrive at the scene of death sooner than they did in England. But surely not the

148

same day. And he couldn't have been dead yesterday or she would surely have telephoned me.

I was standing at the window, staring out but seeing nothing. Gradually, the bottles on the sill came into focus. The little bottle that had held the green pills was empty.

I heard a key in the lock and a few moments later Mercia walked in, wearing her nurse's uniform under a light summer coat. My mind full of questions, I walked towards her.

"The final solution came sooner than expected," she said, slipping off her coat. "Everything has been dealt with."

She turned and faced me and, pinned over her heart, I saw the swastika membership badge of the Nazi Party.

18

I returned from Teltow in a mental turmoil only slightly less acute than the one I'd suffered when I'd made the same journey with the Gestapo. But one thing was obvious: I must face the fact that the Nazis had gained enormously in strength since I'd arrived in Berlin.

I began to see, and understand, how the Nazi faith could divide families, cause children to inform on their parents, and stand quietly aside when the Gestapo came to haul them off to concentration camp. So, much as I wanted to discuss with David the events that had happened at Teltow, I decided not to. He had worries enough. I would simply tell him that Herr Mandelbaum was dead. And I decided not to go to the funeral. It would be an all-male, intensely Jewish occasion at which my presence might embarrass the mourners and would certainly deprive them of the comfort of total fraternity.

But I was neither calm nor philosophical about any aspect of Herr Mandelbaum's death. Much as my relationship with the Mandelbaums had put me under strain and in danger, it had also given point to my life. Now I was back to trying just to stay alive.

My room bell rang out the telephone signal, and when I got down to the instrument Goldgruber looked round the corner and said: *"Herr Vitaker am Fernsprecher."*

So the Telephon had become the *Fernsprecher*, had it? Well, if the bloody Nazis were determined to remove every last foreign word from their holy German language they had a hell of a task on their hands; the older people, at least, would resist. But would they? Would anybody? If everybody was "branded in the mouth" in terms of approval or disapproval of Nazidom, then a new and deeply serious danger was abroad. Perhaps I'd better get used to the idea of the *Fernsprecher* . . .

"Hallo, Eric Johnson here."

"David. I'd be glad of a chat."

"Right. Five minutes. At your place."

"It's Lilli," he said as we walked slowly along the street shortly afterwards. "She's fainting again. I think it must be the tension — on

150

top of the pregnancy, I mean. She won't admit it, but she lives in constant fear.''

"Of course she does."

"So I've been going through the small ads. in the German press, looking for a job with a British connection. Then, if I started here, I could probably get back to the north of England with a job. And I think I've come up with a promising one. It's a German firm that has a Leeds subsidiary. They import British wool cloth and clothing and want somebody to run a branch in Berlin. I have an interview coming up in Bremen quite soon."

"Hm, sounds a bit of a long shot."

"I have to consider long shots, Eric. Anyway, my yarn-selling experience with Mann, Schenker in Fogston till they went west ought to be useful."

"Yes, it ought. And Bremen's fairly close at hand. You should get there and back in a day."

"Not in this case, unfortunately. It's one of those modern smelling-out interviews in which the applicants spend a few days in unrelieved contact with the prospective employer. So I'm booked into a Bremen hotel for three days with no contact with the outside. Can you possibly keep an eye on Lilli?"

"Of course. Glad to."

"And take my pupils? I've postponed as many lessons as I can. Here's a list." I took it, and nodded. "Use the flat here, of course. And it goes without saying that if I get the job, you get my pupils — for keeps."

"Well, that gives me at least two reasons for hoping you do." We grinned at each other.

"I'll tell Lilli. She'll be quite relieved."

A few days later I saw him off, and went straight from the station to Wedding, taking all the usual precautions. There was quite a delay after my coded knock, but eventually the door opened a little, on the chain. "Oh, it's you, Eric," said Lilli, obviously pleased. Even before she opened the door fully, I could see that she had a waxy look and I thought I saw traces of recent tears.

"I've brought something tasty with me," I said. "How do you fancy cheese omelette cooked by my own fair hands?" I'd taken the precaution to ask David what dish she liked best.

"Oh, that would be wonderful, Eric. And you can tell me about England as you cook it — about Fogston." She was already back on the sofa. "Would I feel like a foreigner there? Would I *look* like one? Would they accept me?"

"Steady, steady. One at once. Would you feel foreign? No, they're

151

a bit thick, but friendly. Would you look like one? No — a bit more handsome than the locals, perhaps — in fact, quite a lot more handsome. And would they accept you? Of course they would. Anyway, outside London, Fogston has the biggest Germany colony in England. There's a German pork butcher's on nearly every corner. I hope you like pork.''

"Oh, I thought all the Fogston Germans were rich wool merchants — and mainly Jewish.''

"Well, not quite. Quite a few Germans, including some German Jews, went there in the middle of the last century to teach the locals how to export their wool goods — and how to make music at weekends instead of painting themselves with woad and thumping each other.''

"Eric, how you exaggerate! I'm sure all they beat is eggs.''

"Not so many now — since the Depression came. Yes, I'm talking a certain amount of nonsense, I admit — but not about the friendliness.''

"And what is woad?''

"Body paint. They still use it — though they call it lipstick now, I believe.''

"Eric, I like your nonsense. Tell me more. There is so little nonsense in the New Germany.''

I could see that she was near to tears behind her smiling. And when I thought of her plight I could have wept with her, for she was utterly trapped. Apart from David and me, she hadn't a friend to whom she could speak freely in all Germany. And there must be things from her near-past that she could mention to nobody at all. To her parents she was either missing or dead, and even if she escaped, she could never tell them because to do so would make them accomplices. And she was obviously short of money.

"I'm not much good at nonsense, really,'' I said, handing her the omelette and a fork. "Wrong generation. David's better. You should get him on about his Aunt Hildegard and her cat that does the new German greeting.'' I did the half-arm Hitler salute, but she needed no illustration and looked instinctively towards the window and the door. After she'd eaten the omelette, she suddenly buried her head in her arms and wept bitterly. "I'm just a burden to him,'' she sobbed. "Just a burden. I betrayed him even before I meant anything to him. He was an assignment. And all he did was show me love and kindness. He ought to abandon me!''

"You're quite wrong, Lilli,'' I said when she could hear me. "He needs you just as much as you need him. You're the other half of his life — the half that gives it meaning. And he'll never abandon you. He's not the abandoning sort.''

Soon she regained some control of herself and I did my best to keep up a stream of optimistic talk. But I doubted if I convinced her. I even went so far as to give a toast, in tea, to "Happier Days", linking arms as we had all done at Haus Vaterland. But it was a mistake, and we both knew it. Still, I thought she looked a little happier when I left her, smiling wanly over the back of the settee and waving a hand to me.

In the next three days I gave lessons at Meinecke Strasse, in my own room, and at pupils' addresses, and called several times on Lilli. The travel alone was enough to exhaust any normal person. But I could not afford to be exhausted.

I was in the midst of a lesson in my room with a singularly obtuse German woman who combined the maximum of coyness with the minimum of sexual attraction when my bell rang three times. Then again. And, just to make sure, Goldgruber's voice came booming up the stairwell: "*Herr Yonson, am Franspecher schnellstens! Herr Vitaker ruft von Bremen.*"

My apologies to my pupil could hardly have been briefer, and I bounded down the stairs.

"Hallo, David."

"Eric, I've got the job, and the pay's good — about double what I make now."

"Marvellous."

"But I can't come straight back. I have some sorting-out to do, and a certain amount of learning of the selling technique, getting familiar with the stock, and so on. It'll take about two days, they think, and I don't know just where I'll be. Would you tell my favourite pupil?"

"I will. I certainly will. By the way, your favourite pupil's rather better."

"I'm glad to hear it" was all he dare reply.

It was late in the afternoon when I reached Wedding, having taken all the precautions I could. I knocked gently on Lilli's door, using the code. There was no reply. I knocked again, louder. Still no reply. Perhaps she was asleep. Perhaps she'd fainted. No matter how disturbing this possibility was I could not afford to draw attention, so walked back along the corridor and down to the ground floor to waste a little time. Then, without going out, I climbed back and knocked again. Still no reply.

There was no option. I would have to seek out the woman in flat 23 who, David said, had been exceptionally kind. I knew she had David's key.

I walked along the corridor and knocked. The door was cautiously opened by a woman of about thirty, and I saw the glint of a safety-chain.

"Frau Brandt?" What a mercy I'd remembered the name.

"*Ja?*"

"I'm Herr Mann's friend. I'm seeking Frau Mann. There's no reply from her flat."

"*Ach, ja.*" She momentarily closed the door and I heard the chain slide back. "I was just going along to see her. We usually share a cup of coffee at this time."

She was a bright woman and in no time at all had produced the key to Lilli's flat. A minute later, after knocking and again getting no reply, we went in. Lilli was not there.

The flat was perfectly tidy and undisturbed. Thinking of how I had last seen Lilli, I looked apprehensively at the table, half fearing to see a note there. But there was no note. "Will she have gone out? Shopping perhaps?"

Frau Brandt shook her head. "She does not do her own shopping now. I do it for her. See, I did it this morning." She pointed to a paper bag lying beside the gas oven in the adjoining kitchen.

"You said you usually shared a cup of coffee with her at this time? I looked at my watch.

"In another minute I'd have been here."

There were no signs of any preparation of coffee; so wherever Lilli had gone, she must have gone some time earlier. I walked into the little kitchen and, without letting Frau Brandt see me do it, touched the stove top and the kettle. They were both warm. I would have liked to ask her to telephone me about Lilli, but it was too risky. Somehow I'd have to make time to come again.

When I returned the next day, Lilli was still missing. Frau Brandt knew nothing.

Should I telephone David? I had a number I could ring, but only in dire emergency. He had every right to know, but would it help? The effect on his morale would be devastating. Another day, and he would be back, and so also might Lilli. Reluctantly, I abandoned the idea. I went to bed at midnight but slept hardly at all.

Next day I had a particularly full timetable of lessons, including one with the Baron at ten in my room and another at noon at David's flat. As I faced my first pupil of the day, at eight-thirty, I felt far from bright and effective.

At ten there was the familiar rap of von Steinfels on the door. I opened it, greeted him, and let him in, motioning to the chair. He gave a very curt bow, stepped inside, and remained standing to attention. He did not remove his uniform cap. "Herr Johnson," he said, "I think you should see this." From a side pocket of his tunic he took out a copy of the latest issue of the *Berliner Anzeiger* and handed it to me. It was folded at an inner page, and down near the foot of a column was a small news paragraph ringed in red ink. The heading struck me like a blow: "Body Found." I read on: "Yesterday the body of a young woman was taken from the River Spree in Berlin. According to a note found on the corpse, she was Helga Stern, of Frankfurt. Identification has confirmed this."

"My God," I said. "My God." David couldn't be reached because he would be en route, so he could not even be warned of what awaited him.

"The time for pretence is over," said von Steinfels. "I think you should know that the Authorities know everything: about you, your friend Whitaker and his late wife, formerly Helga Stern. I think you should identify the body as well so that when your unfortunate friend returns he will be in no doubt that his wife is dead. The corpse has already been identified officially. I think also you should see this photo-copy of the note found on the body." He handed me a photostat. I took it and unfolded it. Quite large, it was perfectly clear.

"But it's typewritten!" I exclaimed. "Even if she'd had a typewriter, or access to one, she'd never have typed such a note."

"Not so. She had a most thorough training, including a period in the Document Reproduction Department of the Ministry of Propaganda. She would be well aware that immersion in water blurs or washes out ordinary ink, but not typescript. Anyway, the signature is in ink; it has run, but it's still readable."

That terrifying German efficiency again. But he was right. The signature was smeared as though by water, but I couldn't deny that it was legible. I turned to the message. It read: "I can't go on. It is all just too much. I have tried to be everything to everybody but have succeeded only in being nothing. And all that I have attempted has failed. To those who have loved me, and have been so kind to me, I can only say that I am deeply sorry. What I am doing now is another failure, I know. But it is my last one. Now I shall harm nobody any more. Helga Stern."

"But she wouldn't have signed it 'Helga Stern'," I cried. "That's inconceivable. They really *were* married, she and David Whitaker, quite legally."

"In the sight of death, nothing is inconceivable. She had spent nearly all her life as Helga Stern. She would want to leave it as Helga Stern."

But had she wanted to leave it? She had been depressed when last I saw her. But a girl with courage enough to marry David in such daunting circumstances, and then, above all, to have a baby . . . such a girl would not fling herself into the river. Then there was the suspiciously tidy flat at Wedding and the still-warm stove and kettle, without a word to Frau Brandt, whom she was expecting to call.

Yet people did not advise their friends when they intended to commit suicide. And people *did* take their lives on sudden sad impulse.

These thoughts raced through my mind as the Baron watched me narrowly. And still I could not conceive that she had done it — especially when I recalled his opening words and considered the type-written suicide note. No, it was all too neat, too malign, too super-efficient German. And surely the choice of the River Spree was the last touch of total calculated malevolence.

But why should the Baron trouble to tell me anything? I was back again to the mystery of his whole attitude to me. If he himself had not taken some part in the murder of Lilli, but had come to know of her murder by the Gestapo, then he had good reason for assisting with the ghastly charade of the suicide. In that way, no scandal could arise and no harmful report of Gestapo savagery leak out of the country to places where it might be useful to Germany's potential enemies.

How much did he really know? Did he know who and what had killed Herr Mandelbaum and if, in effect, he was murdered twice? What did he know of Mercia Adam? Well, if he was trying to convince me that Nazi Germany was all-knowing, all-powerful and all-murderous, he had come very near to succeeding.

But the acid test would be my own action related to the field gun. If he knew about that as well, I was finished.

And still he watched me.

Again I raced through the possibilities, and again I could not accept that so brave a girl as Lilli would kill herself just at the moment when life seemed to be opening up for her and she thought she had a chance of being able to escape from Germany. And if the Gestapo really did know everything, this was the time to kill her.

"I do not think she killed herself," I said.

"Before you say anything that you might regret and couldn't substantiate," interposed the Baron, "I would strongly advise you to think again. We all say things when we are under stress of strong emotion that we probably regret later. I would strongly advise you therefore to say no more at present."

Perhaps he was right. If she had killed herself, it was unlikely that she would put the name "Whitaker" on a suicide note if only to spare David complications. And, on the threshold of death, she would find it hard to call herself either Lilli Schultheiss or Lilli Mann. It was probable, or at least possible, that her parents already thought her dead by drowning in the River Spree as a result of the fake suicide note she had left at the Gestapo office when she went into hiding. And even if the Gestapo had never passed on details of this note to her parents, the present finding of her body there would cover all requirements, even the marginal one of preventing her parents making trouble about an unexplained disappearance.

The more I thought about it, the more deeply did I feel she had *not* killed herself. The cold logicality of these facts did not, could not, go with the brave humanity of the girl I had known. But the Baron was speaking again.

"The body is at the mortuary. It will be cremated forthwith and the ashes sent to her parents. I have a car waiting outside. It will take you to the mortuary and bring you back." He must have seen a flash of fear cross my face: "You've nothing to fear," he added. "I give you my solemn word that the sole purpose of the car is to take you to the mortuary to identify the body — for the sake of your friend — and so that you can both be quite sure that Helga Stern, alias Lilli Schultheiss, alias Frau Mann, alias Frau Whitaker, is dead."

This was the first time he had used all these aliases, and I noticed that he did not say "has killed herself." Could it be that he had come to know about her murder only after it was done? Or, if he had known beforehand, was he unable to stop it? In either case, was his action now the only small kindness he dare show in circumstances grim beyond his power to modify? Or was he simply ensuring that there would be no scandal anywhere in connection with the death of a British subject by marriage?

I knew I would have to go. He stood aside and I walked out. The car was there as he had said. We got in and it drove off at once, the driver apparently knowing his destinion. "I told him where we are going," said the Baron, again sensing my fear. What sort of creature was he? How could he be both barbarian and human being? And if he was this terrifying mixture, was he typical of Germany or the Nazis? Or both?

When we reached the mortuary, he gave me a slip of paper, saying: "Show that. Everything is ready. I shall be here in the car when you come out. Then I shall take you back."

The slip of paper did all that he had said it would do, and I was taken at once by a white-coated attendant to the door of a little room in which the body lay on a slab under a white cloth. The feet projected beyond the cloth, and tied to the right ankle by a piece of rough string was a label.

The attendant was courteous and considerate: so much so that I marvelled at it, for his must be a dreadful way to make a living, I thought. He beckoned me forward, and as I stepped into the room I was struck by the intense cold. There was no window, but a powerful electric light shone directly down on to the body. I saw now that on the label was written in block letters: STERN (HELGA), and below this in smaller lettering: Schultheiss (Lilli), Mann (Frau Lilli), Whitaker (Frau Lilli). "If you would be kind enough to look, please," said the attendant, and drew back the cloth from the head and shoulders. The luxurious hair had been roughly tied back with a piece of the same string that tied the label. It was Lilli. "Have you seen enough?" he asked, quite gently.

"Yes," I said.

"No need to report to me," he replied. "Report to the official who brought you."

"Very well."

He replaced the cloth then, nodding towards the obvious indications of pregnancy, added: "Such cases are doubly sad, are they not?"

"They are indeed," I managed to say.

He conducted me back to the entry, holding the door open for me to go out. The car was waiting as the Baron had said it would be, and I got in. "Yes," I said to him, "it is undoubtedly Frau Whitaker."

"Alias Lilli Schultheiss, alias Lilli Mann, born Helga Stern."

"If you wish. It makes no difference now."

On the way to the mortuary my chief feeling had been one of desolation for David, and this had been intensified by what had awaited me there. But now I was overwhelmed with sorrow for the poor girl whose corpse I had just seen lying on that public slab in that ice-cold little room, and I made no attempt to stem or hide the tears that ran down my face. How terrible had been the reward of her optimism! How appalling had been the reality of the New Germany for her.

In my bitterness, I thought that the Baron would bring out some wretched bit of official paper and have me sign it. But he simply nodded. To the driver he said "Back" and that ended all conversation. Throughout the return journey he sat erect and silent, staring straight ahead like a basilisk.

At the house, the car stopped and I got out, closing the door behind me without even looking back. I heard the engine accelerate away. Mercifully I met nobody in the entrance or on the stairs.

Now all my thoughts were with David. What way was there to tell one's best friend — one's only friend — that his young wife and the child they expected were dead?

19

We had arranged that David would first make contact with me when he got back to Berlin, not only because there was no telephone at Wedding, but so that he could be forewarned if there was any radical change. He hadn't been able to say just when he would arrive back, anyway.

After a fashion, I welcomed the need to return to the mental discipline of teaching English. It excluded other thoughts, though my next pupil must have found me a poor and preoccupied teacher.

Just after noon David reached me by telephone at Meinecke Strasse. "I'm back, Eric. In Berlin, at Stettiner Bahnhof. How's everything?"

"I'm not able to speak at the moment, David. I'm in the middle of a lesson. Come straight here. I'll be free by the time you arrive."

It was towards one when I heard his key in the door. At first, I'd thought that I would just have to break the news there in the flat, for a man must have some privacy for grief. But when I heard his key I changed my mind. If I were to tell him in some public place, perhaps the surroundings would help him to restrain his anguish.

I took him, puzzled and apprehensive, to the little open-air café-cum-snack bar which was quite near in the Kurfürstendamm. We sat down behind a thin row of privet-like bushes set in tubs only a few yards from the pedestrians and ceaseless traffic. It was just one o'clock and the animation was at its height. I'd ordered two cups of coffee as we'd walked in and they were placed before us as we sat down.

"Tell me," said David eagerly. "How is she?"

"She's dead, David. They took her body out of the River Spree three days ago. There was a suicide note in a pocket. It was the Baron who told me — the Gestapo seem to know everything, God knows how or why. He came to my room this morning at ten to take me to identify the body. I'm afraid there's no mistake, David. The body has been cremated and the ashes are being sent to her parents." I was appalled by the starkness of my words, but knew it was useless to try to soften them. As their terrible meaning struck him he seemed to go into a trance. How long this lasted I couldn't tell, but the proprietor looked out of his cabin to ask: "Is there something wrong with the coffee?"

"No," I replied. "Everything's in order."

"She wouldn't kill herself," David said quietly and with total conviction. "Not now. No, not now. They've murdered her, and my child. They've murdered them both." For a full minute he was silent again. "I suppose I always knew they would kill her if they found her. She knew it too. She was only lent to me briefly. Then the Gestapo destroyed her because she was no longer any use to them and knew too much."

I was almost sure that he was right, but could not bring myself to say so. Were there, I wondered, Gestapo people and ordinary people? And, if so, were they separate species? Or had Anna-Maria and Helga simply been human, and enthusiastic for the Nazi promise that seemed to hold out so much hope for a reborn Germany? And had they found themselves on a dark path from which there was no turning back? Had they been called upon to be monsters and failed because they were human? It seemed so, just as it sometimes seemed that the Baron had failed the same test, but had managed to survive. Would he — and would Anna-Maria — continue to survive? Would any of us?

* * *

Fortunately, David needed to start on his new job at once to meet a deadline for the publication of the German printed matter. I marvelled that he was able to force himself to work, but he seemed almost to welcome it. In a way, we both used our present preoccupations as a reason for saying little about the immediate past. No doubt a time would come when we would be able to talk and clarify certain aspects that were now obscure.

David had told me that he had been to Wedding, ended the tenancy for the little flat and given all its contents to Frau Brandt. How he had managed to tell her that Lilli was dead I could not imagine, for I knew from Lilli that Frau Brandt had been loving and kind to her, taking a special sort of joy in the pregnancy almost as though it had been her own.

He had removed every trace of Lilli's presence from the Meinecke Strasse flat, not, I felt, because he feared further repercussions from the Gestapo, but simply because he could not bear to be reminded of her by such a neutral object as a nail-brush or a bottle of toilet water.

As August drew to its close I longed for some break in the heat, but none came. In my room, and even to some extent in the street, I was as informal in dress as I could be, hoping that my white open-necked shirts would appear more Byronic than untidy. I felt sorry for the many officials in Germany who seemed to have no summer version of their stout uniforms, and marvelled that they didn't faint with oppression.

As always, the Baron turned up for his lesson in full, unrelenting SS officer's uniform of closely tailored thick black wool cloth and black leather jackboots, though the SS were allowed to wear mufti off duty. Perhaps the Baron never considered himself to be off duty.

I knew precisely the right German phrases for suggesting that he might perhaps care to divest himself of some of his clothes, or at least unbutton his tunic at the neck, but I didn't use them. He endured it to the end of the lesson without having allowed himself the least sign of discomfort. He stood up to go, and said to me in German: "I'm afraid Herr Johnson, that will have to be the last of the lessons. I have found them very useful, but now I have been posted to Danzig. I go tomorrow."

I waited a moment, hoping he would add something. But he simply stood there, stiff and alert — almost at attention — waiting for my reply. "I'm sorry, Herr Baron," I said quite sincerely. "I — I like to think that these lessons have been useful to both of us."

"I'm sure they have. And, who knows? One day we might resume them in another place and another circumstance." He came near to smiling as he said this. Then he made his neat little bow — not a hairsbreadth different from what it had always been — said: "*Leb' Wohl,*" put on his cap with a single movement, turned, and was gone.

My first emotion was one of relief. Surely his going, after all that had happened, would end the mysterious attentions both David and I had received from the Gestapo. But a different emotion overtook the first. Terrifying as the Gestapo were, especially now that the cold-blooded SS chief Himmler was at their head, I'd felt them slightly less terrifying while I'd been in steady contact with von Steinfels. Not that I'd ever doubted, or doubted now, that if he felt it his duty to put a bullet through my head he would unhesitatingly do it. Could "another place and another circumstance" mean in a conquered England? It was as clear to me as it must be to every other normal Englishman in Nazi Germany that Hitler's ambitions included the conquest of England. Was it possible that David and I had been shadowed by the Gestapo because a role was planned for us, working for Germany, in a defeated England? Did it all go back to the German colony in Fogston, with which we both had connections? Was this, and our disenchantment with an England that had no use for us, the key? And if so, was the murder of Lilli — and even in some degree, the posting of the Baron — a sign that they had abandoned the idea?

Next day when I was at Meinecke Strasse, I said to David: "The Baron's finished his lessons and gone. Posted to Danzig. He made no comment about anything."

"No, he wouldn't. There's really nothing to say, is there?"

For no reason I could think of, I recalled David's last, almost gay remark just before his train for Bremen pulled out of Berlin. It had been raining briefly, then the sun came out strongly. Looking up towards the sun, he'd said: "I think it's going to be a fine August in every way, Eric." I'd given a wry smile, marvelling at this faith, but hoping he was right.

Today was the last day of August and it felt like the end of an era. Frau Mandelbaum would never set foot in Germany again. Herr Mandelbaum was dead. Lilli was dead. The Baron was gone. Anna-Maria was gone, too.

August was ended, and with it my second summer in Berlin. Would I see another there?

20

Ever since my first month in Berlin I'd nourished a small daydream of
giving Goldgruber a month's rent with one hand and a month's
written notice with the other. But when I did precisely that the
following day, the first of September 1934, the whole basis of satis-
faction was gone. He was almost an irrelevance.

He must have been curious to know what was in the note, for he
could see his name written on the outside. But he snapped open the
rent book, checked the cash I'd given him, entered it and wrote out
my receipt. Then he turned to my note. Just how bloody Germanic-
efficient could you get? Yet with another part of my mind I admired it.
Perhaps we British were as mixed up about them as they were about
us. He read only the first few lines, then looked up.

"So you're leaving, Herr Yonson. Going back to England, eh?"
Was I wrong, or was he gloating?

"No, Herr Goldgruber. Not England. I'm moving to a garden flat
in the Meinecke Strasse — Herr Whitaker's old flat, in fact."

"Ah, then *he* is going back to England, eh?"

"No. He has taken another flat, a slightly bigger one, in the same
building."

He looked hard at me with his piggy eyes. "Two fine flats, and just
off the Kurfürstendamm! My, my, English must be good now."

I'd deliberately not told him that David had stopped teaching. It
seemed only yesterday since he'd suspected that teaching English was
so poor a prospect that it wouldn't pay the rent of one little box of a
room on the third floor of a third-rate apartment block. Well, some
things had changed, but not Goldgruber.

September advanced with no break in my busy routine. I'd been
teaching David's pupils quite long enough to find out if they would
stay with me, and almost all of them had done. As I continued to use
the lounge of David's flat for quite a number of lessons, I saw much of
him and was relieved to find him putting increasing effort and interest
into his new work. By common consent we avoided much discussion of
the past; but some things had to be discussed: we had to make decisions

that hinged on them. One was Mercia Adam and the part she had played in the death at Teltow. I told David the bare facts, taking care not to suggest a conclusion. He reflected only briefly.

"I see," he said. "I see. In point of fact, I think she's half-German — one parent — but that sometimes makes people come down with a bang on one side. In her case, apparently, it's Nazi Germany. By the way, her name now isn't Mercia Adam, English style, but Mercedes Adam, German style. I don't blame her, though I regret her choice. But if she's helping to rid Germany of Jews, well, that's something else."

"It's possible that she only did an act of mercy, isn't it?"

"Yes, it's possible. But angels of mercy don't usually wear swastika badges."

"Well, we'll probably never know. Anyway, one thing's for sure: we've got to make our minds up about the Nazis and their supporters, Mercedes Adam included. And we've got to stop being such a couple of political innocents."

"Yes, I agree. I don't know how you feel, Eric, but I think the time has come for us to appear to show some favour towards the Nazi attitude, if only to learn what we can, while we can."

"Agreed. For one thing, it might be a form of self-protection, and, marvel of marvels, we're beginning to have something to protect."

"Yes, that's one very sound reason. Another is that we might find ourselves back in England one day actually knowing something about the Nazis and Germany among people who'd thought till then that Hitler was just another Charlie Chaplin playing a part full of bad jokes."

"Perhaps it's time we had an escape plan ready, David. Can you store petrol in your garage?"

"Yes, I suppose so. But the car tank holds plenty."

"Enough to get out of Germany without a refill?"

"No, I see what you're getting at. I'll buy enough cans to fill the boot, and keep them full of petrol in the garage under sacks or something. And while I'm about it, I'll get details of border formalities for taking the car out of Germany into Denmark, Switzerland, France, Belgium or Holland, or by sea ferry to England. And you must learn to drive, Eric. I'll teach you if you like. It isn't my car; it happens, for mysterious book-keeping reasons, to belong to the UK company and I'm sure they'd be glad of a spare driver if it helps them to get their car back in the event of a bust-up; they'd suggest it, never mind permit it."

When I walked down the steps at Haus Odol for the last time on the final day of the month, Goldgruber was not there. He was on parade, his wife said, adding quickly that he had his boss's permission. "I do not doubt it, Frau Goldgruber," I said, but she detected no sarcasm. "You will be sure to impress on him, won't you, how important it is to forward any post without delay?"

"Oh, to be sure, Herr Yonson, to be sure. I know he has your new address; he's stuck it on the wall in the office. Goodbye, Herr Yonson, goodbye. It is to be hoped all goes well."

"Thank you, and for you also."

I picked up my battered fibre suitcase, some loose clothing and a table-lamp I'd made from a bottle, and walked down the entrance steps to the street, where David was waiting for me in the car. Perhaps it had been small of me not only to want Goldgruber to see me go, but to see me go in a brand-new car.

David had left the Meinecke Strasse garden flat spick and span and had even put a bunch of red carnations in a vase in the lounge. He helped me to carry in my few possessions and it took only minutes for me to install myself. "I hope you'll be happy here, Eric," he said.

"And you in your new flat upstairs, David. Thanks for everything."

I went into the kitchen — *my* kitchen — and took two bottles out of *my* 'fridge. It was incredible.

We sat in the two armchairs, quietly sipping the drink and watching the curtains over the french windows occasionally waft to and fro: The same curtains through which Herr Mandelbaum had stepped when I first saw him. Through a half-open door I could see into the bedroom, to the bed that had such poignant memories for me. I'd doubted, when first David suggested my taking the flat, if I'd ever be able to sleep in that bed. But he urged me. "You've got to do it, Eric. We've both got to go on living here in Berlin, facing everything, no matter how bitter — and learning everything we usefully can about the Nazis' intentions without running ourselves into danger. There's no other way." When I'd thought how infinitely more bitter it was for him than for me, I'd felt ashamed.

We finished our drinks and I got up and closed the french windows. As befitted the first day of our new arrangements, we'd decided to relax totally that evening.

"Ready?"

"Yes." He rose and moved towards the door.

We went out and got into the car. "How long," I asked, "do you think this marvellous smell of newness will last?"

He smiled. "How should I know? I've had as many new cars as you have. But I hope forever." He pressed the starter and we moved off.

"Forever's a long time. I know the Third Reich is supposed to last a thousand years. But in a lot less time than that the big balloon might go up and we might have to cut and run.''

''Not run, Eric, remember. Ride — in the car. And I hope there might be time to wear the newness off it first.''

''Even with this bloody lunatic in charge?''

''Yes, even so. You've read his programme in *Mein Kampf*. First he has to annex Austria, then obliterate that 'political and geographical abortion, Czechoslovakia' then Memmel, then Poland . . . Oh, we'll have time to pick up our muskets.''

''*If* we pick them up, David. I hear that the sons of the gentry and the nobility at Oxford aren't at all sure that they'll pick theirs up. So what price poor, ignorant provincials like you and me who aren't supposed to know their arses from their elbows?''

''No price at all. But I fancy we'll be there, win or lose.''

''Well, England's bitched, buggered and bewildered both of us, and clearly doesn't care if we live or die. But it's the only country we've got. So I suppose you're right.''

When we turned into the long straight of the Kurfürstendamm, we saw an endless vista of swastika flags and streamers. Brownshirted Stormtroopers in ones, twos and threes were dotted among the crowds on the pavements. SS men, their black uniforms set off by silver braid and bright daggers swinging on chains, were not so numerous but all the more dramatic in consequence. While these uniformed Nazis were not sweeping people out of their way, I noticed that nobody got in their way.

David slowed down the car and stopped it at the pavement-edge. ''Let's watch the Berliners for a few minutes,'' he said. ''We're in good time.''

Four Brownshirts were approaching in ragged formation. One had a familiar look, and when they drew level with us I saw that it was Goldgruber. I nudged David. Goldgruber had a far-away look and did not see us.

''In a state of double ecstasy I would say,'' said David. ''Once with the Party speeches at the parade, and once with the booze at the beer-hall afterwards. In short: half-mesmerised and half-pissed.''

''They just love the New Germany, don't they, David? Everybody I mean.''

''They certainly do. I suppose it makes them all feel twice as big as they felt before it all began.''

''. . . And Goldgruber four times as big. And ten times as nasty.''
He started the engine and we moved off.

We ran along for a few miles in silence. I couldn't speak for David, but I felt instinctively cheerful. The broad, smooth road, admirably sign-posted, the fine new car, the bright light and the dry atmosphere — even the gay flash of the flags, all brand new and in perfect condition — contributed to my mood. It was all so very different from Fogston, where time was running backwards and organised decay was the policy.

"What are thinking, Eric?"

I laughed. "Oh, I'm just busy kidding myself that we're a lot better off in Berlin than anywhere else available to us."

"Is anywhere else available to us?"

"No."

"Solves the problem, then, eh?"

"Well, it does if the Germans continue to want to learn English . . ."

"And buy English wool cloth and clothes. They're both against the Nazi ethic, you know. For a gang of thieving murderers, they're remarkably touchy about their national dignity."

"Oh, sod all politics and all politicians. Let's talk about more important things, such as the girls we're going to meet, or, to be more precise, the one you say you've got lined up for me." He shot me a quick glance, then looked ahead again.

"Don't be impatient, Eric. In ten minutes you'll be able to see for yourself. So, to quote a famous block-headed British politician, wait and see."

We drew into the car park at Haus Maximillian in Teltow and got out. "Strange that they said they'd meet us here rather than have you pick them up in the car in style, David."

"Not really. One of them — yours — lives near, and they're starting out from her place."

It sounded like an echo, as though I was reliving the past, and the sensation was a little eerie. The band was already in full swing though not yet at full volume, for the garden was only just beginning to fill. We walked under the impressive trees towards the tables where a few parties of relaxed-looking people were already waving large beer mugs at each other and shouting "Prost!" David selected a pleasant alcove far enough away from the band for us to be able to talk, but near enough to everything for us to feel part of the company. As we held out wrists to compare watches, a large light-brown leaf floated down between us to the gravel We were five minutes early.

"Will they be on time, David?"

"What else?" he grinned. "They're German."

A waiter materialised, bowed and said: "Gentlemen, what's your pleasure?"

"We're waiting for friends," said David.

"Certainly. I'll come back later." More people began to saunter in.

They were almost all lightly dressed, as though they took the continuing warm and fine weather for granted. David gave a quick wave. "There they are — and as pretty as paint."

We stood up and I saw as they came towards us that "my" girl was blonde and had beautifully rounded breasts. Both girls were wearing swastika badges. "Hallo, Eric; hallo, David; allow me to present my friend Annaliese Schroeder," said Mercedes Adam in German.

"Delighted!" said David and I in the same language, and almost in chorus, as though we'd rehearsed it.

The introductions over, we all sat down. "What shall we drink, then?" asked David. "I'd thought maybe something exotic and foreign, such as visky-soda, eh?" The waiter had returned and was standing respectfully near us, his cloth over his arm. Printed on it in large letters was the word "Schultheiss." At every place at every table was a beer-mat, and every one proclaimed "Schultheiss." The same word stretched the full length of a banner over the band, and on every wall and every tree-trunk was a sign saying "Schultheiss." Doubtless they were all there that last time we'd been in the garden, but I hadn't noticed them.

"It's still so warm," said Mercedes Adam. "I'd prefer something cool and truly German — beer: dark Schultheiss." The blonde girl smiled agreement.

I tried to catch David's eye, hoping I could relay the order and spare him having to speak the word. But he turned to me and said in a perfectly level voice: "And is it dark Schultheiss for you, too, Eric?"

"Yes," I almost whispered, "ice cold."

A cool little whirlwind hinting at autumn suddenly swirled through the garden and filled the air with leaves. But before they could fall it was gone and the warmth had returned.

The leaves fell gently among us. "Oh," said the blonde girl in mock alarm, "We're being bombed!"

"Only by Nature," I said.

We had planned to be back in Berlin in time for the torchlight procession that the Nazis had arranged for soon after nightfall. Neither I nor David had ever attended one, partly because they were usually through the main streets of working-class areas where Nazis and Communists had fought out their bitter battles before Hitler came to power. Now that Communists had been liquidated, the Nazis were evidently determined to show their strength to elegant, middle-class areas. So this parade would be right through the West End, including a march down the Kurfürstendamm.

The arrangement was that we should drop the girls at Achenbacher Strasse so that Mercedes could, as she said, "change into something more functional''. But I suspected that she didn't particularly wish to be seen at such an occasion with foreigners. And I doubted if our new role of being grudgingly prepared to accommodate ourselves to the inevitablity of Nazi rule had yet made an impact on anybody. I suspected that even Mercedes, with her half-English parentage, was likely to be carefully watched, though it was possible that her dossier at Gestapo Headquarters now carried some approving comment.

Everything went as planned. We dropped the girls, garaged the car, had a snack, and walked the short way to the end of the street in the Kurfürstendamm in good time.

It was as well, for the pavements were already tightly packed with people as far as we could see in both directions. Stormtroopers stood at regular intervals just on the empty roadway, facing the crowds. They had the leather straps of the caps tight under their chins, and they did not smile.

There was not the least sign of rowdy behaviour from the crowds, who talked animatedly about leading Nazis so far as I could gather. Nobody pushed and nobody shouted, and everybody looked happy. David and I stood close together at the back of the pavement, close up to a shop window. By spontaneous agreement we spoke no English.

Eventually, the distant throb of a big drum imposed itself, and the crowd near us fell silent. Now we could hear the throb of the drum more clearly and, on top of it, a noise like the breaking of rough seas on rocks. Soon there came the dull thump of marching feet in heavy boots and, in the far distance, we could see the bright, shimmering band of the flaming torches. The people all around us suddenly erupted into a frenzy of cheering.

As the column drew near, I could feel the pavement tremble rhythmically. Now everybody thrust up an arm in the full Nazi salute and the roar of cheering settled into a steady "*Sieg Heil! Sieg Heil!*" Fortunately, they all seemed too busy watching the column to notice that David and I were neither saluting nor cheering. We had thought before we set out that we would join in. But when the moment came, it was unthinkable.

At the head of the column, which had now drawn level with us, was a military band. I had heard military bands in England, but nothing that could compare with this for style and dash. I felt my skin creep.

Behind the band was a detachment of about a hundred Waffen SS. Every man was well over six feet, young and handsome to a degree. All carried weapons; none carried a torch. Their marching was of parade-ground quality and they looked neither to left nor right. Even their faces, set in a sort of contemptuous determination, were almost indistinguishable from each other beneath the steel helmets. They were human robots and I knew I ought to have found them detestable, but found them superb.

Yet even while I was thrilled, I was also terrified. I could see that David had gone pale, as I felt sure I had. But of his feelings I knew nothing, and dare not ask. What I did know for certain was that if some Stormtrooper, spotting our lack of obvious participation, had said something goading and derogatory, the crowd would have literally rent us. No doubt the great martyrs of history felt elated in such circumstances; I felt only cold fear.

By now the thousands of marching Stormtroopers behind the Waffen SS were beginning to march past, each with his blazing torch. I caught the whiff of naphtha and burning jute, and was a little relieved to find my senses working enough to identify these smells. And still the watchers roared and screamed with enthusiasm.

It was fortunate, perhaps, that the long column of Stormtroopers with its myriad banners now gave way to a column of Hitler Youth and Maidens. They, too, carried countless swastika banners, together with banners of origin, at regular intervals. Selected no doubt for their physical beauty and Nazi fervour, they were handsome in an almost legendary way.

As the military band leading the whole column was now quite some distance away, it was possible for the Hitler Youth to have their own band, playing different music. As it passed us, it began to play the "Hymn" of the Party, the Horst Wessel Lied. The "*Sieg Heils*" stopped and everybody joined the marchers in singing, or rather shouting musically. If there were any non-believers present, apart from David and me, they were wise enough to join in, or at least open and shut their mouths at the appropriate times.

A film camera crew appeared in the space between the pavement-edge and the marchers, snapping on a portable floodlight which intensely illuminated the banners and the ecstatic faces. Passing at that moment was a Hitler Jugend contingent from East Prussia, the cut-off part of Germany behind the Polish Corridor. And marching at the head of her section and singing in a daze of Nazi fervour, was Anna-Maria.

I knew that David had seen her, for he shot me a glance. And I knew, too, that he had had enough. We slipped and shuffled our way back into Meinecke Strasse. Once more in my flat, I poured him nearly half a tumbler of Korn spirit, making no apology for my trembling hand. We sat and drank without speaking, waiting for our emotions and the roar from the Kurfürstendamm to subside.

At last there was a relative quiet and sleep became possible. David stood up, touched me on the shoulder, said "Good night", and went up to his flat.

I continued to sit in the small pool of light cast by the table lamp, thinking about England and my family — and Germany. At that moment I longed to be back in England, but not in the England I'd left. And I longed even more for the embracing warmth of my family, but not as I'd last seen them — cowed and impoverished by the Depression, and diminished as human beings.

I realised reluctantly that I'd been in Berlin long enough to be half in love with the Germany that was being ruthlessly extinguished on every hand. Could one squalid little man with a gift only for vituperative oratory take such a magnificent country back into the Middle Ages, with routine torturings, total intimidation, and even beheadings? It seemed impossible. Yet it was happening. Anyway, the same lack of option that had taken me to Germany held me there. I loosened my tie, stretched myself, and unfastened my watch.

There came a tap on the french windows, light but clear. I jumped slightly, but then realised that no Nazi would tap lightly on a window. I rose, went over, and partly opened one of the doors after I had seen that only one small man in civilian clothes was standing outside. "Forgive the late call," he said softly, in Berlin German, "and the unorthodox approach, but do I speak to the Englishman who teaches English?" Did he want David or me I wondered. It didn't matter.

"Yes," I said.

"Might I come in, please?"

"Yes." I opened the door fully and held back the curtain. An old Jew with a hand pressed to his left side came blinking, shuffling and apologising into the light. He was even uglier than Herr Mandelbaum had been, but I smiled at him, took his free hand, and led him to a chair.

171